# FORBIDDEN

## A DJINN WARS NOVEL

## CHRISTINE POPE

Dark Valentine Press

FORBIDDEN

ISBN: 978-1-946435-00-2
Copyright © 2016 by Christine Pope
Published by Dark Valentine Press

Cover design by Lou Harper

To learn more about this author, go to
www.christinepope.com.

FORBIDDEN

## CHAPTER ONE

JILLIAN POWELL PUT DOWN THE NEEDLE-NOSE PLI-
ers she held and peered inside the device that sat in front
of her on the worktable. Miles had given her this task
because he knew she had a steady hand and a keen eye,
but right then it felt as if all her hours of staring into
the jumbled mess of wiring inside the little box hadn't
accomplished much more than to give her a headache.

Maybe it was time to take a break. Jillian glanced
at the clock that hung on the wall on the other side of
the lab. Nearly five. In the old world, before the Dying,
it would have been almost quitting time, but Miles
Odekirk didn't have much of a clue when it came to normal work hours. He and his partner Lindsay seemed to
spend most of their waking lives in the lab here at the
Los Alamos facilities, although one would think Miles

might want Lindsay to back off a little, since she was now nearly seven months pregnant and couldn't spend hours and hours on her feet the way she used to.

But Jillian didn't really want to think about that. Seeing Lindsay's obvious happiness—and Miles's much more restrained anticipation—only served to remind Jillian of everything she'd lost when the Heat swept across the world and took everyone she'd known and loved with it. Some might say that the passage of time should have begun to heal that pain, now that the second anniversary of the Dying was only a little more than a month away, but instead that inner ache only seemed to grow sharper and sharper as the people around her moved on with their lives and began new ones...something Jillian didn't seem quite able to do.

Damn it.

She got up from the stool where she'd been sitting, then went out of the lab and down the hall to what used to be the break room for this floor of the build-ing. In there was a refrigerator with a pitcher of chilled water, and Jillian poured herself some, glad of the slight relief it gave her from the August heat. Los Alamos didn't get nearly as warm as her native Albuquerque, but it could still be uncomfortable without central air, another amenity that had been lost forever when the old world had died.

Well, actually, she'd heard that they still had air conditioning down in Santa Fe, since the djinn who lived there could keep those systems going without too much effort. Here in Los Alamos, the mere humans who populated the town had to get by with a combination of wind and solar, which meant being frugal with electricity. Tabletop fans on the hottest days, and ceiling fans in public spaces like restaurants and stores, but that was it.

At least Miles and Lindsay had stepped out for a bit, since they had a meeting scheduled late this afternoon with Shawn Gutierrez, the leader of the Los Alamos community. Otherwise, Jillian was sure Miles would be giving her the evil eye right about now for taking a break of longer than a few minutes. Not for the first time, she wondered what would happen if she walked out of the lab, went to Shawn, and told him that he needed to find another work assignment for her. Realistically, she knew she'd never actually do such a thing. She was needed here in the lab, could provide a set of skills that not many others shared. Who could have guessed that her one-time—and somewhat silly and old-fashioned—needlepoint hobby would have lent itself to working with wires and circuits?

Not that she actually knew what she was doing. Miles would give her a meticulously drawn diagram to follow, and she wouldn't deviate from it. In the beginning, she'd helped to increase the community's stockpile of his original devices, the ones that could repel all djinn from a certain area. Having more of the little boxes meant that the safe zone in Los Alamos could gradually be expanded. Now they had a large chunk of Española protected as well, which meant that workers from Los Alamos could come down from their mountain town into the lush valley where the Rio Grande flowed, grow more food there, and continue to scavenge any items that might help to keep their community prospering.

The Chosen, those lucky few whom the djinn had selected from the survivors of the Heat to be their companions and lovers, could come and go basically as they pleased, but the djinn themselves had to avoid any place where the Los Alamos group operated, or face the effects of Miles's devices.

Miles's goal was to modify the devices so they could keep the evil djinn—the ones who had plotted humanity's destruction—away from the human survivors, but allow the benevolent djinn who were inside the devices' area of effect to still have access to their powers. That way, it would be much easier to mingle with the good djinn who lived in Santa Fe.

He'd been working doggedly for over a year now, and so far he didn't have a lot to show for his efforts. Jillian could practically feel the frustration radiating from him most days, although she'd noticed that lately he'd done his best not to be too irritable around Lindsay...now that she could match him in the irritation department, thanks to those pregnancy hormones. But he'd come up with a new angle during the last few days, one he thought looked promising—which was why he needed Jillian, with her deft fingers and sharp vision, to do the actual assembly on the modified device.

Which also meant she should get off her ass and get back to work. It wasn't as if anyone would be waiting for her back at the little two-bedroom house she'd been given for her own.

*And whose fault is that?* she asked herself as she put her water glass down next to the sink in the break room and headed back to the lab. *If you'd really wanted to be with someone here, you could have.*

True enough. People were pairing off all over town. Lindsay's baby wouldn't be the first child born here, nor the last. Jillian had been approached quite a few times, in ways ranging from Brent Sanderson's nervous request asking if she'd like to go to Pajarito's for a drink, to Mitch Kosky's half-drunken assumption that naturally she should be thrilled to be on the receiving end of his not-so-welcome attentions.

She'd gently turned down Brent, who was a sensitive soul and someone she did like very much, if not in a romantic way, and had informed Mitch that she didn't think she'd ever get over her dead husband. He hadn't seemed too convinced by the excuse, but he had left her alone after that.

Those words weren't even a lie. Not really. Jack was in her thoughts nearly every day, even when she tried to tell herself it was time, that no one could blame her for trying to reclaim that part of her life when almost two years had passed since his death.

Tears stung her eyes, and she blinked them away, forcing them back where they'd come from. She couldn't work on Miles's damn device with blurry vision. Anyway, it was stupid to be so upset now, after so much time had gone by. Everyone around her had lost someone. *Everyone*. She wasn't special.

Luckily, Miles and Lindsay still hadn't reappeared. The lab was unoccupied. Jillian sat down on her stool and picked up the pliers in her right hand, then grasped the box with her left. The diagram Miles had provided lay off to one side, and she stared down at it for a long moment so she could commit the complex pattern to memory before she made another attempt. Two days ago, she'd completely fried the circuits in one device because she'd made a bad connection. Yes, the labs here had more components in their storehouses than one might have guessed, but that didn't mean she could be careless.

Jillian pulled in a breath and grasped the fine-gauge copper wire with the pliers, threading it down to the exact spot on the circuit board that Miles's diagram had indicated. At the last second, though, her hand trembled slightly, and the wire touched the circuit just a fraction of an inch to the left of where it was supposed to go. With a curse, Jillian yanked the wire back...and then the box itself began to slip from her left hand. Desperately she scrabbled at it, knowing if it hit the hard linoleum floor, the delicate touch screens that covered its surface would shatter. Her fingers closed on the little box, and she was about to breathe a sigh of relief—until she realized that in her frenzied attempt to grab the device, one finger had pushed down on the power button located on the bottom.

A spark jumped from the exposed wiring to the pliers she held. And then a wave of coruscating, blinding light surrounded her, stealing the breath from her throat so she couldn't scream, couldn't do anything except maintain a death grip on the device while the world disappeared in a flash.

She was falling, plummeting into a dark limbo that seemed to press down on her lungs and made her stomach feel as if it had lodged somewhere in her esophagus. At first she thought she must have been knocked off her stool by the blast, but it shouldn't have taken this long to hit the floor, should it? And then when she did finally land, dropping the device and pliers she held on impact, what she felt under her fingers was rough, gritty sand, not cool linoleum.

Blinking, she raised her head...and then wished she hadn't. The sky wasn't a sky at all, but an ever-shifting maelstrom of colors that flashed in and out of existence, colors she couldn't even begin to name, angry, searing, leaving nightmarish after-images flaring on her retinas. All around were jagged rock formations, some of which were marred by what seemed to be caves. To her confused eyes, those openings looked like dark, hungry mouths.

Her breath caught. Or rather, she realized she couldn't breathe, that when she tried to pull air in through her nose, it seemed to lodge somewhere in her throat and never make it any farther than that. Her lungs ached, were on fire.

She couldn't even scream. No air. The alien landscape spun around her, a red haze beginning to blur her vision. Somehow she found the strength to inch herself toward the device, instincts screaming at her that it was the reason she was here, her only means of escape. But it had fallen so far away...a yard at least. Under these conditions, it might as well be a mile.

No strength. The red haze began to shift to darkness, and she knew her body was giving in, every cell in her being shutting down from lack of oxygen. She would die here...and she didn't even know where "here" was.

Maybe she'd be with Jack soon.

Then, improbably, there came the sound of swift footsteps on the hard-packed sand. Someone knelt next to her, was grasping her by the shoulders and lifting her from the ground. She blinked in shock, saw impossibly blue eyes boring into hers.

No, that couldn't be right. Jack had brown eyes.

The stranger put his hand on the back of her neck and placed his mouth on hers. For a single startled second, she wondered incongruously why he was trying to kiss her. But then a welcome gust of air—*real* air—filled her throat, and she gulped it down, sending the stranger's breath into her oxygen-starved lungs.

And again. And again.

Those eyes remained fixed on hers. After he had shared half a dozen breaths with her, he said, in a deep, rough voice, "Who are you? How did you get here?"

Jillian shook her head. Although he'd brought her back from the brink, she knew if she opened her mouth, she'd release some of the precious, life-giving air he'd provided. Instead, she pointed at the box.

The stranger looked over at it, his heavy brows pulling together. "One of those things? I thought they were only for repelling djinn."

So he knew what the device was. And, although her brain was still befuddled from a lack of oxygen, she realized, looking at the man before her, that he probably wasn't an actual man at all. He was too perfect, from those startling blue eyes to the straight, elegant nose and full, sensual mouth. By all rights, he should be dead in this place, but he looked healthy and strong, muscles sculpted and full beneath the tatters of the clothing he wore.

He had to be a djinn.

Jillian opened her mouth to respond to his words, but immediately choked again on the toxic air. And at once he pressed his lips to hers, so she might take his breath. It flooded through her as she clung to him, knowing that without him she would die.

"Don't speak," he said. "I'm going to get the device." After gently letting her go, he rose to retrieve the box, along with the pair of pliers that lay next to it. Then he came back and put both items in her hands. "Make it work."

Easy for him to say. She didn't even know what the hell she'd done to have the device propel her from the lab to—well, to wherever the hell this place actually was. Maybe the djinn plane, the place some of them referred to as the otherworld? Possibly, although she knew the djinn actually lived there, even if they did prefer Earth, while this hellscape didn't seem like a place where anyone could live and survive.

But somehow the man—the djinn—before her had managed to do that very thing.

She lifted her shoulders and shook her head, trying to make him see that he asked the impossible of her. Apparently he understood well enough, because his full mouth compressed, and his brows pulled together.

"If you don't make it work, you're going to die here," he said. "I can't keep you alive indefinitely. Understand?"

Oh, she understood all too well. In fact, the burning sensation had returned to her throat and lungs, telling her that the last breath he'd given her was just about spent. Tears leaked from her eyes, although that could have just been the toxic atmosphere beginning to work on them as well.

He muttered something under his breath, and once again gave her his version of mouth-to-mouth. She swallowed the air gratefully, then turned the box over so she could inspect the button on the bottom. As far as she could tell, it was still switched on. So it must have been the combination of it being powered and the wire touching exactly the wrong place on the circuit board that had caused it to malfunction so spectacularly, to send her through space into this other dimension.

She grasped the wire with the pliers and began to move it toward the circuit, then paused and glanced up at the stranger. The chances of this working were roughly a million to one, but if by some act of God she was able to reverse the effects, she didn't know how she was supposed to bring him back with her. Which was clearly what he expected.

For a second, he only stared down at her, face hard but blank. Then he nodded, as if he suddenly understood the reason for her hesitation. He moved closer, wrapped his arms around her so his chest was to her back. "Go ahead," he said.

Her hand shook, and she willed it to be still. Another mistake could land them God only knew where. But it was so hard to concentrate with the air scorching her eyes, the stranger's breath rapidly running out in her lungs.

Not to mention his body pressed against hers. No, there was absolutely nothing sexual about the contact, and yet...it had been so very long since a man had held her like this. She'd forgotten how good it could feel.

Crazy.

She couldn't pull in a breath, so she held hers as she guided the wire to what she sincerely hoped was the same place that had caused the reaction the first time around. The stranger's arms tightened against her, as if he braced himself for what was to come next.

This time, she knew what to expect—or at least she thought she did. Still, she couldn't help gasping as light exploded all around them. That gasp sent the djinn world's poisonous air into her lungs, and she began to cough and cough, eyes streaming as she almost lost her grip on the device.

But then the stranger's hands were closing on it, holding it against her so there was no chance of it being lost. He clung to her as they tumbled through darkness for what felt like an eternity. Something was wrong. It hadn't taken this long the first time. An initial blast, and then she had fallen on the surface of that alien world.

At last, though, she felt warm, damp air against her cheeks. Light flowed around them, but not the harsh, glaring light of the malfunction, but sunlight. Blue skies partially obscured by big gray-white clouds.

And then she and the stranger fell into the middle of an ordinary two-lane road. He let out a grunt as she landed on top of him, but he didn't relax his grip on her, or on the device. The impact was enough to start her coughing again, however, and she struggled to pull away from him so she could bend over and cough up the last of the toxic air she'd inhaled before they left.

After a second or two of struggle, he did let her go. She rolled over onto her hands and knees, not caring about the rough asphalt under her palms. Coughed and coughed, and spat foul-tasting mucus from her mouth. At last she sat up, chest still heaving, and saw that the stranger had clambered to his feet and stood a few paces away, hand shielding his eyes from the sun as he looked around.

Jillian thought she should get up as well, although she didn't know if her shaky knees would support her yet. A quick glance told her that she definitely wasn't in Los Alamos—the air was warmer here, the hillsides dotted with the occasional juniper or piñon pine rather than the ponderosa forests that surrounded the mountain town. What buildings she could see looked shabby and rundown, not new and clean and neat the way so much of Los Alamos was. Anyway, if they'd ended up in Los Alamos, the djinn stranger with her would have shown signs of being affected by the djinn-repelling devices placed strategically around the town, and yet he stood there strong and straight, if unsmiling.

A shudder went through her as she sent a quick, sidelong glance in his direction. He hadn't made a move toward her once they'd landed here, and that was something. On the other hand, she didn't quite know what he intended to do. She'd never been around a djinn before. But if he was one of the evil djinn who'd made it their goal to eradicate humankind from the face of the planet, surely he would have killed her as soon as they were away from...wherever that awful place had been.

Not wanting to dwell on that prospect, Jillian made herself look around again. Something about her surroundings seemed halfway familiar, as though she must have come here sometime in the past. With an effort, she pushed herself to her feet, swallowing more of the warm, clean air as she did so. The familiar scent of damp earth came to her nose, telling her that it must have rained here fairly recently. Not that surprising, since it was August, and New Mexico was in the depths of monsoon season.

If they'd actually ended up in New Mexico, of course.

When she turned to look up the street, she saw a building painted turquoise blue, and a line of shops next to it, and she nodded to herself. Of course. She should have recognized the place right away. A glance over her shoulder, and she saw the stranger staring at her, those formidable brows of his pulled together.

"Where have you brought me?" he demanded, hands planted on his hips. He did not look happy with her at all.

Too bad she was too weak to run....

## CHAPTER TWO

ALDAIR HAD NOT KNOWN WHAT TO THINK WHEN the strange woman appeared in front of him. He had spent what felt like an eternity in the outer circles, the place where he had been banished after his ignominious defeat at the hands of his hated half-brother Jasreel. But he knew at once from the way the woman gasped and choked on the poisonous air that she must be human. A djinn could live here, if uncomfortably. A human, on the other hand, would die within the minute.

His quick actions had saved her, but he had not done so for any altruistic reasons. No, he had guessed that if she had the means to come here to the otherworld, then she could also get herself away—which meant she could take him with her. He would be free.

Despite this primary motivation, he could not help but notice that this human woman, whoever she was, seemed as if she would be quite lovely when she wasn't wracked with coughs. Her lips had been lush when he placed his mouth on hers to give her his breath. And the eyes that had stared up at him in gratitude were a dark, smoky gray, quite arresting.

Even so, he would not allow himself to be distracted by her. The important thing was to get away from the otherworld, and she was his only means of doing so. And though at first she had seemed reluctant, or frightened, at the end she did what she must to activate the device and bring them here.

Wherever that was.

Before his exile, and long before the djinn had exterminated most of mankind, Aldair had traveled the world and seen many of its sights for himself. But he could not remember ever being in a place such as this. No grand city of concrete and stone and steel here, nor a wild forest or a lush grassland. They had landed on a narrow road in a valley of some sorts, with the sort of scrubby vegetation he knew grew in the southwestern part of the land that had once been the United States. The buildings he could see appeared quite ramshackle and old, the kind of wooden structures that had to have been built decades earlier, perhaps as much as a century before.

He turned toward the woman, who by that point had gotten shakily to her feet. Even in the plain clothing favored by human females in this place and time, she was enticing enough, with her slim waist and the curves of her breasts, accented by the tight-fitting, sleeveless top she wore.

But he would have to focus on those curves later. For now, he needed to know where they were.

"Where have you brought me?" he demanded. "What is this place?"

For a few seconds, she didn't reply, but kept staring down the street, which, unlike the roads in Taos, had not been cleared of abandoned vehicles. A person could walk around them, but a car could never negotiate the choked pavement. Not that he needed to worry about such concerns; air elementals such as he had their own means of getting around.

"I think we're in Madrid," she said at last.

She pronounced the word strangely, with the accent on the first syllable and a flat "A" sound. Aldair felt his nostrils flare in derision. "Foolish woman," he said, "I have been to Madrid. It looks nothing like this."

At this remark, she turned back toward him, a half-smile playing on her lips. "Not Madrid, Spain," she replied, pronouncing it correctly this time. "Madrid, New Mexico. It used to be a mining town. Now it's a little artist colony, tourist destination." Her smile faded abruptly as she added, "Or at least it used to be... before."

He cared little for that. The Heat had done its work, and he had no energy to waste on the billions the disease had taken with it. "Where in New Mexico?" he asked sharply.

For of course it would not do to be too close to Santa Fe, where a contingent of the One Thousand and their Chosen dwelt. Where that bastard Jasreel lived with Jessica Monroe, the woman who should have been Aldair's own....

"South of Santa Fe," the woman he'd rescued said.

"How far?"

If she was puzzled by this line of questioning, she didn't show it. She did give a little hack of a cough before she spoke, though. They would probably need to find water soon.

"I'm not sure...maybe twenty, thirty miles? Sorry, I only came through here once. Jack and I were driving to Taos, and we thought it would be fun to come up the Turquoise Trail and have lunch in Madrid."

"Who is Jack?"

"My husband," she said, her expression darkening. "My dead husband, that is."

Aldair chose to ignore that comment. If she had survived the Heat, then of course she would also have suffered her own losses. He could do nothing about that. He had not been one of those who had concocted the disease, but he also had not much cared one way or another what happened to mankind. The only reason he had joined the ranks of the One Thousand was that his hated half-brother Jasreel had desired a woman of the Immune to be his Chosen, and Aldair had seen Jessica Monroe as a chance to get his revenge on the brother he despised. Unfortunately, none of those plans had gone the way Aldair had hoped....

The woman coughed again, and he realized they could do little else until they found some water, and perhaps something to eat. If he had been an ordinary mortal, such a task would have been somewhat difficult, as he guessed that any food left behind here in Madrid after its inhabitants had died would be long since spoiled. Bottled water, however, should still be viable.

He imagined holding a bottle in each hand, and in the next moment the wished-for water bottles had appeared. "It appears you need this," he said, holding out one of the bottles to the woman.

Her eyes widened. "What—?"

"It is a power of ours," Aldair broke in. It seemed clear enough to him that she had never been around a djinn before. Not one of the Chosen, then, although she was certainly attractive enough to be one. Perhaps too old? That must be it. At any rate, he guessed she must be one of the survivors from Los Alamos. That made sense, since he could think of no other way she would have had access to one of those infernal devices. "We can summon the things we need for our sustenance. Go on, drink."

She hesitated for a moment, but her thirst clearly overcame her caution, for she went ahead and unscrewed the cap, and took a long drink, followed by another. "Better," she said.

"Good."

The device still lay on the ground where the woman had dropped it. Aldair went over and picked it up. A loose wire dangled from somewhere in its interior. It did not appear to be functioning at the moment, and he could not help but be glad about that.

"I'll take that," the woman said.

He shot her an amused glance. She was standing there trying to look at him quite sternly, but the effect was marred by the smudges of dirt on her cheeks and chin, the way strands of her warm, malt-brown hair had slipped loose from the clasp that held it back from her face.

"I think not," he returned easily. "I want to make sure it cannot send me back to the otherworld."

"It won't," she said. Her fingers tightened on the bottle of water she held. "The malfunction only occurs when the wire hits the circuit board in the wrong place. And it has to be switched on. I pushed the button to turn it off as soon as we landed here."

"Ah." Well, that explained some of it. She'd had no real intention of going to the djinn plane, let alone that world's dreaded outer circles. Only a mishap of some sort. How such a thing could have occurred, Aldair had no idea. He was not a scientist. And at the moment, he didn't much care. The important thing was that he was free...for now, anyway. He had to pray that the elders would not be able to discover that their captive had escaped. "Even so, I will hold on to it." He turned away from her, noted how the sun was beginning to dip behind the hills to the west. "In the meantime, I think it best that we find some shelter. How well do you know this town?"

"I told you, I don't." From the set of her jaw, he could see she wasn't particularly pleased that he had refused to surrender the device to her. "I only passed through once. We had lunch at a place called The Hollar."

Odd name, but he decided to leave that aside. It wasn't important. "Did people live here, or is it only shops and restaurants?"

"Yes, some did, I think. Not many. Probably no more than a few hundred at the most. But I remember seeing houses as we came into town. Mostly on the outskirts."

"Show me," he commanded, and a flicker of irritation came and went in her storm-colored eyes.

However, she didn't protest, only pointed down the road.

"That way, I think. But I'm not sure if I'm up to a hike right now. That crud feels like it's still somewhere down at the bottom of my lungs."

It probably was. While he did not think she had suffered any lasting harm, he knew she would need some time to recover. Any real exertion would only lead to another coughing fit. What she really needed was to rest, to drink more water and have something to eat.

Well, luckily he could prevent her from having to walk at all. Without responding, he tucked the device under his left arm, then went to her and wrapped his other arm around her waist. She let out a startled little gasp, and he said, "You had better hang on tight."

A frown pulled at her fine dark brows, but she did as instructed—after an obvious pause—and wrapped her arms around his waist. Then it was time to take to the air, the ground dropping away from them as he soared upward. She gasped again, followed by a cough, and her arms tightened about him, but she stayed calm and still enough as he flew over the cars choking the streets, past rows of shabby-looking shops and over-grown yards, past a large building that proclaimed itself to be The Mine Shaft. Perhaps another restaurant?

They would have to leave that exploration for later, though. Now they were passing the southern border of the town proper. Aldair's eyes scanned the ground below them, looking for someplace that would serve as a proper refuge. If forced, he would go to one of those ramshackle houses, but he would far prefer something bigger and newer.

There. A dirt road wound off the highway and up a hill, and to a respectable-enough homestead, one with a largish house, a few outbuildings, a windmill.

"That one looks good," the woman said. "There are solar panels on the roof. That means it might still have power."

Such technical issues were not of too much concern to him, for he knew he could spare enough power to maintain a home of that size. Still, if it did have solar power, that meant he would not have to use much, if any, of his own energy.

He brought them down into the open dirt area just beyond the garage. As soon as his feet touched the ground, he set down the woman. She removed her arms from around his waist and stepped away, looking somewhat pale. Had their flight disturbed her, or was her pallor only a result of her exposure to the air of the outer circles?

When she spoke, though, she sounded composed enough. "Well, that made it a little easier." Her voice was still rather hoarse, though, and she lifted the bottle of water to her lips and took a long swallow. "Guess we'd better look around."

"I agree."

Aldair moved past her to the house, which was not the sort of flat-topped stucco structure he'd come to expect in this part of the world, but rather a large two-story building with a sloped metal roof and wide porches that wrapped around three of its four sides. Two chimneys poked their way up from the roof, and well-grown trees—cottonwood and oak, apple and elm—shaded most of its windows.

He went up the porch steps, the woman a few feet behind him. The door was locked, but that mattered little to him; he touched his fingers to the knob, and at once it obediently turned.

The air inside was stale. All the windows were shut, which he found rather surprising. The Heat had struck at the end of September, a time of year when the weather should have been mild and pleasant. One would think the inhabitants of the house would have left their windows open. But he supposed that was a good thing, for at least the interior of the home hadn't been damaged by rain or snow pouring in.

Everything looked clean and neat, except for a layer of dust on all the surfaces. He approved of the interior, open and somewhat spare, with pale golden wood floors and walls painted only a few shades lighter. Abstract art in large splashes of color, a handsome square hearth with a slate surround.

The floor creaked slightly as the woman moved past him, heading deeper into the house. He followed, partly because he wanted to see the rest of the place, and partly because he wanted to see where she was going.

Through a dining area, and then on into the kitchen, which was also more spare and modern than he would have expected, given the overall rundown nature of the town where this house was located. Hard counters of polished stone, steel appliances.

The refrigerator hummed away, and the digital clock on the microwave showed the time as 5:48. So apparently the solar power had held on all this time.

Then the woman paused, her hand going to her mouth as she stared down at the floor in consternation. Aldair followed her gaze and saw a small pile of fine gray dust there, obviously the remnants of one of the home's inhabitants.

His mouth tightened. The place had been so neat and in order that he had found himself thinking perhaps no one had been here when the Heat struck, that possibly this had been someone's second home.

Apparently not.

"I can take care of that," he said, and waved a hand. Instantly, the back door opened, and a small breeze whisked the dust outside where it could trouble them no longer.

Except…the woman appeared very troubled indeed. Her hand shook as she pushed one of those stray strands of hair away from her face, and she'd gone even paler. "Did you really have to do that?"

"Yes," he said evenly. "What else would you have me do? That dust has been lying in here for almost two years. At least out in the wind and the sun it can become one with the earth again."

Apparently she hadn't thought of it that way. Her eyes still looked haunted, but after a moment, she gave a reluctant nod. "I suppose so."

Good. At least it didn't seem as if she meant to argue with him. He moved to the refrigerator and opened it, then wrinkled his nose at the foul smell that greeted him. Yes, the power had stayed on all this time, but most refrigerated items were never meant to be kept for several years.

A wave of the hand, and it was all gone as well, the odor along with it.

The woman made a shocked little sound before offering him a somewhat rueful smile. "Sorry," she said. "I'm just not used to seeing a djinn in action."

"You come from Los Alamos, don't you?"

"Yes," she replied. "I was about to ask you how you knew that, but then, I guess it's the only place around here with humans who aren't Chosen, isn't it?"

"That I know of, yes."

She nodded, looking resigned. Perhaps she had hoped there would be other survivors, but Aldair certainly knew of none.

"I am Aldair al-Ankara," he told her. "What is your name?"

"Jillian. Jillian Powell."

"Well, then, Jillian," he said. "I suppose we should see what else there is to find here."

Something about his name had sounded halfway familiar, although Jillian couldn't quite place it. Maybe she'd overheard it in a conversation once. The djinn of Santa Fe couldn't visit Los Alamos, for obvious reasons, and although Julia Innes returned there every few months to have a convo in person with Miles and Lindsay, and sometimes Shawn Gutierrez, it wasn't as if Jillian had ever been invited to participate in those conversations. She had a semi-useful function in the lab, but she didn't have anything to do with actually running the town.

At any rate, she supposed it didn't matter. This Aldair had saved her life, and she had to be grateful to him for that. Why he hadn't been able to return to Earth under his own power, when it seemed as if the djinn could move back and forth between the planes with relative ease, she didn't know. Something to ask, if she ever worked up the courage to do so. But since his name was at least a little familiar to her, she guessed he must be one of the Santa Fe djinn as well, which meant he had to be one of the good guys. Good djinn. Whatever. Her limbs still felt shaky, but the fear that he was going to hurt her had retreated a little. Even so, she had to admit it was sort of overwhelming to be this close to a djinn. She'd known they were perfect...she just hadn't quite realized *how* perfect.

In the meantime, they explored the house, which felt a lot more state-of-the-art than the sort of place she would have expected to see in little out-of-the-way Madrid. It had central air, for one thing, even though it wasn't running at the moment. Would the solar be enough to support the system? Jillian had no idea, and she realized it was far more important to keep the refrigerator going and the pump for the well—which she'd spotted as they'd made their descent toward the property—running than it was to prevent her from sweating in the heat. Besides, it really wasn't that hot today. Once they'd opened all the windows, the temperature in the house became nearly tolerable.

Three bedrooms and two baths upstairs, along with a nearly empty room toward the front of the house, filled with natural light. Propped up against the wall were a number of canvases in various stages of completion, and another nearly finished painting rested on an easel. All the works were of the same style as the pictures that hung on the first floor, so clearly the artist had lived here.

Had those been his—or her—ashes on the kitchen floor? Neither Jillian nor Aldair had encountered any remains up here on the second story, so it seemed that the artist must have lived alone, or at least was alone when the Heat burned its way through the population.

"I will take this room," Aldair announced as he stood in the middle of the master bedroom and surveyed its simple but handsome furnishings, the flat-weave wool rug on the floor. "You may have one of the other two."

High-handed bastard, wasn't he? Jillian reminded herself she would be dead if it weren't for him, and so she bit back the retort that rose to her lips. Anyway, why was he assuming they would stay here at all? Yes, she was feeling tired and would like to put her feet up and drink some more water, but at the same time, it seemed wiser for them to head to Santa Fe. He could be reunited with his people, and then one of the Chosen there could drive her back to Los Alamos. Or they could send word to have someone come fetch her. If only Aldair hadn't secreted the device somewhere. As soon as they'd entered the house, the little box had disappeared into thin air. Another djinn trick, she supposed.

"Um…we're staying here?" she ventured.

He gave her another of those fearsome frowns. "Of course. Why else would I go to the trouble of selecting a house?"

"Well, you did say I should rest a little. But—"

"Yes, you should rest. Choose a room that suits you. I will get you more water."

"But—"

The syllable fell on empty air, because even as she'd spoken, he'd disappeared. Was it typical of the djinn to just come and go like that, without a word of warning? Maybe. But she couldn't help thinking it was pretty rude. She tried to remind herself that she didn't have much context for djinn behavior, but she still found the way he'd melted into thin air as she was speaking more than a little annoying.

Fighting back a sigh, she headed out into the hallway and peered into the other two bedrooms. Not much choice, really, since one of them had been set up as a home office, with a big 27-inch iMac on the desk and a large table that was covered in a scatter of papers, most of which boasted sketches or small watercolors, many of them startlingly realistic renderings of the landscapes around town. So apparently the artist dabbled in other styles when he or she wasn't creating the large abstracts that decorated the walls.

The other room clearly had been intended as a place for guests to stay, with a double bed and a nightstand and a low dresser topped by a mirror. More paintings hung on the walls here, and a terra-cotta pot containing what had probably once been a philodendron was set to one side of the dresser.

Jillian went to the bed and sat down, for the first time really stopping to assess how her lungs felt. Sore, and raw, but now she could take a deep breath without coughing, which had to be an improvement. It did seem like the best thing to do was put her feet up and rest for a while. After she was feeling more like herself, she could talk to Aldair and convince him to take her to Santa Fe.

As she bent down to untie her sneakers, a horrible thought crossed her mind. Maybe he wanted to keep her here alone because he wanted...well, because he wanted her.

*Don't be ridiculous,* she told herself as she pulled off her shoes. *If he wanted to try something, he could have done it already. Anyway, he's barely given you a second glance. What would someone who looks like that want with a human woman, anyway?*

That sounded logical enough. But clearly there were djinn who found themselves attracted to humans, or none of them would have been with their Chosen. True, but that didn't mean Aldair was attracted to her. When he'd given her mouth-to-mouth, when he'd flown her to this house...at no time had he acted the least bit interested in her, even with the close contact they'd shared.

No, there had to be some other reason why he didn't want to go to Santa Fe. Maybe he'd had some kind of a falling out with the djinn there. Oh, yeah, that was a reassuring thought.

Doing her best to push those suspicions aside, Jillian plumped up the pillows and shook them to get rid of any dust, and then settled herself against their soft surfaces, realizing in that moment how much her body really did ache. Each breath awoke a series of new pains in her back and shoulders, probably from that violent coughing fit she'd experienced when she arrived here. It did feel good to have her feet up, to have her body supported by those cradling pillows.

A small creak out in the hallway made her turn her head in that direction. Aldair stood there, holding a glass of water. More importantly, he'd somehow managed to outfit himself in new clothes, a djinn-style outfit in shades of blue and gray. It looked as if he'd brushed his hair as well, although the expanse of chest revealed by his open robe was distracting enough that Jillian couldn't tell for sure.

He entered the room and handed her the glass of water. "Here."

"Thank you," she said, taking it from him so she could wet her still-dry throat. The water tasted good, sweet and cold and clean.

"From the well," he said. "It is functioning properly, so there will be no shortage of water."

"That's good." She hesitated, hands wrapped around the glass, as if feeling its smooth, cool surface was enough to give her courage. Even though she couldn't quite rid herself of the tension that ratcheted up when she was around him, she wanted to sound as normal as possible. "But Aldair—why do we even need to worry about a shortage of water? You can just fly me to Santa Fe, and then—"

"We will not go to Santa Fe," he cut in, blue eyes flashing with sudden anger. "This is a safe place. We will remain here."

"But—"

"You will not speak of it," he said. "Rest now."

And then he was gone again, this time in a swirl of those blue and gray robes, so he looked something like a departing thundercloud. At least, his expression had been positively thunderous.

Now, what the hell was all that about?

## CHAPTER THREE

ALDAIR SAT AT THE DINING ROOM TABLE, A BOTTLE of wine he had found in a rack in the kitchen placed off to one side. He had worked through nearly half the bottle already, but he thought he would need far more alcohol than that to ease his roiling thoughts. The stray notion passed through his mind that perhaps he should conjure some food to go with the wine, although at the moment he did not feel himself inclined to do so.

The silence from upstairs discomfited him. He had expected Jillian to come down here in search of him so she might continue to argue about going to Santa Fe, but apparently she was not inclined to do so. Perhaps she was afraid of him. She would do well to fear him, if she but knew what he was capable of.

However, in his brief acquaintance with her, she had not seemed particularly intimidated by his presence, had spoken up for herself, even though she must know he could blink her out of existence with a snap of his fingers, should he so wish.

Not that he did wish such a thing. Her tongue might be sharp, but it was contained within a very lovely mouth.

He told himself not to be foolish. Unlike the djinn in Santa Fe, he had never felt any particular desire for a human woman, had thought such entanglements to be foolish, when one considered the ramifications of encouraging a serious connection to anyone not of his own race. He had been with Katelyn purely for expediency's sake, and he had only sought out Jessica Monroe because she was someone his brother desired. Yes, she was certainly comely enough, with her big dark eyes and long dark hair, but there were many women of the djinn who were far more beautiful.

No, the situation with Jillian Powell was slightly more complicated. Without her, he would still be back in the outer circles, so he knew he must be grateful to her for that. And also...well, he supposed he could admit to himself that it was good to hear another voice again, even if that voice belonged to a human woman. In his exile, he had not seen another living soul for... how long had he even been there? Time had no meaning in that hellish landscape. He had been sent away in the early spring, and he thought now he had returned in the late summer, so it had to have been at least a number of months, if not more.

The other rogue djinn, Khalim and his followers, had also been sent to the outer circles, but Aldair had never seen any sign of them—by design, he was sure. The exile he'd had to endure had been made far, far worse by his utter solitude. Perhaps those other djinn were dead. Not from the harsh conditions they had to endure, but by their own hand. That was the usual fate of those banished to the outer circles. After enough time had passed there, death began to seem like a welcome relief.

Not that he would have ever stooped to do such a thing. Hate had kept him going, had filled his veins with a fire that sustained him far more than the foul water and meager plants he'd found to live on. He'd sworn that one day he would be free, and would seek his revenge. Yes, no one had ever escaped the outer circles, but he had told himself he would be the exception.

And so it appeared he was. He had escaped, and sat here now in a comfortable refuge, with a roof over his head and a beautiful woman lying in a bed upstairs.

The thought awoke a flicker of desire, but he pushed it away. He could not allow himself to be distracted by such inconsequentials. He had told Jillian he would not take her to Santa Fe, but that did not mean he didn't intend to go there himself, once he had devised a foolproof plan. For he had unfinished business in that place, with the half-breed who unfortunately shared his family name.

A soft whisper of a sound made him look up from his wine glass, and he saw Jillian standing in the doorway to the dining room, her expression an odd mixture of diffidence and need. For one wild second, he thought that need might be directed at him, but then he realized she was staring at the wine bottle on the table.

"Oh, God," she said. "Wine? And it's okay?"

"It is fine," he replied. "I think those two years it waited for us only served to improve it. Would you like some?"

"Yes, please." She came up to the table, pulled out the chair opposite him, and sat down.

Watching her, he thought she looked somewhat improved. Color had returned to her cheeks, and her eyes were no longer bloodshot. Her hair was even messier than the last time he had seen her, though, with more strands slipping out of the clasp that held it—perhaps because of the way she'd been lying against the pillows in her borrowed bed.

His groin tightened at that mental image, and he pushed it away and made himself instead summon a wine glass for her from the cupboard in the kitchen. It appeared on the table before her, and she gave a little start.

"I suppose I should try to get used to that," she remarked. "Is that how you brought the wine here, too?"

"No," he said as he poured a healthy measure into her glass. "It was in a rack in the kitchen, with not quite a dozen other bottles. I will not have to summon any for a good while."

Her eyebrows lifted at that comment, and he wondered if she was going to press him again about how long he intended them to stay here. But she said nothing, instead raising the glass to her lips so she could sip from it.

"Ah," she said, once she had savored, then swallowed the wine, "that helps."

"So will this," he said, spreading one hand toward the center of the table. A platter with bread and cheese and grapes appeared there. Light fare, true, but something to cushion the wine.

This time she didn't even blink. "Yes, I think it will."

She set down her wine glass, and reached over to pick up a slice of bread and place a square of cheese on top. Aldair did the same, somewhat amused by her willingness to ignore his djinn powers if it meant she would be provided with food and wine. But he was glad to have distracted her, for that meant she might leave the subject of Santa Fe aside for now.

They ate quietly for a moment. He savored the taste of real food, of the rich red wine slipping over his tongue. Jillian seemed to appreciate the offering as well, although of course she could not have suffered the same deprivations he had over the past...well, however long it had been.

"There's probably a good deal more here in town, too," she offered, and Aldair lifted an eyebrow.

"A good deal more?"

"Wine. They had a pretty decent wine list at The Hollar, and then across the street is the Mine Shaft. Although I have a feeling they were more into hard liquor over there."

"That was a tavern?"

"Yes, a restaurant and bar. Jack and I didn't eat there when we came through, but we did poke our heads in to take a look." She'd been wearing a slight smile before she spoke, no doubt one brought on by the food and the wine, but it melted away as she appeared to recall the trip she had taken with the husband she'd lost.

Aldair felt a stab of irritation. The Chosen he had known in Taos had certainly seemed to have little problem moving on with their lives, even with all that they had lost, so he had no idea why such a concept would be so difficult for the woman sitting across the table from him.

*Ah, but she was not Chosen,* he thought. *Perhaps she has spent this time alone, without a new partner. However long it has been.*

He felt compelled to ask, "What month is it?"

"August," she said, and gave him a curious glance. What she saw in his face, he couldn't be sure, but she added, her tone gentle, "It will be two years since the Dying at the end of next month."

So that meant he had been imprisoned in the outer circles for nearly a year and a half, human time. Such measurements were not precisely applicable to life in the otherworld, but it always helped to have some context.

"Ah." He lifted his glass of wine and allowed himself a large swallow so he wouldn't have to make any further comment.

She was silent, too, as she reached for some more bread and cheese, then washed it down with her wine. At last she said, "Aldair...what were you doing in that place?"

He stiffened. "I fear that is none of your affair."

An eyebrow lifted, and she settled against the back of her chair, arms crossed. "Oh, really? Because you seemed pretty eager for me to get you out of there."

Of course he was. Who would not have been, when presented with such a chance for deliverance?

"It is part of the djinn world," he said curtly. "And that is all you need to know."

"Okay," she said, tone even enough, although from the way her eyes narrowed slightly, he thought she was more than a little annoyed by his reply. "Then maybe you can answer this. If you had no intention of going to Santa Fe to be with the rest of your people, then why did you ask how far away it was? What difference could that make?"

Damn her. She was not going to leave it alone, was she? He poured himself more wine, pointedly ignoring the lowered level of the alcohol in her glass. "I wanted to know because I wanted to make sure they could not detect my presence here."

"You're hiding from them?"

He didn't answer, only drank some wine.

"But...why?"

Aldair began to think there might be some limits to his gratitude. In his past, he had had very few dealings with mortals before he pretended to be part of the One Thousand who had taken human lovers for their own, so they might be spared certain death at the hands of those who wanted all of mankind annihilated. However, those rare times he had been forced to meet with humans, they had treated him with the deference deserving of one of his kind. He was not used to women who stared at him with arms crossed and who demanded answers as if they were equals.

"Let us just say there is no love lost between myself and the djinn who dwell in Santa Fe," he said at last.

She didn't respond for a moment. Her fingers tapped on the stem of her wine glass. "That place where I found you...was that some kind of djinn prison?"

He did not much like how she had been able to make that particular logical jump. Despite the ordeal she had just suffered, her mind appeared quick enough. He would have to watch what he said around her.

Because she didn't seem particularly worried by the prospect of his apparent incarceration at the hands of his own kind, Aldair only shrugged. "Perhaps that is as good a word as any. The outer circles are more like...a place of exile."

She was silent then, appearing to consider his words. However, she did not ask the next logical question, which would be why he had been sent there in the first place. She drank some more of her wine and then raised her head so she could look at him directly. For the first time, he realized she must have been wearing some kind of cosmetics when her mishap with the device propelled her into the otherworld; he noted dark smudges along her lower lashes, blurry black marks that had nothing to do with the skin itself being bruised.

"So...since we're more than twenty miles away from Santa Fe, the other djinn won't be able to tell that you're here?"

He shrugged. "Most likely not. If they had known I would be in the vicinity, they might have been able to reach out and detect my presence. But I doubt any of them thought I would ever return to this world."

That comment made her eyes widen. "That place you were sent—they expected you to be there forever?"

"That was the intention. However, most of those who are sent to the outer circles do not survive there for very long."

Her dark lashes swept down, hiding her eyes as she appeared to digest that particular piece of information. "That's...barbaric."

The same thought had crossed his mind once or twice—it would have been far more merciful to simply execute those whose transgressions warranted exile—but again he merely lifted his shoulders. "Perhaps. But effective. At any rate, no one expects me to be here. And also, the topography of this place can function as an effective shield. Being hidden away in a valley like this will make it more difficult for them to realize I am no longer in the outer circles."

Her expression was troubled. However, Aldair did not know her well enough to determine whether her worry was for his sake, or arose from a simple concern for her own well-being. After all, she must have guessed that the outer circles were a punishment of last resort, not something given lightly. And so she must also be wondering what kind of monster she had been trapped with.

"I see," she said at last, which did not give any indication of her feelings. One finger traced the wood grain of the tabletop. She wore no polish, or any rings on her right hand, although he had noted the plain gold band on the ring finger of her left.

That reminder of her dead husband must be with her always. No wonder she clearly had spent her days since his passing alone.

Aldair would not allow himself to feel any guilt over that death. Men had had ample opportunity to become better stewards of this wonderful world that had been given to them, and they had squandered its riches. No, he had not been one of the mad geniuses who devised the disease, nor one of those who cheerfully volunteered for the task of spreading the Heat among the population, but neither had he mourned the passing of humankind...especially not when its aftermath had given him such a ripe opportunity for revenge.

Then Jillian said, "Thank you for the wine, and the food. I'm feeling a little tired now—I think I'll go upstairs and lie down again."

"Of course," he replied, although in the back of his mind he thought her excuse was merely that—a logical reason for removing herself from his company. Perhaps she had realized that she was trapped here with a criminal, and no ordinary one, but a djinn, someone who could overpower her in a number of unpleasant ways.

She had no way of knowing that he did not intend her any harm. At least, not unless she gave him some provocation.

An uncertain smile touched her lips, and she rose from the table and left the room. A moment later, Aldair heard her light footsteps on the stairs, followed shortly thereafter by the soft *thump* of her bedroom door closing.

Well, at least it seemed as if she had no immediate plans to flee. Then again, perhaps she wanted to be alone so she might devise some stratagem for getting away from him.

Unfortunately, she could have no idea how difficult it would be to escape from an air elemental.

Jillian leaned against the door of her borrowed bedroom and pulled in a deep breath, one that rasped on its way down and seemed to burn slightly at the bottom of her lungs. Yes, she was feeling much better, but it appeared as if she'd need some more time than she'd thought to fully recover from her ordeal in the outer circles.

The outer circles. Now she could put a name to that hellish place, although she still had no idea why it was that the malfunctioning device had sent her there. Yes, intellectually she understood why she might have gone to the djinn plane itself, because Miles had told her that his devices worked by detecting djinn energy and subverting it somehow, turning it against them. So maybe there existed some strange connection between the devices and the djinn otherworld, some way that the little boxes would find themselves drawn there. But the outer circles were something else entirely.

Well, she couldn't let herself worry about that right now. Somehow she'd made it back to Earth, and now that she was here, she had much bigger problems to deal with—the biggest one being the djinn who sat downstairs at the dining room table and was even now drinking wine and eating bread and cheese as if nothing particularly untoward had just occurred. And soon someone in Los Alamos would be sure to note her absence, although there wasn't a whole hell of a lot she could do about that. To them, it must seem as if she'd vanished into thin air...which in a way she supposed she had.

What could Aldair have done, to be sent to the outer circles? It must have been something pretty awful, because a race of beings that could nonchalantly exterminate all of humanity had to possess very different morals from the ones she'd been raised with. Maybe he'd killed another djinn. Or several djinn. Or maybe....

No, she wouldn't let her mind go there. Not that she'd ever had anyone make unwanted sexual advances toward her, except that one creep at an office party years ago, but even with her lack of experience, she hadn't

picked up anything like a predator vibe from Aldair.
Or at least not that sort of predator. Anyway, he'd had
ample opportunity to pounce if that was his true intention, and he hadn't made a single move. Whatever his
history, she didn't think it included assaulting women.

Unless part of his game was to make her think she
was safe, and then get some sort of twisted pleasure in
savoring her betrayal.

*Stop it,* she told herself. *Just stop it.*

To calm herself down, she made herself walk
around the room and inspect it closely this time. Even
though it was a secondary bedroom, it was still nearly
as big as the master she'd shared with Jack back at their
townhouse in Albuquerque. She'd never been all that
great at estimating square footage—kind of a joke
for someone who'd worked as an office assistant at a
real estate broker's—but she thought the house here
in Madrid probably had to be around three thousand
square feet. A lot of space for just one person, but then,
Jillian reminded herself that she didn't know for sure
that the artist whose dust they'd discovered downstairs
had lived here by him- or herself. Maybe the other
members of the family had been out when the Heat
descended.

But she didn't want to think about that, either,
didn't want to think about how Jack had gone into
work during that terrible time, even though she'd
begged him not to. That had been the second day after

the illness had first begun to spread through the population, although at that point they still hadn't gotten any real confirmation one way or another that it had struck Albuquerque yet. But even the rumors had been enough to set Jillian on edge; she'd called in sick, although she felt fine, and she'd pleaded with Jack to stay home.

He hadn't, of course. He loved his students and believed he had a duty to them, and had told Jillian that he would be letting them down if he didn't show up for work that day. So he'd driven off in the used Prius they'd bought the year before, and that was the last she ever saw of him.

By now she was used to the way the tears seemed to come out of nowhere, and, just as she had countless times before, she blinked fiercely until they subsided. There, that was better. She had to keep it together right now.

The room didn't contain any other furniture beyond the bed, nightstand, and dresser. Jillian opened the top nightstand drawer and found it empty except for a rectangular box of tissues. The drawer below that contained nothing at all, and the dresser was similarly empty.

Definitely a guest room, then, which seemed to shoot down the idea that whoever had lived here might have had a family. Jillian ran her hands over the thighs of her stained jeans and realized she had absolutely nothing to change into. Aldair had apparently magicked a new set of clothes for himself out of nothing, but she didn't possess that particular gift. And since the djinn had claimed the master bedroom for himself, that meant Jillian wouldn't have much opportunity to go in there and see if there was anything she might scrounge for herself. At least not without asking permission.

Well, she'd just have to get by for now, and then maybe tomorrow she'd feel up to roaming around Madrid to see if she could find a change of clothes. It didn't exactly thrill her to know she'd be taking items that once belonged to the residents here, but she didn't have many options. This wasn't like Santa Fe, where the Chosen had all those boutiques to raid, along with a Target, two Walmarts, and the stores in the mall at the southern end of town. Or even like Los Alamos, which didn't have a ton of shopping options, but did at least boast a Beall's Outlet, not to mention the places down the hill in Española.

She sat down on the bed and pulled off her socks; she'd already taken off her running shoes earlier, and had gone downstairs in her sock feet. Had Aldair noticed? Probably not. He'd seemed pretty focused on the wine.

That wine had helped her a little as well, if only to ease some of her aching muscles. The food had also soothed her somewhat acid stomach, although she wished now that she could brush her teeth. It was very early, probably only six-thirty, and yet Jillian felt as if she could sleep for a hundred years. But doing that without brushing her teeth didn't sound very appealing.

Moving quietly, and hoping that Aldair wouldn't be able to tell that she hadn't yet lain down as she had said she would, she opened the door and went down the short hallway to the bathroom. Like the bedroom she'd just left, the bath seemed intended for guests, as she couldn't see any personal items, just extra rolls of toilet paper and another box of Kleenex under the sink.

But there in one of the vanity's drawers was an untouched tube of toothpaste, and a toothbrush still in its packaging, along with a few bars of glycerin soap and a jar of Oil of Olay. Thank God. Jillian had no idea who had lived here once, but she silently thanked them for being so thoughtful, and prepared.

Water came out of the faucet when she turned it. Aldair's doing, or just another indication that the solar panels on the roof were still capable of doing their job? She'd never lived anywhere off-grid like this, so she had only a very fuzzy idea as to how everything was supposed to work.

In the meantime, she should just be glad there was water at all.

She brushed her teeth, doing her best to get rid of the residual sourness of the outer circles' acrid air, and then washed her face as well, using the soap and following it up with the moisturizer she'd found. Afterward, she thought she felt almost human, although when she looked in the mirror, she wasn't too thrilled by her reflection. Shadows showed under her eyes, and she noted a tension to her mouth that hadn't been there before.

Well, what did she expect? After everything she'd just gone through, she supposed she should be glad that she didn't look like about fifty miles of bad road.

When she turned away from the mirror, though, she couldn't help letting out a gasp. Aldair stood in the hallway just outside the bathroom, leaning against the wall, his expression curious.

"So you were not that weary after all?"

Damn it, how had he managed to appear there without making the slightest sound? Another kind of djinn trick, she supposed—an extremely unnerving one. She gathered herself and replied, "I didn't want to go to sleep without getting cleaned up first. If you don't mind."

A small smile played around his lips. "No, I don't mind. But I heard water running, so I wondered."

"Well, now you know." She put the moisturizer back in the vanity's drawer, then hesitated. Aldair showed no signs of moving, and she realized she'd have to push past him to get to her bedroom. The prospect of bumping into him didn't seem very appealing. On the other hand, she didn't want him to think he'd intimidated her, even though of course he had. Jaw set, she began to make her way out of the bathroom, and wouldn't allow herself a sigh of relief when he shifted slightly out of the way so she could pass.

But then he said, "You plan to sleep in those clothes?"

His words brought her to a halt. Reluctantly, she turned back toward him and shrugged. "I don't have much choice. I didn't find any spare clothes in the bedroom I'm using."

He glanced past her to her open bedroom door, and then farther down the hall to the room he'd claimed as his own. "Perhaps you should try my room."

Was this his way of trying to be helpful, or was he only inviting her to look there as a way to get her in his room? No, that was ridiculous. She really needed to stop looking at him as some sort of otherworldly sexual predator. Otherwise, she was going to end up driving herself crazy.

"You don't mind?"

"If I minded, I would not have invited you to look."

Well, true enough. She almost asked him why he couldn't simply conjure some clothing for her, the way he'd done for himself, but decided it was better to leave the topic alone. Did a djinn even know anything about women's undergarments, bras and panties and all that? Attempting to explain all that to him would be mortifying.

So she murmured a thank-you and went on into the master bedroom, which was quite large, with an en suite bathroom and a little sitting area near the dormer window. The furniture here was also simple, probably to showcase more of those colorful abstract paintings, which hung on every wall.

Jillian went to the dresser and began to carefully go through the top drawer. Here she found tank tops and yoga pants and sweats, all of which would be helpful for sleeping. Well, maybe not the sweats; the weather was far too warm for that. She pulled out a few of each and began to make a pile on top of the dresser, uncomfortably aware of Aldair watching her the entire time.

The drawer next to that contained underwear. Not all that appealing to take someone else's undergarments, but still better than wearing what she had on for lord knows how many more days. But lo and behold—there was a pack of cotton underwear, still unopened. A size bigger than what she normally wore, but she'd take it. A bra with the tags still attached—her cup size, but a larger band size. Still, if she put it on the smallest hook, it should work.

Then a pair of jeans and a T-shirt, again bigger than what she wore, but at least they were clean. They'd keep her going until she could go raid some of the little town's boutiques. She remembered there actually had been several places in Madrid that sold women's clothing, although she hadn't done anything more than look in the windows when she and Jack visited here. Boutique clothing really hadn't been in their budget; back before the Dying, she'd shopped at places like Ross and Marshall's and T.J. Maxx. And then she realized she was distracting herself with those thoughts, because that way she didn't have to think about the djinn who stood a few feet away and watched her with hard blue eyes.

She made a neat pile of everything she'd found and then picked it up. "Thank you," she told Aldair, who had waited in the middle of the room while she went through the dresser. "This should be enough for now."

"Good." He didn't say anything other than that, but the half-amused expression he wore irritated her for some reason. Did he think she enjoyed having him watch her pick out her new underwear?

"I'll just go to sleep now," she said stiffly, and went back out to the hallway and on into her room. After she set her plunder on the bed, she closed the door, wondering as she did so whether he would protest.

But he didn't. From the room down the corridor, she heard only silence.

Even so, she wondered whether she'd be able to fall asleep at all, knowing he was just a few yards away.

# CHAPTER FOUR

THE WOMAN DID NOT VENTURE FORTH FROM HER room after that. Whether she slept or not, he couldn't know for sure, since his abilities did not include the power to see through walls, or doors.

All the same, he did not wish to go too far from this house, just in case she might make an attempt to leave while he thought she was asleep. He could not risk her getting away and going to Santa Fe. She would be sure to tell the djinn there of his presence in Madrid, and then no doubt that do-gooder Zahrias al-Harith would inform the elders. They would send him back to the outer circles without a second thought; Aldair was certain of that.

So instead he took the time to become more familiar with this place that would be his shelter—and Jillian's— for the foreseeable future. It would do him no good to attempt to locate a refuge farther away from Santa Fe, as he would only run the risk of encountering more of his kind. At least here he knew where his enemies were. He could not say the same thing for the rest of the world.

He'd already cleared the refrigerator of any spoiled food, and he did the same with the items he found in the kitchen pantry. Normally, he would have required more of a meal than the bread and cheese he'd shared with Jillian, but it had been so long since he'd eaten anything fit for djinn consumption that the meager repast was quite enough to satisfy his hunger. They would need more, of course, although he had no worries on that count, for he knew he could summon what they needed directly from the stores in Santa Fe. No one would notice those items missing, he guessed. At least not for a while.

By then full dark had fallen, but the absence of light was no real impediment. Djinn eyes were sharper than human eyes, and could see well enough even in total darkness. Anyway, a large yellow moon had begun to rise in the east, and its light helped to illuminate his way.

The house did not have a cellar, but it did possess several outbuildings in addition to the garage, which still contained a largish vehicle—a truck with a shell, he thought. One shed held gardening equipment, and indeed, he saw the remains of what had probably once been a flourishing vegetable garden off to one side of the property. Unfortunate that it had not survived, and Aldair knew he would probably have little luck coaxing it back to life. That was the province of the earth elementals, who could create an oasis from a dry desert.

Or at least they could here on Earth, a world suited for sustaining life. Very little grew on the plane where they had been exiled, save those specimens that were carefully nurtured in protected courtyards and atriums.

The other shed contained only a jumble of discarded machinery and household items. Odd, since the interior of the house itself was so spare and neat. But perhaps the owner of the home had managed to keep it tidy by relegating any unwanted bits and pieces to this cluttered little storehouse.

He did not find anything of any particular value, though, and so he went back inside. The air in the house felt stuffy after the evening breezes outdoors. While the day had been warm verging on hot, with the sun gone behind the hills to the west, the atmosphere outside had cooled rapidly, even as the house trapped its heat indoors.

Well, he could do something about that. Turning on the cooling system might tax the solar-supplied energy, but he would supplement it with a boost of his own. It would be worth the expenditure, to sleep comfortably after so many tortured days and nights in the outer circles, where his only pillow had been a lump of molded sand.

Cool air began to blow from the vents, and he nodded in satisfaction. Much better. While he was forced to admit to himself that he was still in exile, this house provided a far more pleasant situation than the one he had just escaped. He would do well enough here for a while until he could think of a way to regain his true freedom, the freedom to leave this place and make his own home in the world...and take his revenge on Jasreel.

For he knew that whatever else happened, he would never be a prisoner again.

Jillian opened her eyes, unsure as to why she should have awakened. Yes, it had taken her longer than usual to fall asleep, partly because of the thought of Aldair being in such close proximity, and partly because she was sleeping in a strange place, but normally that sort of thing didn't faze her, even with a possibly hostile djinn across the hall, asleep in his own bed. That is, she assumed he must be sleeping. If djinn didn't sleep, then Aldair would have had no reason to claim a bedroom as his own.

Cool air moved over her face, and she realized that must be what had awoken her. The room had been stuffy and warm when she went to sleep, despite the wide-open window. However, she'd been so tired that even the heat hadn't been enough to keep her from eventually passing out, her body craving the rest it so desperately needed. There wasn't a clock in the bedroom, so she didn't have any idea how long she'd been asleep. At some point, though, the air conditioning had come on.

She doubted it had magically turned on by itself. Aldair must have activated the system. Did djinn have poor heat tolerance? Probably not all of them, since some, she knew, were fire elementals. Aldair hadn't specifically said what his talent was, but, judging by the way he'd lifted her into the air and flown her here, he must be an air elemental.

Well, whatever the reason, she could only thank him for turning on the A/C. Already the dark room around her felt much more comfortable. She rolled over and stared into the darkness, which wasn't quite as dark as she'd expected, not with that pale silvery moonlight flowing in past the sheer curtains at the window.

She knew she should go back to sleep. Her head ached slightly, a clear signal that however long she'd been lost in slumber, it certainly hadn't been long enough. Yes, the situation was beyond weird, to be trapped in this house on the outskirts of Madrid with a djinn who might or might not be some kind of hardened criminal, and yet she told herself that only meant she should get as much rest as possible now, just in case the opportunity presented itself to get away.

*And get back to what, exactly?* she thought as she rolled onto her other side and hoped maybe she'd be more comfortable that way. *Who is even going to miss you?*

Well, that wasn't entirely fair. She'd had a few acquaintances in Los Alamos, but she didn't know if any of those relationships were intimate enough that the people in question would truly mourn her absence. Her own fault, because the hurt from Jack's death had translated into her not wanting to get too close to anyone else, not even as a friend. When you kept people at arm's length, you didn't have the right to expect them to miss you when you were gone.

What she'd had with Jack...it was special. Sure, everyone always thought that about their relationships, but deep down she'd known how lucky she was, had known the way she and Jack had clicked from the moment they met that there would never be anyone else for her. Even the silly way they'd joked about their names, Jack and Jillian. An outsider probably would have thought their lives pretty ordinary, the high school biology teacher and the office assistant at the real estate firm, but they'd been happy. It had been enough.

She'd thought it would always be enough, that nothing could ever separate her from the only man she'd ever really loved.

Right then the ache inside was almost unbearable. More than once, she'd thought if God was really merciful, then He would have taken her along with Jack. At least then they would have died together.

But then, how could God be merciful when He let the djinn do this to humanity? He'd stepped aside and let a bunch of vengeful elementals hit the reset button. A latter-day flood, she supposed, only much cleaner. A few billion piles of dust, and it was time to start over.

Jillian did what she could to shove those thoughts to the back of her mind. They'd already played in her head over and over again, and brooding over what had happened and could never change wasn't going to improve her current situation. She needed to save her strength and then do what she could to get away, get back to Los Alamos. Aldair certainly didn't need her here; she'd already done the one thing he needed most—getting him back here on Earth. After that, he could go it alone.

At last her eyes shut, and she fell into an uneasy slumber.

The muffled cries and whimpers had no context, waking him as they did from deep sleep. He pushed himself upright. His surroundings were unfamiliar, but he knew where he was—a human-built house in this strange little town called Madrid. And when he sent his senses ranging out into the night, he could tell he was the only djinn within many leagues. No humans, either, except the one who slept across the hall from him.

Which, he realized, was where those noises were coming from.

He pushed back the covers and stood, then wondered if he should let it alone. It sounded as if the human woman was having a bad dream. Surely it would end sooner or later, and then she would subside.

In the meantime, though, she would keep him from sleeping, and he would not tolerate that.

Her door was shut, but that mattered little. He would not let courtesy prevent him from going inside.

She thrashed on the pillow, her eyes tightly shut. In the moonlight, he saw the glitter of tears on her cheeks. Murmurs of "no" and little hiccuping cries escaped her lips, but he could tell she truly was asleep, that she had no idea how much noise she was making.

"Jillian," he said sternly, hoping the sound of her name would be enough to rouse her, but she gave no sign that she had heard him.

Biting back a sigh of frustration, he moved closer to the bed. Although the room was now cool enough, thanks to the air conditioning, she had pushed back the covers, was now exposed against the pale sheets.

It was easy enough to see that she had taken off the constricting undergarment human women wore to support their breasts. They now pushed against the thin knitted fabric of the top she wore, dark in places with splotches of perspiration. Again he experienced a sudden unwanted and unexpected tightening of the groin, a burst of sudden need. Not for her in particular, but for any female. It had been far, far too long since he had experienced that kind of exquisite release.

He pushed the desire away, burying it for now. When he had cleared his name and could think of himself as truly free, then he would find a djinn woman to be with. Certainly he could do better than this human female, however superficially attractive she might be.

"Jillian," he said again.

She was crying outright now, little hitching sobs even as she gasped with terror at a threat only she could see. Wherever she was, it must be far, far away from the sound of his voice.

Since it seemed obvious enough to him that merely speaking to her was having no effect, he went over to the bed and touched her arm, shook her. "Jillian, you must wake up. You are having a bad dream."

She startled then, eyes flying open, pale in the darkness, even as she pushed herself up to a sitting position. "Jack—what?"

"No," Aldair said, thinking that he was being remarkably patient, "I am not Jack. You are safe, here in Madrid. Do you remember?"

For a long moment she said nothing, only stared at him as if she had never seen him before. Then she let out another of those scratchy-sounding sobs and bent over, her entire body shaking, her hands pressed against her face. Before he really even realized what he was doing, he sat down on the bed, put his arms around her, and pulled her close. He stroked her hair, thinking the caress might comfort her. At the same time, he had to do what he could to ignore the sensation of her full breasts pushed against his bare torso. The fabric of the top she wore was so very, very thin....

Then she pulled in a breath, even as she drew away from him, her eyes still wide. "I am so sorry," she said, her voice hoarse. "I didn't—I forgot where I was."

"Apparently," he replied dryly. He needed the sarcasm, needed it to prevent his body from reacting to hers. One part of him wanted nothing more than to push her down on the bed so he might take her then and there, but he forced himself to stay calm and cold. The last thing he wanted was to have a human woman make him so completely lose control. "What was it, anyway?"

She had backed up against the pillows, thus putting as much distance between them as possible without her actually getting up off the bed. "Nothing. A nightmare."

"I gathered that. Perhaps it would help if you told me?"

A shake of the head. "No, that's—it's nothing. I have them sometimes. It's probably just from sleeping in a strange bed. That's all."

From the way her voice shook, Aldair didn't think it was nothing, but he wouldn't bother to press the issue. She was a stranger, and her fears and night terrors meant very little to him...except when they disturbed his sleep.

"Very well," he said as he got to his feet. "Perhaps it would help if you told yourself you are safe here."

"Am I?" Still with that little tremor in her tone.

"Of course," he said curtly, glad that mortals could not read minds, that she could know nothing of the desire which had coursed through him only a few seconds earlier. He went to the door and paused there for a second before saying, "Why wouldn't you be?"

And then he shut the door firmly so she would not have the opportunity to reply.

God. Oh, God.

How could she have lost it like that in front of that hard-faced djinn?

What made it worse were those blissful few seconds that had passed when he held her but she hadn't recalled who he was, had only felt the comfort of a man's strong arms around her. It had been so good to be held like that...before she realized it was Aldair who was doing the holding.

The nightmare was always the same. She'd been having it ever since she got to Los Alamos, about a week after the Dying had ensured that the haven in the Jemez Mountains would be the only refuge for humans left in the region, possibly in the entire world. Before then, on the frightening trek from Albuquerque with a few survivors she had met, she'd been too terrified to let herself relax deeply into sleep. After that, though, once she'd been given her house and had been assured that the djinn could not touch anyone living in the mountain town, she'd relaxed enough that the demons of her subconscious could let loose.

She was back in Albuquerque, running through the ruins of the city where she'd been born and where she'd spent her entire life. Crazy, too, because in reality, the djinn hadn't destroyed the city itself, only the people who lived there. But in her dream the place looked like some hellscape out of a post-apocalyptic vision, buildings shattered, skies gray and lowering. And she ran through those ruins because she'd caught a glimpse of Jack, had discovered that he wasn't dead, that he must be Immune, just as she was. For what felt like hours she chased after him, but he always stayed far enough ahead that she could barely see him, only caught a flash of his sandy hair and the blue polo shirt and khakis he'd been wearing when he drove off for work that warm early autumn morning.

At last, though, she got close enough to call out his name. Then he paused and turned toward her, wearing the easy, friendly smile she loved so much. And she went to him so she could hold him, but he dissolved into dust at her touch, flying apart into millions of particles that fell all around her, choking her, making her fall to her knees as she coughed out her life, the way so many others had....

Sometimes she could wake herself up before she got to that point. Sometimes, but not always. Just like tonight. She'd probably been too tired, too overwhelmed.

And then Aldair had come in. Just the realization that he'd seen her sobbing and terrified was bad enough, but to let him hold her, to be pressed up against his bare chest while she was wearing nothing except that skimpy tank top....

She didn't know if she'd be able to face him in the morning.

The worst part, though, the one she really didn't want to acknowledge to herself but knew she must, was that she'd *enjoyed* it. Not consciously, true, but... it went beyond merely the reassurance of having a presence there, someone to hold her and tell her it was only a dream.

No, a thrill had gone through her body...a sexual thrill. Just for a second, until she came to her senses, but in that second she'd felt her nipples start to go hard, a warm, familiar ache between her legs. She'd wanted him, before her higher functions kicked in and told her that was about a thousand kinds of wrong.

Had he been able to tell? She prayed not, because that would make everything so much more awkward. Bad enough that she'd acted like such a terrified idiot in front of him. But if he'd sensed her arousal, well, he must be thinking she was a weak human, unable to keep herself from lusting after a djinn even in the aftermath of a horrible nightmare.

She didn't want him. Of course not. All that had been was a physical reaction, one easily explained away. It had been a very long time for her. No one since Jack. She hadn't wanted anyone, because no one she'd met had been able to measure up to him. Or at least measure up to how she remembered him.

These days, she really wasn't sure which was the real truth anymore. And that made it even worse, because she'd begun to wonder how accurate her memories of Jack really were, whether she'd started to idealize those recollections as they began to fade more and more with the passage of time.

Did this happen to everyone? She didn't know, because the survivors at Los Alamos didn't want to talk about what they'd lost. They only wanted to look forward to the future. That made sense, perhaps was the wiser course, and yet Jillian didn't know how to let go.

How could she, when she'd had the love of her life and lost him?

## CHAPTER FIVE

JILLIAN WAS TAKING A VERY LONG TIME TO COME downstairs this morning. Aldair didn't find her behavior all that unusual, however. After the events of the night before, she was probably embarrassed to be around him. He knew he would be, if their positions had been reversed. Not that he would have ever allowed himself such a loss of control. A nightmare was a silly thing, compared to what he had endured in the outer circles.

At any rate, she lingered upstairs for a good deal of time after he heard the water in the bathroom shut off. They did seem to have a good supply here, thanks to the well, and so that was one less thing to worry about. He himself had also showered, washing away the dirt and dust of his exile. Djinn tended to favor baths, long, luxurious affairs with scented oils and other comforts, but he had to admit there was also something quite satisfying about the human invention of the hot shower.

As was the tradition of morning coffee, something the djinn had adopted millennia ago. He found a stash of it in the pantry, in a large airtight canister, so it had not gone too stale. And besides the pre-ground coffee, he had also located several bags of whole beans and a grinder. It would be a long time before they had to go in search of a supply to supplement what they had here, or he had to take what he needed from the stores in Santa Fe.

Of course, speculating on how long the coffee would last led his thoughts to precisely how long he intended to stay here. Not forever, no, he did not think he could stomach that. But djinn could be patient—they must, in lives measured in centuries and even millennia, instead of the short decades allotted to mortals—and so he thought it would be some time before he felt compelled to venture forth from this sanctuary. Certainly enough of a span for the hue and cry to die down.

If there even was a hue and cry. He had never detected any kind of surveillance while he was trapped in the outer circles, so he had no idea whether the elders even knew that he had managed the impossible by escaping from his exile. They saw a great deal, but he tried to reassure himself that they certainly did not see everything.

So he thought he should be safe enough here for the interim. Or rather, he hoped he would be. Since he had also never encountered any of Khalim's group during his time in the djinn world's equivalent of a prison, he also guessed there was no one who could report him missing. All he had to do was live quietly here for a time, and then move out to the greater world when a sufficient span had passed.

The slight creak of the stairs told him that Jillian had finally deigned to come down to the kitchen. He had just finished pouring a cup of coffee for himself from the French press he'd found in the cupboard when she appeared in the doorway, looking diffident.

"Is that really coffee?" she asked, her voice a little too studiedly casual.

"Yes," he said, careful to keep his own tone neutral. "Would you like some?"

"Yes, please."

She came farther into the kitchen and waited a few feet away while he fetched another mug and filled it as well.

"I drink it black," he said. "There is sugar, but if you wish for cream, I will have to summon it."

"No," she said hurriedly. "Black is fine. I got used to drinking it that way in college."

She took the mug from him and wrapped both her hands around it, then blew on the liquid inside. Aldair took that opportunity to study her more closely. She'd put on some of the clothes she'd found in the master bedroom the day before; they didn't fit her very well, being rather large, and he hoped she would be able to locate something else here in the little town, something that wouldn't do so much to obscure her form. Even if he had no intention of doing anything about it, he would prefer to see her looking like a real woman, not someone made sexless by baggy garments.

No, he realized even the unflattering clothing was not enough to render her sexless. Not with that fall of warm brown hair, or those full lips, pursed now as she blew once again on her coffee. She must have washed her hair, because it still looked damp, although it had already begun to dry into long, loose waves. He had thought they must have come from some artifice, created by one of the innumerable devices mortal women used to alter the texture of their hair, but he realized those waves must be natural. And while it did not seem as if she wore any cosmetics, he saw she had no need of any, not with those long lashes, and the smooth creaminess of her complexion.

Then he realized he was staring, and drank some of his own coffee. No need for him to wait for it to cool down, since his kind could endure heat and cold far better than humans.

"I thought we could explore the town today," he said. "I want to see what is here, what we can take for our own use."

Something in her expression altered, although he could not tell exactly what it was. Perhaps she was merely relieved that he had not brought up the embarrassing events of the night before.

"That's a good idea," she said. "I don't know how much we'll find, but there's got be some usable stuff in the shops and the restaurants. Some of those boutiques probably have clothes that will fit me."

"Good," he said.

He'd thought he had kept any kind of inflection out of his voice, but he couldn't miss seeing the way her eyebrows lifted slightly at his remark. "What, the djinn fashion police don't approve of baggy jeans?"

Refusing to be baited, he replied, "We believe clothing can be both functional and beautiful. Those jeans are anything but beautiful."

She actually chuckled. "No, I guess not."

They fell into a small silence after that exchange, but Aldair did not find the lack of conversation awkward. Rather, he was relieved that she did not attempt to continue their discussion. Jillian sipped her coffee, and he drank some of his as well. He had pushed aside the curtains at the kitchen window and so was able to see the yard beyond—overgrown, but lovely in its way, with cheerful yellow sunflowers waving in the morning breeze, and other flowers he didn't recognize—tall spikes of orange blooms, and low, spreading carpets of pale purple—adding to the beauty of the day.

It had been a very long time since he'd seen a land-scape he could consider remotely beautiful.

When Jillian spoke next, she did sound rather hesitant. "So...do djinn eat breakfast?"

"Of course we do. But I like to have my coffee first. Are you hungry?"

She nodded.

"There are chickens here. They seem to have survived well on their own, and have multiplied. So we can have eggs. There are components to make bread and such. I will assemble them shortly."

"Just like that."

He tilted his head at her. "Just like what?"

"You make it sound so easy."

"For a djinn, it is. I will admit that there are some among us who find it amusing to make their food as you humans do, without the help of magic. But since we have these powers, I see no reason why I should not use them."

"No, I suppose not." Then she gave a rueful smile. "Just as well, I guess. I was never very good at cooking. Jack—well, let's just say I was usually the one doing the washing up, not the meal prep."

"You will not have to do that here," he pointed out. "I can use my powers to take care of cleaning up afterward."

"Handy."

Was she being sarcastic? He shot her a sideways glance, but her expression seemed almost bland, as if she wanted to make sure he couldn't see much of what she was thinking. Well, perhaps she was doing her best to guard herself after her breakdown of the night before.

He drained the last of the coffee in his mug, then set it down on the countertop. "Let me see about that breakfast."

In a way, the whole situation was utterly bizarre. How could she have sat there at the dining room table with him, eating scrambled eggs and buttered biscuits—all of it the lightest and fluffiest and tastiest she'd ever had—and acted as if there was nothing strange about sharing a meal with a djinn?

Especially a djinn who had held her the night before as she sobbed into his arms.

Well, he seemed inclined to pretend that whole incident had never happened, and she was all too happy to follow his lead. They hadn't spoken much, but had both eaten with good appetite. Not that surprising, since their small meal of bread and cheese at dinner wasn't exactly the sort of thing that had a lot of staying power. And at the end, he'd made a small waving motion with one hand, and their dirty plates immediately gleamed as clean as if they'd just been sent through the world's most state-of-the-art dishwasher, right before they all vanished back into their cupboards.

As she'd said, handy.

Now they were venturing out into the town, the air warm and friendly as it touched her still-damp hair, ensuring that it would finish drying soon enough. By late afternoon, temperatures would probably be downright hot, but Jillian resolved to enjoy the morning's mildness while she could.

From off in the distance, she heard the clucking of chickens. It sounded as if a whole flock of them had congregated somewhere behind one of the buildings. So Aldair hadn't been making that part up. She wondered how the chickens had survived all this time, since she knew coyotes roamed these hills.

Something else was roaming the streets of Madrid as well. They hadn't gone more than a hundred feet or so before a smallish black and white dog came bounding up to them, tail wagging, ears flying, mouth open in a happy doggy smile. Astonished, Jillian bent down to scratch the dog behind the ears, and he promptly nudged her knee so she wouldn't stop.

Aldair paused and looked back at her. "It seems you have found a friend."

"I guess so." She fondled the dog's ears, feeling his fur soft against her fingertips. Amazing that he was in such good shape—he didn't appear to be hungry, or dirty or mangy. Maybe regular soakings from the late-summer monsoon storms had helped to keep him clean. "I'm just surprised he managed to survive here for so long. A dog this size, you'd think the coyotes would have gotten him."

Her heart twinged at that thought. What had happened to all the cats and dogs and other pets when all their masters perished during the Heat? In Los Alamos, the residents had taken in the abandoned animals, but there was no one here in Madrid to have done the same thing. Miles had once estimated that approximately .002% of the world's population had survived the Dying, which meant that, statistically, Madrid was just too small for any of its residents to have lived. The animals here would have been on their own.

"We made sure they would be safe," Aldair told her, and she looked up from the dog to meet the djinn's hard blue eyes.

"What do you mean?"

"I mean that the animals were innocent. They have been provided for. I am not saying that some haven't perished from old age or disease or accident in the time since the Dying, but we have made sure that they would continue to flourish, just as they did when they had human masters."

Jillian tried her best to wrap her mind around that idea. So the djinn thought nothing of wiping out nearly all of mankind in one fell swoop, but they had done what they could to protect the animals left behind? In some ways, the two behaviors seemed completely contradictory, but then, from what she'd heard, djinn didn't always act the way one might think they should. She supposed she should be glad they could show that much mercy at least.

And when the Heat struck, she and Jack had still been mourning the loss of their little dog Alfie, a chihuahua-mix rescue who'd died only a few months earlier. At the time, Jillian hadn't known whether it was better that she didn't have to worry about Alfie's fate after the Dying, or whether it might have helped to have a dog to focus on. She'd missed him, but she hadn't quite come to the point in her life in Los Alamos where she was ready to take on a new dog.

Well, it looked like a dog had found her, for better or worse.

"Do you mind?" she asked Aldair. "I mean, it looks like he's glommed on to me. Is it all right if he sticks around?"

"I don't mind if he stays with you," he said, then added, to her surprise, "I like dogs."

If asked, Jillian would have said that she didn't think Aldair seemed like a doggy person in the slightest, but she wouldn't argue. Not when it meant she could keep the dog with her. Maybe she wouldn't feel so trapped here if she had a dog to focus on. He trotted along at her side as she followed Aldair, who had resumed walking briskly toward town. Now they passed an art gallery on one side, and then a cluster of smaller shops across the street, an eclectic mix of more galleries, clothing boutiques, even a chocolate shop.

Of course, none of the chocolate would be edible anymore. Too bad, although Jillian realized Aldair could probably magic up some chocolate, if she asked nicely. Surely djinn had to like chocolate, too. How could anyone *not* like chocolate?

He paused in front of the Mine Shaft Tavern. "This was the bar, correct?"

"Bar and restaurant," she said.

"Then it could have some items we might use."

A long, sloping ramp led up into the bar. Jillian followed Aldair, and the dog followed her. She would have to come up with a name for him. He wasn't wearing a collar, so he didn't have any tags to let her know what his real name might be.

Aldair opened the door to the Mine Shaft. Inside, it was so dark that the place might as well have been inside a mine, just as its name indicated. And even though she couldn't see much of anything, Jillian detected a faint odor of decay, probably from failed refrigerators. Her nose wrinkled. She didn't much like the idea of going in there, but she also didn't want Aldair to know that the place had her spooked. Back when she'd first come to Los Alamos, she'd been assigned to one of the details that went around the town and swept away the dust of its former inhabitants and cleaned out the refrigerators and freezers of any contents that had spoiled. That hint of decay she'd detected was enough to bring back all those horrible memories.

A wave of Aldair's hand, and the lights flared on, even as the ceiling fans overhead began to turn lazily, churning at the thick air. Across the room, a jukebox came to life, playing a twangy country-western song, something Jillian didn't recognize.

As she looked around, she sort of wished the lights hadn't come on. Because she spotted four or five piles of the ominous gray dust ranged along the base of the bar, as if those victims of the Heat had decided they would rather spend their final moments here having a last drink before the deadly fever overcame them altogether.

Aldair appeared not to notice, or possibly he just didn't care. He walked over to the bar and surveyed the contents of its shelves.

"Throwing a party?" Jillian quipped, and he turned partway toward her and gave her a sour look.

"Of course not. But it is good to know what is here, even if we don't intend to use most of it."

That was for sure. She'd never been one for hard alcohol. She and Jack had mostly drunk wine, unless they went to a ballgame or something, where they'd always order beer. True, their wine consumption was mostly of the box variety, or Trader Joe's cheaper offerings, but she still had preferred it over mixed drinks.

Aldair looked over at the jukebox and waved his hand again. Abruptly, the music shut off.

"Not a country-western fan?"

He frowned. "Hardly."

Then he crossed the room and went out the door that led from the bar to the mining museum, a kitschy little space separating the bar from the restaurant itself. The dining area was small, and overflowed into an outdoor eating area on a deck.

The djinn surveyed all this with his arms crossed, his expression unsmiling. Jillian waited a few paces away, her new dog at her side. She could tell Aldair was less than thrilled with what he had found, but really, what had he been expecting? They were basically in the middle of nowhere. It wasn't like you were going to find a Zagat four-star restaurant in tiny Madrid, although The Hollar's food had been damn good.

He stopped in the middle of the deck and looked around. From here you could get a fairly decent view of the main part of the town—the only part of the town, Jillian thought, since basically Madrid consisted of this tiny stretch of Highway 14 and not much else. There were a couple of side streets, and then outlying homesteads like the one they currently occupied, but this was mostly it.

The wind caught at Aldair's longish hair, ruffling it around his face. Jillian had never met a djinn before him, so she didn't know if they tended to wear their hair long, or whether his had been cut shorter and then grown out during his time in exile. If asked, she would have said she wasn't much for long hair on men, but something about it suited him, suited the high cheek-bones and almond-shaped eyes and sensual mouth.

Really, he was kind of ridiculously good-look-ing. But then, all djinn were supposed to be, weren't they? That was why the people they'd selected as their Chosen were also extremely attractive, she supposed... they had to match.

"There are more shops down that way," she said as she came up to stand next to him. "And I think maybe a coffeehouse or something. I don't remember how many more restaurants there are besides this one and The Hollar—that's across the street—but I know there aren't many."

"The coffeehouse should have some supplies we could use," he said, still staring down the street. The wind also played with the hem of the open silk robe he wore, making the fabric shimmer like sunlight on water. Finally, he glanced down at her, and his mouth pulled into a slight frown. "And weren't you going to look for something else to wear?"

"Yes," she replied, acutely aware of how shabby she must look in contrast to his djinn-ly splendor. "Why don't you check out the coffeehouse, and I'll head over to one of those shops across the street. I think there was some kind of a boutique that might have something."

He nodded. "That should do."

Without another word, he strode across the deck and then took the steps that led down to street level. Jillian shrugged and followed suit, the dog at her heels, tail wagging the whole time.

Her recollection had been correct—there was a place called The Heavenly Boutique just a few doors down from The Hollar. When she stepped inside, Jillian couldn't see any of that terrible dust, and she let out a sigh of relief. In fact, it still smelled good in there, probably because of the open baskets of potpourri that sat on the antique dressers being used as display items. The potpourri was pretty much used up by this point, but she could tell it had done its work for as long as possible.

A brief look around told her the clothing here was probably more what Aldair would have liked—romantic tops, flowing skirts, lots of pretty scarves. And a lot of high-end soaps and body lotions, that sort of thing. She'd have to pick and choose, since there was a limit to how much she could carry. No, none of these clothes were exactly practical, but she doubted she would be doing much manual labor while she was here in Madrid, either.

*But what about if you have a chance to make a break for it?* she asked herself as she took a few items into one of the dressing rooms. *Are you going to walk twenty-five miles in wedge sandals and a gypsy skirt?*

Well, probably not. But she had the jeans and T-shirts she'd gotten out of the master bedroom back at the house, and there were the clothes she'd been wearing when the lab accident had turned her world upside down. There must be a laundry room at the house; she'd just run a load when it seemed appropriate.

In the meantime, there was something almost decadent about being able to choose the things she liked here without having to look at the price tag and worry how she'd ever be able to afford it. The world didn't work that way anymore. Maybe some people would have called this sort of casual appropriation looting, but really, how could it be looting when you weren't actually taking it from anyone? At least now these beautiful things would get a chance to be enjoyed.

She decided on a long, flowing skirt in a shade of dark teal, accented with silver sequins, and to go with it a lacy white camisole top. The wedges she'd first spotted probably weren't the most practical thing to wear around here, because of the uneven ground and complete lack of sidewalks in Madrid, and so instead she went with a pair of flat natural-colored leather sandals with silver beadwork. Hanging from one of the open wardrobes was a large beaded purse, and she pulled that down so she could load it up with some of the choicer-looking soaps and lotions, along with a few more changes of clothing.

That seemed to be enough for now. Jillian emerged onto the porch, and the dog got up from where he'd been waiting there, tail wagging. She would never know who his owners had been or where exactly he'd come from, but clearly he'd been well trained.

"What would you like for a name?" she asked him. His head cocked to one side, and one ear went straight up while the other remained flopped over. His left eye had a large black spot surrounding it, making him look as if he was wearing an eye patch. Well, that would work. He definitely did have patches all over. "Does Patches sound good to you?"

He let out a short, sharp bark, and even got up on his hind legs and danced around, the feathers on his tail flying. One paw almost caught on her sequined skirt, and she took hold of it before it could do any damage.

"Be careful," she warned him, but clearly he wasn't too put off by her tone. His tail wagged ferociously, and he shared another of those happy doggy smiles with her. Looking at his obvious enthusiasm, she wondered if the name she'd chosen for him was actually the one that had been his all along. It was kind of obvious after all, considering his coloring. She couldn't quite figure out what he might be, though. Part terrier, definitely, but with a few other things mixed in. Possibly Papillon, too, because of those lopsided ears. Definitely one-hundred-percent good old American mutt, and there was nothing wrong with that.

She looked down the street and saw Aldair approaching. Unlike her, he was empty-handed, and she wondered if his trip to the coffeehouse had been less than fruitful. When he drew near, she asked, "Were they out of coffee?"

"Not at all," he replied. For the barest second, his gaze moved over her, clearly taking in her new and improved appearance, but he didn't comment on it. Instead, he went on, "I found a number of useful things, but I sent them on ahead. Why carry them back uphill if there is no need to?"

"Of course." Yes, that would be useful. Locate the items you need, and send them instantaneously to your house. No loading and unloading, no schlepping shopping carts around.

"As I can do for you," he added.

And the heavy purse she'd been carrying was suddenly gone, the weight of it disappearing from her shoulder. She gasped, then told herself to relax. He had told her what he intended to do, even though it had happened much more quickly than she'd expected.

"Um...thanks."

"It is not a problem. But there are more places to explore while we're here. Shall we?"

She nodded, and followed him down the street to the mercantile building, which probably would have some things they could use. As she walked, though, she had to wonder what his plans were. Right now he was acting like he wanted to stock up for the winter.

And winter was still a long ways off....

## CHAPTER SIX

He was doing his best not to be distracted by her. Difficult, after she'd made such a transformation as the one he'd just witnessed. When he approached her as she waited outside the boutique, he had to keep his eyes from widening in appreciation. The clothing she'd selected wasn't particularly snug or revealing, but it fit her well, hinting at the curves beneath. Her bare arms were slender, with just a suggestion of the toned muscles under her lightly tanned skin. And then there were her feet, nearly bare in the beaded sandals she wore. He hadn't been expecting the dark pink polish on her toes, since her fingernails were bare and cut fairly short.

Something about that polish, and the delicate ankles and toes the skirt revealed, made him want to stare. Again he had to fight back a surge of desire, telling himself he had no time for such things, especially not with a mortal woman.

Luckily, he had other matters to distract himself with, such as going through the mercantile building so he could create another pile of possibly useful items to be sent back to the house. All of the food stocked in the store had long since rotted, and he certainly had no need of any of the bottled sugary drinks in the now-dark refrigerated case, even if they were still viable. But he collected bags of nuts that might still be good, while Jillian gathered a group of pillar candles from the display on a table placed up against one wall.

"We have no need of those," he pointed out. "The house has solar power, and even if that should fail, I can keep the lights going."

"True," she replied, "but if the power does fail and it's really hot, I'd rather you used that djinn energy to keep the air conditioning on. That's where candles could be useful."

He thought that prospect rather unlikely, but he didn't argue. If she wished to have a batch of useless candles cluttering up the place, then so be it.

At length they had gleaned everything that looked remotely useful, and he sent it all on to the homestead as well. He glanced down at the pretty but flimsy sandals she wore and asked, "Would you prefer to have me fly you back to the house?"

Her eyes widened in surprise, but then she shook her head. "No, I'm fine walking. Besides, I've got Patches to worry about. I doubt he'd enjoy flying through the air, fifty feet above the ground."

The dog, of course. Aldair had almost forgotten about him, because he'd been waiting patiently on the porch while they searched the mercantile. A well-behaved animal, it seemed, and so he wouldn't argue the point. "No, I suppose the dog would not enjoy that very much." He paused and sent Jillian a quizzical look. "Patches?"

"Well, I had to name him something, and it seemed to fit. And you know, we've scrounged all this stuff, but I didn't see any dog food. I might have to start looking in the other abandoned houses."

"No need for that. I can summon that as well if necessary. It helps to have certain items on hand, because that way I don't have to expend as much energy to get them. But it would be easier for me to bring the dog food here rather than have you go on a house-to-house search looking for it."

She gave a dubious nod, as if she was still trying to work out the mechanics of his djinn powers, and what they were and weren't capable of. But she didn't argue the point, which was the important thing. Aldair did not want to have to continually explain himself to her.

They headed back toward the house, Patches running on ahead. It seemed clear enough that the dog was thrilled to have found new masters. Where the rest of the town's canines had gone, Aldair didn't know. Perhaps they were still out foraging in the hills, happy to be free now that they had the run of the place, could go from house to house with impunity. For some reason, though, this dog had chosen to come to them, and he wouldn't argue the matter.

After all, if Jillian had a dog to look after, then perhaps she would be less inclined to push him about returning to Los Alamos.

The walk back to the house was uphill the whole way. Aldair gave Jillian a sidelong look, but she appeared to be managing well enough, even in those flimsy sandals she had chosen. Not that he minded the footwear; it was good to see her looking like a female.

*Or perhaps not,* he thought as she ranged a little ahead, smiling as Patches circled back to her and wagged his tail once again. *Because having a beautiful woman around all the time may prove to be difficult.*

Perhaps. In the meantime, he found he enjoyed watching her, seeing the way her cloudy gray eyes lit up as she stopped and bent to scratch the dog's ears, noting how the sunlight caught ripples of gold and warm copper in her long brown hair. Some weight seemed to lift from her shoulders as she played with the dog, and Aldair could not help but be glad of that. He had enough burdens of his own to carry; he did not wish to suffer hers as well.

Putting away their haul didn't take much time, because Aldair whisked everything into its respective cupboards and drawers before Jillian could barely blink an eye. However, he hadn't touched the items she'd procured for herself, and so she took some time hanging up the lovely new garments she'd found, arranging them by color and type, although even that didn't take too long, either. It wasn't as if she'd cleaned out the whole store, only selected items for three or four days' worth of wearings. She could always go back tomorrow for more, if she felt so inclined.

Maybe that wasn't such a good idea. She should be figuring out a way to persuade Aldair to let her go, not stocking up on her wardrobe...as fun and frivolous as that might be. Her gratitude must always go to the people of Los Alamos for their efforts in making the town a safe and viable community, but she had to admit that day-to-day life there ranked fairly low on the frivolity scale.

From the open window—because it hadn't yet warmed up enough to warrant turning on the air— she heard a dog's excited, happy bark. Startled by the sound, Jillian placed the scarf she had been holding in one of the dresser drawers, then went to the window and looked outside. Down in what had been the yard but was now mainly a scrubby collection of weeds, interspersed with late-summer wildflowers, she caught the incongruous sight of Aldair apparently playing ball with Patches. Aldair held a neon-green tennis ball in one hand and hurled it so the dog would have to go bounding after it. Obviously thrilled by this game, Patches tore after the ball and then trotted back, his tail with its modest black and white feathers flying like a banner in the breeze.

Now, where in the world would a djinn have learned to play tennis ball with a dog? True, Aldair had admitted he liked dogs, but still, she didn't think she could have pictured him doing something as prosaic as throwing a ball and playing catch. He seemed far too dignified for that. But there he was, face brightened by a rare smile, as he reached down and wrestled the ball from Patches' teeth and threw it again.

Something tight and painful within her seemed to relax somewhat as she watched them. Jillian hadn't even known she was that tense until she felt herself pull in a breath of warm, sweetly scented air, letting it flood through her whole body. This was good. Yes, it seemed crazy to even admit such a thing to herself, but she couldn't remember the last time she'd witnessed anything as silly and joyful as a djinn and a dog playing ball together. Maybe she just hadn't allowed herself to. It had been easier to ignore the few bits of beauty and happiness in this new world, so she could stay shrouded in her cocoon of grief.

She descended the stairs and emerged into the kitchen, then went out the back door so she could stand in the porch in the shade. "Having fun?"

Aldair turned toward her. He'd been in full sun, and she noted a faint sheen of sweat on his forehead… and on the sculpted muscles of his chest and stomach, although she didn't dare let her gaze linger there for very long. "I thought it might be good for Patches to get used to me. He is quite energetic."

"Yes, I think he's a pretty young dog." Young enough that he'd been born wild, after the Heat had removed all the humans from the town? No, that didn't sound right. The dog seemed far too acclimated to people and their behavior. Still, she guessed he hadn't been much more than a puppy when the world changed forever. No wonder he'd attached himself to her and Aldair so quickly.

At her words, Patches came bounding up to the porch, tennis ball in his mouth. When she reached down to take it from him, he pulled away slightly, tail going a mile a minute. She couldn't help smiling, since her dog Alfie had liked to play much the same game. Not that the little chihuahua mix could manage a tennis ball, since his mouth was so small. But he'd had a special-sized ball of his own, one that he guarded fiercely…except when it came time to play fetch.

"Oh, so you want to play keep-away?" she asked with a grin.

The dog feinted backward, and she hurried after him, determined not to let him get away. Yes, maybe this would have been easier in tennis shoes, but she and Jack had played with Alfie in the depths of summer when Jillian only had on flip-flops, so it wasn't as if she couldn't manage. Although she had to admit that Alfie, with his much shorter legs, had been a lot easier to catch up with.

Aldair looked on in some amusement as she stumbled through the weeds, once or twice having to stop and rescue her skirt when it got caught on an overgrown stalk. But then Patches paused for a second to smell something interesting, and she was able to grab the ball from his jaws and throw it out onto the gravel driveway that led toward the garage. He chased after it while Jillian watched him in some triumph.

"It seems you've played this game before," Aldair remarked as he came to stand a few feet away from her.

"Yes," she said, her tone casual. At the same time, she did what she could to keep her eyes somewhat level with his. Those open robes he wore showed off way too much. She wasn't used to being around a man with that much skin exposed. That much warm, gleaming skin.... Damn it. She gulped in a breath and added, "We used to have a dog. He was a rescue, so we got him he was older. We lost him about six months before...well, before."

That revelation only elicited a nod, although Jillian thought she could see the way Aldair's jaw muscles tightened. Was it the reference to the Dying that had bothered him, or the life she'd had with her husband?

No, that was definitely flattering herself. To hide her discomfort, she turned back toward the driveway and called out, "Come here, Patches!"

The dog bounded obediently toward her, but, true to form, he dodged out of the way the second she reached for the tennis ball. Aldair chuckled.

"Perhaps I should show him that we djinn have a few tricks up our sleeve."

He curled his fingers slightly, and at once the ball came flying out of Patches' mouth and landed neatly in Aldair's palm. The dog's eyes widened, as if even he had realized that something wasn't quite kosher here.

"Isn't that cheating?"

"No," Aldair said. "I am merely using my own skills to counter his. I do not see that as cheating."

Apparently neither did Patches, whose tail was wagging so hard that his hindquarters moved along with it. Jillian thought he looked delighted at this wrinkle in the age-old game. But she also realized how hot it was standing out here, how her hair had begun to stick to the back of her neck. And she wasn't wearing any sunscreen. She was going to get fried if she stayed out in the yard for much longer.

"Well, you kids have fun," she said. "It's getting too hot for me out here. I'm going inside."

Aldair glanced up at the sky. The day had started out cloudless, but a few big puffy clouds had begun to appear, promising rain by evening. That was how things usually went during monsoon season. "We will be in shortly," he said. "I think another five minutes will ensure that Patches will take a long nap this afternoon."

"Probably," she agreed, then turned and headed back inside. The air in the kitchen still felt comfortably tepid, although not for much longer. When Aldair came in, she'd check to make sure if it was all right to turn on the air conditioning. She didn't know whether it would work properly without him there to oversee it.

From outside came another of Patches' excited barks, and Jillian shook her head. Obviously the dog didn't find anything strange about their situation, but she didn't know what she was supposed to think. For a few minutes there, life had felt fun. Normal. And oddly domestic.

She decided it was probably better not to think about that at all.

As Aldair had guessed, the dog fell asleep on the rug in the living room within minutes of coming inside. He'd stopped to swallow what looked like almost half the contents of the bowl of water Jillian had thoughtfully set out for him, nosed around the floor for a short time in case anything interesting to eat had been dropped there, and then collapsed in blissful exhaustion soon afterward.

It was good that he'd had water, but he would need food when he awakened. Aldair reached out with that sixth sense all djinn had, questing outward for something the dog could consume. As it turned out, he didn't have to look very far, since it seemed that many of the households here had dog food in their pantries, along with canned and dry goods. He summoned a large unopened bag from a ramshackle house up the canyon, then opened it and poured a measure into a bowl he fetched from the cupboard.

At the clatter of the dry food into the bowl, Patches came running, all wagging tail and excited grin. He put his head in the bowl and started crunching away, just as Jillian appeared in the doorway to the kitchen.

"So you found some."

"Yes. There is a good deal available in town. Your idea to look for dog food here was a good one, although I believe I saved you some walking in the hot sun."

"You did." Her head tilted slightly at his words, as though she was not sure why he would have shown her such solicitude. "I still don't know why we went poking through those stores if you could just bring anything we needed directly here."

"Sometimes it is good to see things for oneself," he replied. "I do not know this town. Now I know it a little better." He raised an eyebrow at her, and allowed himself to give her new ensemble a rather piercing glance. "Besides, I did not think you would wish for me to select your new garments."

A flush rose to her cheeks, one he did not think could be blamed entirely on the sun she'd been exposed to a short while earlier. "No, I suppose that's something I needed to do on my own." Appearing to gather herself, she went on, "I found out who this house belonged to."

"Indeed?" he asked, trying to sound polite. Truthfully, he could not think why that mattered. Whoever had lived here, they were long gone.

"Her name was Natalie Marquez. I guess she was a fairly well-known artist. In that room upstairs, the one that must have been her studio, I found a stack of brochures that had been printed for an upcoming gallery show. It was supposed to be on October fifth."

Jillian paused there, and wouldn't look him in the eye. For a few seconds, Aldair could not quite comprehend her sudden quiet. Then he understood the reason for her silence. The Dying had begun less than week before that. There would have been no show, for the artist and anyone who would have attended had surely perished days earlier.

And what did Jillian expect him to say? He would not offer her words of reassurance or condolence. Certainly not of apology. What had happened, happened. He could not change any of it…and indeed, he did not know if he would, even if he were suddenly given the miraculous power to go back in time and change the events that had led up to the Dying. Mankind had nearly ruined this world. Why would he wish to have all those teeming billions back, just so they could continue their work of destroying God's creation?

True, he thought as he gazed down into Jillian's lovely, troubled features, some humans were probably worth saving. Perhaps even the artist who had once lived here. But again, he could not change what the world had become.

"That would explain the art," he said, his tone as dispassionate as he could make it. "And the house, I would suppose, if she was successful. This home would have been rather costly, would it not?"

For a second, Jillian's lips pressed together, as if she was annoyed by his response but didn't want to show it. "Yes, I think so. Not that I ever priced real estate in Madrid. But still…it's large and fairly new, and sits on a lot of land and has its own well and solar power. It's certainly nothing that Jack and I—well, our place in Albuquerque was nothing like this."

Was she saying that she had been poor, back in that world before the Dying leveled everything? Now there was no such thing as rich and poor. Only djinn and human, alive or dead.

Aldair had the perverse thought that he was glad he had been able to offer her a place so much better than what her late husband had provided for her, and then told himself that was a ridiculous notion and thrust it aside.

"It is well suited for our needs," he admitted, although he would say nothing more.

But even that inoffensive statement appeared to annoy her. Once again he saw that tightening of her mouth, and her brows drew together. "And what exactly *are* our needs, Aldair? How long do you plan to stay here?"

Another unspoken question hung in the air. *How long do you plan to keep me here?*

He would not answer that, for he did not know himself. He only knew it was far too early to set her free, or for him to venture forth from this place. If he went too close to Santa Fe, the djinn there would surely detect his presence.

"For as long as is necessary," he said curtly. Because her lips parted slightly, he knew she wasn't about to let it go, was going to ask another of her infernal questions.

Annoyed by her persistence, he blinked himself away to the place she had called the Mine Shaft before she could ask any further questions.

He might have been a djinn, but in that moment he was experiencing an all-too-human-urge to have a drink.

## CHAPTER SEVEN

Jillian stared at the space Aldair had just occupied, then remembered to close her mouth. Typical. Ask a question he doesn't want to answer, and off he goes. She'd dated a few guys like that in college before she met Jack. They'd annoyed her back then, and Aldair was annoying the crap out of her now. Some things never changed.

Her irritation only increased as she realized it was beginning to be truly hot in the house. Did she dare turn on the A/C? Probably not.

Instead, she went to the refrigerator and got out the pitcher of cold water and poured herself a glass. Patches, who had finished his kibble, watched her with some interest but then wandered back to the living room when he realized she wasn't going to produce anything except water.

Jillian realized it was probably around lunchtime, but her appetite seemed to have disappeared. Just as well, since she didn't know how much of what they had would be edible without having Aldair around to fix it. Or conjure it. Or whatever the hell it was that he did.

Glass of water in hand, she went to the living room window and looked out. The porch was still deceptively shady, since the sun now hung almost directly overhead, but she knew it would be much cooler in here, even with only the ceiling fans going. Outside, everything seemed dead quiet, not even a bird in sight, the only sign of life the fluttering of the leaves in the trees that surrounded the house.

She was alone. Did she dare leave?

Problem was, she didn't know where Aldair had gone. He could just be out in the shed, poking around, or he could have blinked himself away to the next town over, tiny Cerrillos, site of a former turquoise mine. She doubted he would have gone any farther than that, not with his obvious reluctance to get close to Santa Fe.

But if he was still here in Madrid somewhere, then it was far too likely that he'd see her trying to make her way out of town. There was only one road in and out. Maybe an ambitious hiker could have headed up and over the hills that ringed Madrid, but Jillian had no real experience when it came to that sort of thing.

Beyond the town lay miles and miles of open country. Most likely, she'd wander there, hopelessly lost, until Aldair caught up with her...or the coyotes did.

Neither prospect sounded very appealing. An angry djinn might be just as frightening—if not more—as a pack of hungry coyotes.

So she stepped away from the window and sat down on the couch. Patches, who had been sleeping only a few feet away, opened one eye and then shut it again when he saw that she didn't plan to do anything more interesting than sit on the sofa.

At least in here there was the ceiling fan to keep things from getting too uncomfortable, and the porch and the trees just beyond it also helped to shield some of the room from the late August glare. If they were lucky, the few clouds hanging around the area would continue to gather, and storms would develop to help tone down the heat of the day.

Some time passed. Jillian wasn't sure how long, since the clock sitting on the mantel had long since wound down. It was too dim in there to read, but she'd just about decided she would grab something from the bookshelf in the upstairs hall and go into the family room—which wasn't as shaded as the living room—when the quiet of the space was broken by an odd little *pop*. Aldair stood in the opening of the hallway that led toward the dining room, arms crossed. As his gaze fell on her, though, a small smile touched his lips.

"You did not try to leave."

"Would there have been any point?"

The smile broadened. "No."

"That's what I thought."

Her reply only made him shake his head. "You are an unusual woman, Jillian Powell."

"Not really," she said. "I'm probably the most ordinary person you'll ever meet. But maybe that's the problem." She got up from the sofa and smoothed out her skirt. "Can we turn on the air conditioning now?"

He had been so certain she would at least make the attempt. No, she would not have gotten very far, since he had sat at one of the tables by the window in the bar while he consumed his brandy and would have seen her the second she came down the street...and probably sensed her before that, since his kind had the ability to detect when a mortal was in the vicinity. But still, he found it interesting that she hadn't even tried to escape. Fear of his reaction, or...?

Or perhaps she was intelligent enough to realize that a single human woman simply didn't have the resources to outrun a djinn, especially an air elemental such as himself.

Whatever her measure of intelligence, it didn't seem to be enough to prevent her from being angry with him. After he had made the cooling system turn on, she thanked him briefly and then went upstairs.

Almost immediately afterward, the door to her room was shut with sufficient force to be almost a slam, but not quite.

He did not much care whether she was angry with him or not. Had she really expected him to tell her the truth? How could he, when he did not know for himself how long they would linger here? He supposed he should be glad that she had not continued to press the issue, but instead had taken herself off to her room.

Where he guessed she must be sulking now. No matter. She was still here, and that was the important thing. Their refuge had not been compromised.

Jillian did not seem inclined to come downstairs, even though the noon hour had passed and he assumed she must be hungry. Again, her choice if she did not want to eat. He went ahead and put together a light meal of fruit and sausage and bread, at the same time giving a few pieces to Patches, who watched the entire procedure with great interest and an equal amount of hope.

And afterward he went to the living room, because it was cool and dim in there, and he needed to think. More than anything, he wanted to know what had been happening in Santa Fe during his absence, and also in Los Alamos. Clearly, the survivor community there still thrived. He wondered if the two settlements cooperated in any way, or whether they led entirely separate existences. Probably the former, just because he knew that Zahrias al-Harith possessed a soft heart and would wish to provide whatever help he could to the humans who still lived. A weakness, but perhaps one that could be exploited, if Aldair could only think of the correct way to go about things.

Which, he decided, could be best served by prying more information out of Jillian. She had not said much about Los Alamos, or her life there, so he would have to coax those details out of her. Unfortunately, she did not appear to be in a very coax-able mood at the moment. That should be easy enough to remedy, however.

He would make her a fine dinner, and open some of the wine he had found in the kitchen. Humans had nowhere near the capacity to hold alcohol that djinn did, and so he thought he should be able to get her in a relaxed and biddable state easily enough. Then she would tell him whatever he needed to know, and he could formulate his plans from there. Most likely she would not even be able to decipher his real reasons for giving her such a good meal. All the better. He did not wish for the two of them to be perpetually at odds. She might not believe it, but he did not wish her any particular harm. He only wanted to be done with this place so he might reclaim his life.

And after that, she could do what she wished with hers.

Once upon a time, Jillian would have been glad of the luxury to be able to read uninterrupted for hours.

There was always so much to do in Los Alamos—the long hours she put in at the lab, and also the volunteer work she did with the children. She didn't have the training to be a teacher, but she loved kids and helped out where she could, teaching them some of the needlecraft her own grandmother had taught her. With things the way they were now, sewing was a skill they could all use one day. Sooner or later, the world's human survivors would have to learn how to make their own clothes, and not continue to rely on what they could scrounge from the items their former civilization had left behind.

At any rate, in Los Alamos many days had passed where she felt as if she was running from dawn to dusk, helping out where she could. By the time she returned to her house, she barely had the energy to scrape together something to eat before she collapsed into bed. Her situation here was exactly the opposite. She didn't know if she could come up with enough activities to keep herself occupied all day long.

Now, however, the book she'd retrieved from the bookcase in the hall outside her door—a political thriller, set in a world now gone forever—couldn't do much to hold her interest. Was it silly of her to have sequestered herself upstairs like this? Maybe she should have taken the book and gone downstairs to the family room, put her feet up on the couch and read her book there, acted as if none of this was unusual at all. Aldair didn't seem overly inclined to share her company, so he probably would have left her alone.

Possibly.

From outside she heard a muffled bark. The windows had been shut tightly to keep the cool air inside, but they weren't exactly soundproof. Jillian set down her book on the bed and went to the window so she could peer out into the yard.

Aldair stood there, moving his hands in graceful arcs so he could...well, at first she wasn't quite sure what the hell he was doing. Then she realized that with each wave of his hands, another clump of weeds became flattened and fell to the ground, as if he was using the air itself as a sort of scythe. When he finished one area, the fallen vegetation rose into the air in a single mass and then drifted away from the djinn, presumably being sent to the no-man's-land beyond the property lines.

This whole procedure seemed to fascinate Patches, who ran after the weeds as they drifted away from the yard. His tail wagged like crazy, and he even snapped at the airborne vegetation, as if he wasn't quite sure what it was but had determined he might as well let it know that he was watching closely.

And Aldair—well, he stood in profile to her, so she couldn't see his expression fully, but she at least was able to tell that he smiled, and even appeared to chuckle as Patches circled back and pawed at his leg.

The djinn bent down and scratched the dog behind his ears, which of course made Patches writhe in ecstasy.

Watching them, Jillian couldn't help smiling a little, too. She didn't know what impulse had driven Aldair to tidy up the yard, but maybe he was a neat freak who wanted the house's grounds to match its interior. Or maybe he simply didn't want Patches picking up any more goatheads and prickers from the rough scrub. She'd plucked out several already today as she was petting the dog.

Whatever the reason, she found herself liking Aldair a bit more because of it. And also because of that smile, which, even in profile, looked genuine and unforced. Around her he always wore an air of faint superiority, even when he smiled, but in that moment, he couldn't know she was watching. He was merely being himself.

Jillian wondered if she should go down to be with them, play with Patches some more, now that a clear area had been created. More clouds had gathered, dimming the bright sunlight just a little, so maybe it wouldn't be so unbearably hot in the yard.

But no. She didn't want to watch Aldair's smile fade into something far too close to a smirk, with that slight lift at the corner of his mouth and the way those bright blue eyes of his seemed to look at her and detect every fault, every flaw.

Better to stay up here and try to read, and let him enjoy his time outdoors. She still had no idea what his crimes had been, precisely, but she thought he'd earned a few moments of happiness in the sun.

Jillian did not come downstairs, which suited Aldair's plans. After he had cleared the yard so they wouldn't have to see such an overgrown jungle every time they glanced out the windows, he went back inside, glad of the rush of cool air that greeted him as soon as he entered the kitchen. Patches went over to his bowl and began gulping greedily at the water within, consuming so much of it that Aldair was compelled to refill the bowl with more water from the tap.

By that point, late afternoon had come upon them, and the sky grew darker—not because the sun would set anytime soon, but because the clouds he had been watching all day had thickened noticeably. He could feel the energy within them, the building moisture. By the time full dark came, they would probably let loose with thunder and lightning, but Aldair did not mind that so much. If anything, a thunderstorm might create a more intimate atmosphere for the dinner he had planned, a sense that he and Jillian were very much drawn together in this place of shelter.

He had mocked her for the candles, but in fact he thought they would serve him very well. The sideboard in the dining room boasted a number of candle holders in varying shapes and sizes and materials—dark bronze, and ceramic gleaming with glazes of deep red and brown, and carved wood, and even slightly tarnished silver. He set them on the table and the sideboard itself, and judged the effect rather interesting.

A deep red cloth to cover the table, handsome against the dark stoneware the owner of this house had selected for her own. Simple, heavy silverware. Compared to the more ornate styles of his people, these items could be thought of as lacking in sophistication, but when viewed together, they did have a certain charm. He hoped Jillian would see them in the same light.

The same with the meal he planned to serve. Nothing too elaborate, because then she might become suspicious that he had gone to too much effort, although of course he did not need to use much energy to summon the components he required. He did not know what they ate in Los Alamos, but surely she should welcome a dinner of roast chicken and almond rice and squash with butter dill sauce.

In the middle of these preparations, he paused to allow Patches outside so he might relieve himself before the storm hit. The dog ran outside, sniffed around the newly cleared yard yet another time, and then took care of things before trotting back inside. Not a moment too soon, for he entered the kitchen just as the first roll of thunder rumbled overhead.

Good. Aldair glanced into the dining room one last time, assured himself that all looked well, and then headed up the stairs so he might knock on Jillian's door.

She did not answer right away, and he wondered if she was still annoyed with him for disappearing to the Mine Shaft in order to avoid her questions. Her opinion did not matter all that much to him, but he did wish to avoid having to coax her out of her room.

But then the door opened, and she looked up at him, one eyebrow lifted at a quizzical angle. "What is it?"

"Are you hungry?" he asked politely. He knew he must act as pleasant as possible so she would have less of a reason to demur. "Because I thought you might like some dinner, especially since you had nothing for lunch."

"I—" She hesitated for a long moment, so long that Aldair feared she might refuse, even though that surely meant she would go hungry. "I suppose I should eat something." Thunder crashed overhead, and she winced. "I guess it's not the sort of night to be alone."

Was she bothered by the storm? She seemed as if she was made of tougher stuff than that. In any case, she had agreed to come eat, even if in a rather grudging manner. "No, I suppose it is not. And," he added craftily, thinking that perhaps he should appeal to her obvious affection for their adopted dog, "I do think

Patches would like it better if we were both downstairs with him during the storm."

She didn't quite sigh, but he noticed how she let out a small breath. A quick backward glance over her shoulder at the book she had left lying on the bed, and she nodded. "You're probably right. My dog Alfie wasn't bothered by thunder, but I know a lot of dogs are."

Aldair nodded. "Then let us go downstairs."

He led her to the dining room. All those candles created a warm glow in the space, gleaming on the smooth glaze of the stoneware and reflecting warmly from the knives and forks and spoons. The curtains were closed, but a bright flash of lightning glowed behind them, followed by another rumble of thunder not long afterward. From overhead, the rain pounded on the metal roof, a dull roar muted somewhat by it being two stories above them.

"It's lovely," Jillian said, although she slanted him a half-suspicious glance, as if attempting to determine the real motivation behind such a spread.

*Not a seduction, I assure you,* he thought, although he could see why she might have that impression. Surely a woman as lovely as she had to have been on the receiving end of more than one attempt to get her into bed. However, the only thing he intended to seduce from her was more information.

"Please sit," he told her, indicating the chair to the right of the one at the head of the table. Hearing their voices, Patches entered the room. He did not appear terribly discomfited by the storm, but he did curl up in a corner and watch them expectantly, as if waiting for the main event to begin.

Again one of those hesitations, before she shrugged slightly and took the seat Aldair had indicated. The sequins on her skirt reflected some of the candlelight as she arranged the fabric so it would drape gracefully to either side, and the candles' soft glow woke warm shimmers of gold in her brown hair.

Realizing he should not pay any attention to those distracting details, Aldair sat as well, then reached for the bottle of wine so he could fill Jillian's glass. He had opened the bottle nearly a half hour earlier so it would have plenty of time to breathe. She watched him still with that quizzical expression on her face, as if she was attempting to decide exactly what his motivations for all this show might be.

"I thought we got off rather on the wrong foot," he said as he poured an equal amount of merlot into his own wine glass. "It was not my intention to make you feel uncomfortable, but I have my own reasons for needing to stay hidden."

"So you said." She wrapped her fingers around the stem of her glass, but she didn't lift it to take a drink.

"But I still think I should be able to go back to Los Alamos. I promise I won't tell anyone about you."

Perhaps she wouldn't...or at least she wouldn't intend to. But he could not trust her to keep her mouth shut indefinitely. "So what would you tell them?"

"Basically what actually did happen...except I'd leave out the part about the outer circles, and meeting you. Only that the device malfunctioned, and that I found myself transported miles and miles away and had to find my way back to Los Alamos."

"And they would believe this?"

"Probably." Now she did lift the glass to her lips so she might take a sip. Her eyes shut briefly, and she nodded, as if in approval of the quality of the wine. "Why wouldn't they believe me? As far as they're concerned, I would have no reason to lie. And they couldn't get many details out of me, because I'm not a scientist. Even Miles wouldn't expect me to be able to explain what happened."

"Miles," Aldair repeated. He already knew Miles Odekirk was the scientist who had created those fiendish djinn-repelling boxes, but of course Jillian could not know that.

"He was a scientist at the Los Alamos Laboratory... before. Anyway, the devices are his invention."

"So why were you working on one of them, if you are not a scientist?"

She sent him a sideways glance, but it wasn't precisely suspicious. More...embarrassed, for some strange reason. "Because I'm good with my hands. That is, I'm good at detail work, and that's what they had me doing—assembling things. I didn't know what I was doing, not really. Miles would give me a diagram, and I'd follow it." She stopped there, wine glass still in her hand, and a corner of her mouth twitched. "Did you actually intend to have dinner, or was this just an excuse to get me down here and fill me with wine?"

"My pardon," he said immediately. For he had been so intent on opening the conversation with her that he nearly had forgotten about the food. "You must be famished."

He waved his hand, and the dinner he had imagined appeared in front of them, the chicken a warm golden-brown and studded with rosemary, steam rising from the bowls of rice and vegetables. A basket sat off to one side, folded white cloth revealing just a hint of the fresh-baked rolls beneath.

A startled flicker from Jillian's storm-colored eyes, and then she grinned. "I should have known it would be no problem for you. This looks amazing."

"I hope you find it so." He turned toward the chicken on its platter and cut off a piece, balancing it on the end of the large serving fork. "Your plate, if you would?"

She set down her wine glass so she could pick up her dinner plate and extend it toward him. He deposited the large chunk of breast to one side, and she busied herself with filling the rest of the plate with rice and vegetables, and finally a roll.

While she was occupied, he cut off a rather larger piece for himself, and then set down the serving fork and carving knife. And after she was done with the side dishes, he took a portion of each of them as well.

"Better?" he asked, once both their plates were filled.

She had been just about to take a bite of chicken; she popped it in her mouth, chewed, and then nodded. "Much better."

"Good."

Aldair decided it would seem more natural if he allowed her to eat quietly for a few moments before he asked any more questions. After she had had a few mouthfuls of everything on her plate, and washed them down with wine, he said, "You had done that sort of work before? Assembling machinery, I mean."

"God, no." She offered him a rueful little smile. "I'm good at needlework. My grandmother—my mother's mother—taught me. Sewing, of course, but what I really preferred was needlepoint and petit point. I even won a blue ribbon at the state fair once. I suppose it seems like a silly, old-fashioned thing to do, but I enjoyed it. Anyway, because I was used to working on very detailed pieces in small spaces, and because I had very good eyesight, Miles thought I would be a good person to assist him in the lab. That's all. But that's also why he wouldn't be able to get any technical details about the accident from me. I wouldn't know what to begin to tell him."

This explanation did seem plausible enough. Still, Aldair could have no way of knowing that Miles wouldn't continue to press Jillian for more information, and that eventually she would not blurt out something she knew, even if she did not do so out of malice.

He simply could not take that risk. "I suppose not," he said carefully. "Was there anyone else who could do similar work?"

"Lindsay helped, but she wasn't as good at it as I was."

"Lindsay?" The name also sounded somewhat familiar, although Aldair could not recall exactly who she was.

"Lindsay Adarian. Or I guess Lindsay Odekirk now, although she and Miles aren't officially married. But still, she's started going by that because they're going to have a baby in a few months."

This revelation was enough to make Aldair's head spin. Now he recalled where he had heard Lindsay's name. She had been one of the Chosen in Taos. Her djinn partner was Rafi, who had been killed by some of Khalim's men when he attempted to escape to the djinn otherworld in search of help. Yes, that death would have left Lindsay alone in the world, without a djinn mate, but never in all his long lifetime would Aldair have thought that she would turn from a magnificent specimen like Rafi to that spindling scientist, Miles Odekirk. He was the sort of man who could be broken in half by a djinn. But Lindsay had transferred her affections to him, was having a child with him?

Clearly, a great deal had occurred during those months when Aldair was trapped in the outer circles.

"I see," he said, although he still couldn't quite understand what could have attracted a beautiful woman like Lindsay Adarian to someone such as Miles Odekirk. "Do you have many children in Los Alamos?"

"A few." Jillian swallowed some more wine, her gaze turned inward, as if the question had upset her somehow. "There were nine of them among the survivors who first came there, but now people have started having babies, too." Her mouth tightened, and she drank again, so much that Aldair felt compelled to pour another measure of wine into her glass.

Ah, a sore subject. Had she also lost a child when she'd lost her husband? But she had made no mention of such a tragedy touching her, and Aldair rather thought she would have said something. He paused, wondering if he should probe at the wound, then decided he might as well ask.

"Are any of those children yours?"

She startled at the question, then shook her head. "No. I—Jack and I didn't have any children. We tried, but...."

So she was barren? Unfortunate...or perhaps not, given how uncertain the world was these days. Aldair could not help marveling at the human survivors who would take the risk of having children, when none of them could know for certain that the shield Miles Odekirk had devised would actually continue to keep them safe.

Aldair was not certain of the expression that crossed his face, but Jillian must have guessed something of what he was thinking, because she said, "No, it wasn't me. The doctors checked us both out. It was Jack. We were trying to decide what to do next. Adoption was way too expensive. Jack wanted to use a donor, but I didn't know if I really wanted to go that route. Then the Heat took that decision right out of our hands."

For a moment, Aldair didn't say anything. Her confession surprised him, but then, she had had a good deal of wine with not much food. And also, he had to stop and decipher what she had just told him, since infertility was not an issue with djinn. A man and a woman of his people would decide together when to have children. Such things did not happen by accident, but they also occurred on schedule, with no worry that the outcome would be other than what they expected, once they had decided they wanted to conceive. He'd heard that for humans the process could be far more difficult, however. And a donor? He had to puzzle that one out as well, and then realized she must have meant a surrogate to provide the father's genetic material, since her former husband had apparently not been up to the task.

Would she believe him if he murmured any words of sympathy? Probably not. Even now she sat there wearing a troubled, closed-off expression, as though she realized that she had just said far more than she should.

"That is...unfortunate," he allowed at last. "But perhaps a blessing in the end. Immunity from the Heat was not genetic. But at least the disease also erased itself from the world once it had done its job."

"We guessed as much," she said, still appearing far too stony and cold. She did not look at him as she added, "That is, it seemed logical to us, considering no families survived together, and yet the children born afterward were healthy enough." A brief hesitation, and then she said, "Could I have some more chicken, please?"

He cut off more of the breast and deposited it on her plate, then watched as she ate silently, her gaze still obviously averted from him. Had he angered her somehow, or had his questions brought up memories she would rather have avoided?

"Sorry," she said after an uncomfortable few minutes had passed. "I've tried really hard not to think about any of that."

"It is all right," he replied, more to reassure her than because the words were actually true.

"Is it?" She set down her fork and finally looked over at him—*truly* looked at him, her gaze meeting his. "I should forget about it. Jack's gone. I can't change anything about what might have been." She reached for her wine glass but didn't drink, instead held it cradled in the palm of her hand. "So why don't we talk about you for a while?"

"I am afraid that would be a very dull topic."

One eyebrow lifted slightly. "I find that hard to believe. Tell you what, Aldair," she added, leaning toward him just a little. "You tell me something about yourself, and I won't bother you about letting me go back to Los Alamos for...well, let's say a day. Deal?"

He didn't like the sound of that. "Only a day?"

"Two days?"

It was his turn to raise an eyebrow.

"Three," she conceded. "I think that's being pretty generous."

He regarded her carefully for a moment. She gazed back at him, expression guileless, although he did not know how much he could really trust her. Still, three days was a good span of time. Given the three days she had just offered, he should be able to devise a way to free himself of this place, especially if he did not have to suffer Jillian's incessant demands for him to let her go.

"Very well," he said at last. "What did you want to know?"

## CHAPTER EIGHT

She really hadn't thought he would go for it. And maybe allowing him three days was too much. Right then, though, she was feeling a bit reckless. Possibly she'd had too much wine, or possibly she was just doing her best to push back the inner turmoil those memories of Jack's infertility had evoked. She'd been so sure they would have a family together, that they'd be able to have that special physical embodiment of their love. Because Jack wanted a family as much as she did, they'd started looking into alternatives. Even the most no-frills adoption would have cost them nearly twenty-five thousand dollars. They didn't have that kind of money saved up. Not even a quarter that. And no one in either of their families had those sorts of disposable funds...even if

Jillian or her husband could have swallowed their pride enough to ask for a loan.

So Jack had tentatively suggested a sperm donor. At least that way the child would be hers genetically, and they could choose someone with his physical traits and ethnic background in the hope that the child would look as if he or she could be the product of their union. But something in Jillian had balked at the idea. She didn't want another man's child. She wanted Jack's baby. Barring that, better a child who needed a home, rather than trying to create one who might fool their friends and neighbors into thinking the child had been conceived naturally. In her mind, adoption would have been better...if they'd only had the money.

Anyway, she wasn't sure what had made her blurt out such a confession to Aldair, of all people, but she couldn't take it back now. Neither could she take back the bargain she'd just made with him...if she even wanted to. After all, he'd been extremely close-mouthed this entire time, and she definitely wanted to learn more about him.

"You said the djinn in Santa Fe know who you are," she ventured, and he nodded.

"I lived among them for a time, but not in Santa Fe. They first settled in Taos, and then moved to your capital city after our elders told them they could not remain in Taos after all."

"Why couldn't they stay there?"

Aldair's gaze slid away from hers. "Let us just say that a certain power exists in that region, a power which comes from the land. It is the sort of power that could give a group of djinn an unfair advantage, should they decide to explore its secrets. The elders decided it was better that no djinn could dwell there at all, and so the group moved to Santa Fe."

"And you went with them?"

"No." The muscles in his jaw tightened, but he answered evenly enough, "By then I had already been sent into exile."

Jillian allowed herself to digest his statement for a moment. It was clear enough to her that Aldair hadn't much liked divulging that one little detail—but, as far as she could tell, he had told her the truth. So he was doing something to hold up his end of the bargain.

All right, so he'd been in Taos with the members of the group there. But from what she'd heard, all those djinn were paired off with humans, their Chosen. Did that mean Aldair had a partner back there? What happened to her when he was sent to the outer circles?

"You were with the djinn in Taos," she said slowly as she tried to decide on the best way to phrase the question. "So that means you must have been another conscientious objector."

"One of the One Thousand, yes." Again with the clenched jaw. Yes, he was giving her the answers she wanted, but she could tell he didn't like it much at all.

"And you had a Chosen."

He let out a breath, then picked up his wine glass and drank, swallowing so much that he almost emptied the vessel. Not that the glass remained empty for very long, since he reached for the wine bottle and replaced what he had just consumed. The candlelight didn't reveal everything, softened the edges of the room and lent a magical glow to the space, but Jillian could tell that they'd almost finished off the bottle.

She had a feeling he'd summon another one as soon as that occurred.

"Yes," he said at last, the one syllable so grudging she was somewhat surprised he'd uttered it at all.

"What happened to her?"

"I don't know. I was in no position to know anything of what was occurring here on your plane after I was banished to the outer circles."

Which brought them to the question she wanted to ask the most. "So...why exactly *were* you banished?"

The fingers of his free hand drummed on the table-top. "I find I weary of this game. I think what I have told you is worth at least two days free of your importuning. We should leave it here, I think."

Jillian crossed her arms and shot him an irritated look. "Are you serious? We had a deal."

"And now I am rethinking that deal." His eyes narrowed, and she couldn't help experiencing a small thrill of fear at the glare he sent her. For just a moment there, she'd almost forgotten he was a djinn, and so she'd forgotten her own fears and pushed too hard. She needed to remember that he could blast her into next week if he wanted to. Not that she really thought he would.

But she also didn't want to find out for sure.

All the same, she refused to let him intimidate her. He'd already called all the shots so far, and she was damned if she was just going to sit there and take it like a doormat. "I suppose that's typical of you djinn, isn't it? You can twist things any way you like, just because you think you have all the power." A particularly loud burst of thunder crashed overhead, and she couldn't keep herself from wincing. *Way to look tough, Jillian,* she thought, but she wouldn't let that momentary hint of weakness prevent her from adding, "And maybe you do have all the power. But that still doesn't mean I'm going to play your games."

"Jillian," Aldair said, her name a clear warning, but she ignored him, and instead took the napkin from her lap and laid it down on the table, then stood.

"Dinner was lovely," she told him. "But I think I'm going to bed now."

"Oh, are you?" he inquired, his tone silky.

She began to take a step away from the table—and realized she couldn't move at all. It was as if an invisible barrier had been erected all around her, one she couldn't push her way past, no matter how much she tried.

"Stop it," she gritted from between clenched teeth.

"Stop what?"

"You know exactly what," she retorted. "Whatever it is you're doing right now. All you're doing is proving me right—throwing your weight around, using magic on someone who doesn't have any of her own to defend herself. That doesn't make you strong. It makes you weak. A bully."

As soon as she spat those words, the barrier around her vanished. Because she'd been pushing against it, she stumbled slightly, then regained her footing with as much dignity as she could muster. Although she really didn't want to look at him, she forced herself to lift her chin and meet his angry stare. Those blue eyes glaring at her were so hot with anger, they might as well have been the cobalt-tinted center of a welding torch.

"You know nothing," he growled.

"Maybe not. I do know one thing, though—I've had enough of you tonight."

And she stalked out of the dining room, back taut with worry the entire time, certain that he would throw another of those barriers in front of her, or call the winds to swirl around her and make her stumble and fall. Or even that he would come after her and grab her by the arm, force her to return to the dinner table. If he tried anything physical, she knew there wasn't much she could do about it. After all, he was a djinn, and she was only human...and a very ordinary human at that. She had never taken any kind of martial arts, or even the sort of self-defense classes that used to be offered for women at the local community college.

However, Aldair didn't do anything of the things she feared. She felt his angry stare beating on the back of her neck, but he didn't stop her as she made her way to the stairs and headed to her room. Neither did he stop her as she went inside the bedroom and slammed the door. Hands shaking, she turned the lock. No, that probably wouldn't do much to keep him out if he was really determined to get in, but at least it made her feel as if she'd done something to protect herself.

And then she sat on the bed, her trembling knees finally giving way so she actually dropped onto the edge of the bed rather than lowering herself with any kind of grace. She couldn't believe she'd just gotten in a djinn's face and practically yelled at him. That wasn't like her. Not that she couldn't get damn angry when pushed, but she'd never been one for confrontations. And to act like that in front of someone who could erase her existence as if she was nothing more than a gnat...well, she must have been drunk. Or seriously tipsy.

As she sat there, shaking hands clasped around one another, she wondered what on earth Aldair was going to do next.

He remained at the table for a long moment. It was the only thing he could do, because he feared if he went upstairs and confronted Jillian over her insolence, he would lose his temper completely, and that would not be a good outcome for either one of them.

How dare she? Who did she think she was? Only a mortal, only a foolish, pestilential woman whose entire existence was little more than a single breath to a djinn. She had no right to say such things to him. She knew nothing at all.

Scowling, he waved an angry hand at the table. Immediately, all the dishes and silverware crashed to the floor, including the platter that had held the chicken. Patches had been hiding in a corner of the room, doing his best to avoid the conflict between his two people, but as soon as he saw that chicken carcass fall onto the rug, he leapt into action. His mouth had just begun to close on one of the drumsticks when Aldair came to his senses and realized the dog could hurt himself badly if he crunched down on one of the chicken bones.

At once the entire mess disappeared. Patches took a startled step backward, then let out a disappointed whine, his big brown eyes staring imploringly upward at the man who had snatched such a tasty treat right out of his mouth.

Aldair let out a curse and all but fell on the chair where he'd been sitting previously, his hands hanging at his sides. At once, the dog came over and laid a head against his knee, and Aldair began to stroke him behind the ears, letting the reassuring feel of his soft fur help to calm him down, bring him to his senses.

How many times had he let his anger get the better of him?

Too many to count, he feared.

A few more breaths, and Aldair began to feel something more like himself. "No fears, my friend," he told Patches. "I think I can give you something better than a chicken carcass." He extended his hand, which now held a large meaty rib bone. The dog's tail began to beat frantically, and he took the prize from Aldair's hand and settled down in a corner so he could work on the bone in earnest.

*Well, I have mended one bridge,* Aldair thought. *Unfortunately, the other one will be far more difficult to repair.*

He got up from his seat and went out into the hall so he might look upward, toward Jillian's room. All seemed quiet enough up there, although with the way the thunder continued to crash and roll, he found it difficult to tell for sure. This was quite a violent storm, one of more strength than he might have imagined. Would it continue to rage all night, or would it finally die away once its energy was all spent?

An elemental of the air, he could sense something of a storm's patterns, of what the wind and the rain might be doing. However, all he felt now when he reached out into the atmosphere was utter chaos. The storm would do as it willed, and would not tell Aldair anything of its intentions.

Since there seemed to be little else he could do, he ascended the stairs, slowly, one at a time. Usually he would never notice such a mild exertion, but now it seemed as if those stairs had doubled in height since the last time he had climbed them.

When he came to the landing, he hesitated for a long moment. Perhaps it would be best if he went directly to his own room and left Jillian alone. After a night to sleep on her rage, perhaps she would not be as angry in the morning. On the other hand, he did not wish for this tension between them to fester. He knew all too well what long-simmering resentments could do to one's soul.

So he went to her door and knocked softly. "Jillian." No answer.

Well, he should have expected as much. It would have been highly unlikely for her to appear quickly and be all smiles, an apology on those lovely lips.

He tried again. "Jillian."

Again he heard nothing. It seemed she intended to freeze him out. But if she was going to turn this into a contest of wills, she would soon discover that she had chosen the wrong opponent. Djinn knew all about patience.

To his surprise, however, the door opened a few seconds later. Jillian stared at him, face nearly expressionless—except for the too-bright glitter of her gray eyes. No, it didn't appear that she had been weeping, but she did seem to be on the verge of losing what little control she had left.

"What do you want?"

Her question took him aback. What *did* he want? Not to be at odds, for one thing. And to have his freedom again—true freedom, not the spurious sort he had achieved by hiding himself away here in Madrid.

But Jillian could not do much to help him with the second matter. As for the first, well, he would have to offer her the olive branch. Doing so went against everything he believed about himself, but although he disliked admitting that fact, he was the transgressor here. Perhaps she had overreacted, but she would have had nothing to react to if he had not reneged on his promise in the first place.

"I want to apologize."

Her eyes widened. "You—what?"

"You heard me." Anger rose in him again, but he pushed it down. He had already allowed it to master him once this evening, and that was one instance too many. "Do not make me say it a second time."

Her gaze seemed too sharp as she studied his face. Then she nodded. "That's hard for you, isn't it? Apologizing, I mean."

"Possibly." That was as much of an admission as he was willing to make.

A little silence then while she continued to watch him. He did not much like being subjected to such scrutiny, but he did not look away. At last she said, "Are you going to tell me?"

"Tell you what?"

"Why you were exiled."

His jaw clenched, but he forced himself to reply. "Yes. But not tonight," he added quickly, when he saw her open her mouth to speak. "Let me come to it in my own time. Do you understand?"

"Yes." Improbably, she offered him a smile. "We've probably both had enough tumult tonight. Whenever you feel like you're ready, Aldair."

So gracious, like a queen deigning to bestow upon him a great gift. But no, he should not think of her response in such a way. Truly, he hadn't detected anything of condescension in her tone. She was trying to be reasonable.

Why was such a thing so hard for him?

"Thank you, Jillian," he said. "I will say good night, then."

"Good night," she echoed, and closed the door to her room.

He let out a breath and made himself go across the hall to his own bedroom. While he had been speaking with Jillian, Patches had come up the stairs and settled himself a few feet away. He followed Aldair into the room, then jumped up and curled himself into a ball at the foot of the bed.

"Please, be comfortable," Aldair said, his tone wry. Despite those words, he did feel oddly comforted by the presence of the dog. At least Patches would not call him to task for his bad behavior.

He thought of the short distance that separated this room from Jillian's. So very close, and yet she might as well be a million miles away. She did not approve of him at all, that much was clear.

Unfortunately, he knew that her disapproval would only increase a hundredfold once she learned precisely why he had been sent into exile in the outer circles.

## CHAPTER NINE

JILLIAN LAY AWAKE FOR A LONG WHILE, STARING UP at the ceiling. Yes, the storm had proved itself to be both ear-splitting and long-lasting, and yet she knew that wasn't the real reason why she was so wakeful. No matter what she did, she couldn't seem to keep Aldair al-Ankara out of her thoughts.

In just about every way, he was the exact opposite of Jack. Her late husband had been kind, thoughtful, the sort of person who didn't think twice about offering to help a friend move, or to stay extra late after school to give one of his students some unofficial tutoring. Friendly, too, able to strike up conversations with just about everyone he met. Even the frostiest of strangers generally succumbed to his charm, but there had never been anything of a player about Jack. He just genuinely liked people and wanted to be there for them whenever he could.

Then there was Aldair. Rude, condescending, secretive...right then, Jillian was pretty sure she could come up with an extremely comprehensive list of negative adjectives to describe him.

And yet....

He'd come up here to apologize to her. She could tell from his stiff manner that such behavior wasn't exactly familiar or pleasant for him, and yet he'd done what he could to patch things up between them. What his motivations truly were, she didn't know for sure, but he'd seemed almost genuine right then.

The weird thing was, she had the impression that many of his actions were driven by some kind of long-buried hurt, the sort of thing he didn't want to admit even to himself. She somehow doubted he would admit such a weakness to her, either.

She wouldn't push. Right then, she wasn't even sure whether he'd carry through on his promise to tell her the story behind his exile. She hoped he would, because she wanted to know the truth. However, she also knew that she didn't have a great deal of leverage. Really, she didn't have a single thing he could possibly want. She'd done him the service of getting him here and away from the hell that was the outer circles, but now all she could really offer was some local area knowledge, and that had been pretty much tapped out as well.

So she was here on his sufferance. About all she could hope was that he wouldn't decide she was a liability, something to be disposed of because she presented too much of a risk.

No, he wouldn't do something like that. At least, she very much hoped he wouldn't. There had been more days than she wanted to count when she'd found herself on the verge of wondering if life really was worth living, but at the same time, she didn't want to have that life snatched away from her.

*If you're trying to make yourself fall asleep, you're not doing a very good job,* she told herself in some irritation, then rolled over on her side. *Aldair isn't going to do anything to you. Look how angry he was tonight, but nothing happened.*

Well, nothing except being pinned in place by a weird invisible force field. She guessed he must have used the air itself against her, forming a barrier that was impossible to break through. And if he could do that, he probably could do a great many other things as well.

*Not helping,* she thought, and punched the feather pillow to make it plump up a little beneath her cheek. She'd always hated the damn things because of the way they went perpetually flat. Good thing she didn't have allergies on top of everything else.

She knew she was distracting herself. Or at least trying to. Because the one thing she didn't want to face, didn't want to admit, even in the darkest depths of her soul, was that while Aldair frightened her in some ways, she also found herself oddly thrilled by him as well. It wasn't just his looks, although they were probably part of the weird attraction. Never in her life had she ever met anyone remotely like him. Which made sense. He was a djinn, after all.

He was also trouble. She knew she had to stay on her guard around him. If she played this right, maybe she'd survive and make it back to Los Alamos.

Somehow, though, that prospect didn't seem quite as appealing as it had just the day before.

They tiptoed around each other the next morning. Oh, Jillian was being very polite, thanking him for the coffee and breakfast, being careful to fill Patches' water and food bowls, but Aldair could see how on edge she was. She hadn't forgotten his actions of the previous evening, that much was certain.

As though the thunderstorm had never been, the day outside the windows was bright and clear and sharp, the sky a perfect cloudless blue. The only evidence of the rain that had pounded down on the house were a number of puddles in the newly cleared area just beyond the front porch.

Although the weather didn't exactly cheer him, Aldair was glad to see the storm had passed. He wished to do some more exploring this morning—more to get out of the house than because they actually had need of anything—and such an activity would have been complicated by another downpour.

He watched Jillian from beneath his lashes as she blew on her coffee and drank some, then broke off a piece of her biscuit and handed it to Patches, who'd been waiting patiently under the table for any choice morsels that might come his way. Aldair wanted to raise an eyebrow at this indulgence, but after all, he had provided a bone for the dog the night before, so he wasn't precisely blameless when it came to spoiling the animal.

During their mainly silent meal, he kept wondering whether Jillian would press him to talk about his exile, even though he had told her the night before that he would not bring up the topic until he was ready to. However, she seemed to understand that she should hold her tongue, because she said nothing except she hoped the storm might have helped to cool things down a bit.

"That would be good," he said, then swallowed the last mouthful of eggs on his plate. Jillian need never know of the destruction he had caused the night before, as he had made sure all the broken plates and glasses were repaired and returned to their proper places in the cupboards before she even came down-stairs. "I think I will look around the town a bit more."

She nodded but didn't reply. Her expression turned somewhat thoughtful, however, and he wondered what she might be thinking. Was she pondering her chances for an escape? No, he somehow doubted she would take such a risk, especially after their confrontation last night. She had had a little taste of what he might do when provoked, and he doubted she wished to explore that subject further.

Very well. He did not much care for the brittle courtesy which now lay between them, but he had no one but himself to blame for that. Or rather, he might believe Jillian had led him to that outburst because of her questions, and yet he could have prevented himself from losing his temper, if he so wished.

He rose from the table and set his dishes in the sink. Later, when he had a mind to it, he would clean them up and put them away, but for now he only wished to be out of the house, away from Jillian's presence for a while. Some fresh air would clear his head.

As soon as he went to the back door, Patches sprang out from under the table and ran to go with him. Aldair glanced back at Jillian, but she only gave a resigned lift of her shoulders. It appeared clear enough that she would not prevent him from taking the dog along on today's explorations.

The air was still cool, and smelled of wet grass and damp earth. He inhaled deeply as Patches went bounding forward, apparently determined to anoint every clump of weeds he found. Being outside did feel better; the house had seemed heavy with the weight of words unspoken, tension thick as humid air.

Because he did not have any particular goal in mind, Aldair meandered, crossing from one side of the street to the other, going into shops as it pleased him. He could tell right away that no looting had occurred here; all the stores' wares still remained where their owners had left them, nothing moved or touched or disturbed. The chief items for sale seemed to be jewelry, which surprised him somewhat, for he hadn't thought a small, poor-looking settlement such as this would be able to support so much costly merchandise. But then he remembered how Jillian had told him this was once a tourist town, and so he guessed that most of these gleaming silver pieces were intended for people other than those who actually lived here.

Some of them would be very beautiful against the smooth skin of her throat, or wrapped around her slender wrists or hanging from her delicate ears. In the past, he had enjoyed giving gifts of jewels to his lovers, of seeing their personal beauty enhanced by the beauty of the jewelry they wore. Perhaps he should take something to Jillian, a sort of peace offering, even though she most certainly was not his lover.

Ah, but would you mind very much if she were?

He recalled how she had glared at him last night, how her breasts had heaved with the angry breaths she'd huffed out. There had been something almost magnificent about her rage, about her fearlessness as she faced him down. He might have expected such bravery from another djinn, for they would have been evenly matched in such a confrontation, but a human? Most definitely not.

And she had looked so very beautiful.

His gaze fell on a heavy necklace in one of the display cases before him. Fashioned of silver, it was set with turquoise stones of a clear, exquisite blue, almost the color of the sky overhead. If he hadn't known better, he would have said those perfectly matched cabochons must have been mined in Persia, but he doubted that. Everything here looked as if it had been made in the Southwest, probably by members of the local indigenous tribes. They had been very skilled in silversmithing, from what he recalled.

Wherever the necklace had come from, it was beautiful, and would suit Jillian very well. He would take it to her, and hope she would understand the gesture.

*And if she asks about your exile?*

Then he would tell her the truth. She would probably despise him afterward, but at least he would not be keeping any more secrets from her.

Well, not too many, that is.

He slipped the necklace into a pocket of his robe and headed back to the house, Patches trotting along happily ahead of him. Although it would have required far less time to take to the air in the manner of his kind, Aldair walked instead, because of the dog. And also, there was something to be said about a good, brisk walk, especially on a fine summer morning such as this one.

Some part of him had feared that Jillian would not be there, would have taken the opportunity to flee, but those fears had been for nothing. She sat on a red-painted bench in the shade of the front porch, the same paperback book she'd been reading the day before open on her lap. As he approached, however, she closed it and offered him a tentative smile.

"Back already?"

Was that disappointment in her tone? No, he didn't think so, more that, in an attempt to make inconsequential conversation, she had blurted out the first thing she thought of.

"It began to grow warm."

"Yes, I guess so."

They gazed at one another for an awkward moment. Today she had on another flowing skirt, this one in a warm red, although the pale brown top that accompanied it was closer to the type she'd worn when he first met her—sleeveless, of a fine knit that clung to her body. The contours of her full breasts were clearly visible.

He swallowed. "I thought you might like this," he said, and pulled the necklace out of his pocket.

Her eyes went wide. "I—where did you get it?"

"From one of the shops in town."

That reply seemed to discomfit her; her mouth pursed, and she glanced away from him. "Isn't that kind of like stealing?"

A spark of anger flared in him. Here he had attempted to do something nice for her, and she was accusing him of being a thief? "Hardly," he returned, voice cold. "The person who once owned that shop is long gone. There is no one left to inherit these pieces. So from whom, pray, am I stealing?"

"I—" She shook her head. "Sorry. I guess that was sort of hypocritical of me. After all, I took these clothes from a shop here, too." Setting aside the book, she rose to her feet and came toward him. "It's very beautiful, Aldair."

Yes, a definite olive branch. He knew she would take it. Anyway, he had the impression that her first response had been only an automatic reaction, that she hadn't stopped to reason out what she was saying. Still, he wanted to see how far he might push things.

"Will you wear it now?" he asked, then undid the clasp and held the necklace up, end to end. He meant for his intention to be very clear—he wished to fasten the piece around her neck himself.

A long pause. She looked from the necklace to him and back again. Was that a shiver he saw move through her body? Perhaps. But then she nodded. "Of course."

Only a few feet separated them at that point. He moved closer to her and draped the necklace around her throat, then pushed her heavy hair out of the way so he could fasten the clasp. As he did so, a shiver of his own touched him. How soft her hair was, so thick and sweet-smelling. In that moment, he wanted nothing else but to bury his face in it and breathe deeply, then turn her around so he might touch his mouth to hers.

But he did not. He made sure the clasp had caught, and released her hair so it could fall down her back before stepping away.

This whole time she had held herself very still, as if to make sure that she would not move and therefore initiate any more contact than necessary. Did his touch repulse her? No, he didn't think so. For some odd reason, he thought she was more afraid of her own reaction than his.

As soon as he was done, however, she stepped away, offering a smile he didn't believe for one second. One hand went up to touch the necklace. The stones gleamed brightly blue against the tanned skin of her throat, and seemed to awaken an echo of blue in her eyes, although they had always appeared to be a pure, foggy gray until that moment.

She was exquisite.

"Thank you, Aldair," she said, the words hardly more than a whisper. Then she went to the bench and retrieved her book, and fled inside.

He didn't try to stop her.

God.

Jillian stood in front of the mirror in her bedroom, hand once again moving to touch the turquoise necklace she wore. Never in her life had she owned anything so expensive, except maybe the half-carat diamond Jack had bought her for her engagement ring—a ring safely stowed in a box at her home in Los Alamos, because she'd worried that the diamond would get hung up while she was wiring one of Miles Odekirk's devices— but the costliness of the piece wasn't what had her so unbalanced now. No, it was the memory of Aldair's touch, the sensation of those strong hands moving her hair aside so he could fasten the necklace for her.

He'd done it on purpose, of course. Why, she wasn't sure. To mess with her head? If that had been his intention, he'd done a damn good job. She shouldn't be dwelling on the way it had felt to have him stand so close, to sense the heat of his body on the bare skin of her arms and neck. A few inches more, and he would have been pressed right up against her.

And some part of her wouldn't have minded that at all. Not one bit.

*You are losing it,* she told herself. *You can't let yourself be attracted to him. No matter how gorgeous he might be.*

Problem was, her mind might be telling herself these things, but her body just wanted more. Wanted him to pull her close so she could feel those amazing muscles pressed against her. Without even trying, she could recall the touch of his mouth on hers. Yes, at the time he'd only been giving her mouth-to-mouth, had been doing his best to keep her alive, but that didn't seem to matter right now. She knew the shape of his lips, knew what it felt like to have his longish hair brush against her cheek as he bent close.

"Stop it," she said out loud, glaring at her reflection. It didn't help that right then she appeared dewy and aroused, perspiration gleaming on her forehead and chest. Damn it, she looked like—well, she looked like someone who really, really wanted to get laid.

She wouldn't lie to herself. It had been a very long time, and even though she missed Jack every second of every day, from time to time she'd entertained the thought of having a one-night stand with someone reasonably attractive in Los Alamos, just so she could scratch that biological itch and get back to mourning. However, she'd never given in to that impulse, knowing she'd hate herself afterward. Her heart had to be engaged for her body to fully appreciate the experience.

So how did that explain the attraction to Aldair? She certainly wasn't in love with him. She didn't even like him very much. But for some reason, her body seemed to crave him the way an addict might crave another hit of heroin.

Wait, though...didn't the djinn have the ability to make humans fall in love with them, or at least in lust? She'd heard rumors to that effect, although of course she'd never had a chance to have those reports proved one way or another.

Until now.

Maybe.

She wished this room had been built *en suite* like the master bedroom. That way she wouldn't have to leave to go to the bathroom. Right then, she desperately needed to splash some cold water on her face.

*Well, you can't hide in here forever,* she told herself sternly. *You just need to get up and go out there like nothing happened. Nothing did happen. He fastened a necklace for you. End of story. You don't need to act like he suddenly sent you into heat.*

Problem was, it did feel almost exactly like that.

She pulled in a breath, then another, and opened the door. Aldair's bedroom door stood open as well, which meant he was probably downstairs. Good. Maybe she wouldn't have to bump into him at all.

Five steps down the hallway to the bathroom, and then she was safely inside. She plucked a washcloth off the rack, wetted it, and pressed it against her feverish cheeks and forehead. That did seem to help, so she repeated the process again, following up with a fresh application of lip balm from the little tube in the top drawer of the vanity.

After she had put the lip balm away, she opened the bathroom door. Aldair stood immediately outside, and she gave a little gasp.

"I am sorry if I startled you," he said.

"No—I mean, yes, you did startle me, but that's all right." God, she sounded like an idiot. Also, it didn't help at all that she was now in such close proximity to him once again. He towered over her, and it seemed like the more she tried not to look at the muscles of his chest and stomach, the more her gaze was inexorably drawn to that very dangerous region.

"I thought we might try something different tonight," he said, and she raised an eyebrow.

"Different?" Damn, her voice sounded terrible. Just that single word had come out all strangled, almost cracking on the last syllable.

"Yes." If he was amused by her discomfiture, she couldn't detect any sign of it. "Will you have dinner with me at the Mine Shaft?"

"The bar?"

"The very one. A change of scenery, as they say."

"Well, I—" Jillian floundered for a minute, then decided the suggestion sounded fairly harmless. When you got right down to it, the atmosphere in the dining room here at the house was far more intimate. The eating area at the Mine Shaft was quite large and sort of kitschy, with that mural on the wall behind the small stage, and all the dollar bills pasted to the walls next to and behind the bar itself. Why Aldair had asked her to go there, she had no idea, but it seemed safe enough. "Sure," she finally replied. "That sounds like fun."

"Fun," he echoed, and nodded. "Yes. Will you come there at seven tonight?"

"Sure," she said again. It wasn't as if she could really respond any other way.

"Good. I will see you then."

He turned away from her and headed back down the stairs while Jillian stared after him in some mystification. Even two days spent in his company had told her that he could be unpredictable, but she had absolutely no idea what he might have planned now.

She supposed she would find out in a few hours.

## CHAPTER TEN

PATCHES TAGGED ALONG WITH HIM TO THE MINE Shaft, probably because the dog seemed eager to seize any chance to get out and about. Aldair didn't mind; he enjoyed the company, which was far less problematic than Jillian's.

The idea to come to the Mine Shaft had occurred to him as he puttered around downstairs. They'd shared rather a scene in the dining room at the house, and he thought the atmosphere there might still be loaded with tension. The tavern seemed like far more neutral territory. At any rate, they had the entire town to themselves, so why not use those parts of it that might be appealing?

However, he had to revisit the "appeal" of the former restaurant and bar as he stood in the space that had once served as a dining area and the bar itself. And also a place for entertainment, judging by the small raised stage at the far end of the room. In fact, several amplifiers and a guitar remained there, covered in dust.

Not the gray dust that signaled someone had succumbed to the Heat in that spot, but only an accumulation of grime from being neglected for nearly two years.

Indeed, the whole place needed a good cleaning. For a djinn, that was only a minor concern—a flick of his hand, and unseen winds gathered up the dust and the cobwebs, and blew them out a side door. The mirror behind the bar sparkled, and the chrome on the taps shone as if it had been newly applied.

Much better. He thought there were far too many chairs and tables in the room, and so he had them stack themselves and then move outside, to be piled up under the remains of a large canvas pavilion. What purpose the tent had served, he had no idea, but it still provided some shelter, even though it was now stained and beginning to show rips and tears in the fabric.

He kept one table, setting it off to the side, near one of the windows, which overlooked a substantial porch. The room had already been hung with the sorts of small white lights mortals used to decorate for Christmas, so all he had to do was touch a finger to the wire to wake them up again. They came to life, lending a festive air to the space, for even though the sun still shone brightly outside, the bar remained rather dark.

During all this, Patches sat off to one side, watching as Aldair wrought his subtle transformations. But when his master went behind the bar to fetch himself a drink as compensation for his efforts, the dog cocked his head to one side and whined.

"I fear there is nothing here that I can give you," Aldair said, pouring himself a shot of brandy. "But I do think there may be some table scraps to come later tonight."

Patches' tail began to wag at that remark, almost as if he had understood every word. Or perhaps all he needed to hear was "scraps" to realize that his reward would come, if he would only be patient.

Aldair, however, was thinking of an entirely different kind of reward. He'd seen the arousal in Jillian's flushed features when he went to speak with her, knew that his touch had made her react in a way she probably found most unwelcome. But he wouldn't let her reluctance deter him. He had been with far too many women not to recognize the obvious signs of attraction, no matter what she might do to push them away.

And indeed, although at first he had told himself he had no desire for her, either, now he knew better. Yes, she was a mortal. That did not matter, compared to her beauty or the fire of her spirit. She would realize soon enough that they were meant to be together, if only for a short while. Once she'd experienced his touch, she'd forget about the man she had lost. Such devotion was to be applauded, he supposed, but there was no reason for her to make a martyr of herself because of it, allowing her beauty to fade as the lonely years went on. She deserved better than that.

He smiled, and nodded as he downed the rest of his brandy. Yes, this would be a night that Jillian Powell remembered for a long, long time.

Ridiculous that she should be this nervous. Jillian glanced at the clock on the nightstand. Since the house didn't seem to have lost power the entire time it was unoccupied, because of its solar panels, she guessed the hour must be fairly accurate.

Six fifty-five.

Aldair had said to be at the Mine Shaft at seven. It would probably take her about five minutes to walk down the hill and into town. She hadn't seen any sign of Patches all afternoon, and so she thought he must have been with Aldair the whole time. She just hoped that he'd remembered to feed the dog.

Another brief glance in the mirror to make sure her hair wasn't too much of a mess, and then she made a minute adjustment to the necklace she wore. All right. She couldn't stall any longer, not if she didn't want to be late.

No point in locking the front door, not when they were the only two people in town. She closed it quietly behind her and began to make her way down the drive, walking carefully on the loose gravel. The sun had just touched the hills on the other side of the small valley where Madrid was located, turning everything to burnished gold. Although the air was still warm, a light breeze had started to pick up, ruffling at her hair and playing with the full skirt she wore. It felt delicious, and right then she was glad Aldair had decided to move the venue for tonight's dinner. No reason to stay cooped up in the house, especially on a fine evening such as this.

As she walked, though, she kept telling herself that she needed to keep things cool between them. Friendly, but nothing more than that. She still couldn't quite explain her visceral reaction to him, but at least she knew the strange attraction existed, which meant she could work consciously to fight against it. If she'd been the type of person to easily fall into bed with someone, enjoy the physical sensations, and then move on, maybe she'd be looking at Aldair in a whole new light. In a way, that would have made things a whole lot easier. She could give her body the release it needed without having to compromise her heart—or her love for Jack—in any meaningful manner.

But she wasn't that person. Never had been. All she could do was find a way to coexist with Aldair until he had determined the best plan to leave her behind while still avoiding the djinn in Santa Fe. Then she could go back to her life in Los Alamos, and he could—well, he could go off and do whatever it was that djinn did. She was still a little hazy on that part. Surely they must do something to fill up all those long, long years, but she had no idea what that something might be. It would be a long walk to Santa Fe, but once there, she knew she could get one of the Chosen in town to drive her to Los Alamos.

As she approached the Mine Shaft, she saw that little white fairy lights glistened from the porch just outside the bar. Had those always been there? She didn't know, because the one time she'd driven through town with Jack, it had been daylight.

She sort of hoped the lights had always been there. That would mean Aldair hadn't put too much effort into this dinner.

The ramp that led into the bar creaked slightly underfoot as she made her way inside. Almost as soon as she entered the building, Patches ran up to her, tail wagging. Obviously he didn't have any particular misgivings about the evening that lay ahead.

In here, too, were more of the little white Christmas lights, hanging around the edges of the room. Everything looked much shinier and cleaner than the last time she'd been in the tavern, so she guessed Aldair had tidied things up. Even so, there was only so much you could do to shine up a place like the Mine Shaft. It had a patina of age on its furnishings that could never be erased.

Music played softly in the background. The juke-box, Jillian realized, although the song wasn't the sort of loudly twangy country-western Aldair had disdained earlier. Still country, but a lot mellower. Not Patsy Cline, but something of a similar vintage.

Aldair emerged from the door that led into the kitchen, looking completely out of place in his stormy blue and gray robes. These seemed more blue than the garments he'd worn earlier, almost a cobalt color, with shimmering silvery silk pants underneath. The fabrics were very beautiful, but nothing could quite erase the incongruity of a man wearing something that looked straight out of the Thousand and One Nights while he stood in a dive bar in Madrid, New Mexico.

"Jillian," he said with a smile, then gestured toward the room around them. "How do you like it?"

"It looks a thousand percent better," she replied. "I'm glad you thought of it."

"Good. Here—this is where we will sit."

He gestured toward a table near the window. For the first time, she realized that he'd cleared the room of all the other tables and chairs. It felt much bigger, although she wasn't sure she liked the arrangement. Removing most of the furniture and only leaving them the single table and two chairs just seemed to point out how they were the only two people in town.

But she wouldn't comment on that. She managed to smile as she sat down at the table. From somewhere he'd located a tablecloth—they weren't exactly standard issue here—and an old blue-tinted bottle was filled with the sunflowers that grew in every vacant lot and along the roadsides. They added a cheerful note, one that Jillian appreciated.

"I should do that back at the house," she said, pointing toward the flowers. "They grow everywhere, so it's not as if I have to feel guilty about cutting a few."

"They are rather ubiquitous," Aldair agreed. "But I am glad you like them." From nowhere he produced a bottle of wine, and she blinked. Yes, he was a djinn and could conjure items out of nowhere as he liked, but it was still rather disconcerting to watch.

But she didn't make a comment as he poured dark wine into the glasses on the table, then sat down. Patches, who'd been lying down off to one side, came closer as soon as he realized that his chances of begging some table scraps were about to increase exponentially.

And then plates appeared before both of them, each with a perfectly formed ribeye steak topped with melting bleu cheese, and spears of asparagus off to the side, and a stack of au gratin potatoes to the other. It was the sort of meal Jillian hadn't had since before the Heat, and not very often then. Maybe something very special, like a birthday or an anniversary.

"This looks wonderful," she said.

"Good. I have tasted many of your people's dishes, but this was a meal I had several years ago, and wanted to replicate."

"So—so you spent time here on Earth...before?"

He nodded as he picked up his steak knife and fork. "Yes. We djinn could come and go on this plane. We were not barred from that. But we could not make our permanent homes here. It was a place of respite, away from the otherworld."

"Is the otherworld all like the outer circles?" If that was the case, then she could begin to understand why the djinn had been so driven to take this world back for themselves.

"No. But it is not nearly as pleasant as it is here, either. We took most of our resources from your world—there are so many fewer of us, your people never noticed the lack. But it is not all an empty desert like the outer circles. We have palaces, structures with enormous enclosed courtyards planted with trees and flowers, so we might believe ourselves elsewhere."

"That sounds beautiful."

A frown creased his brow, and he set down his fork after taking only a single bite of his steak. "It is only a counterfeit of beauty. It is not the real thing, for that can only be found here."

As he spoke, he watched her, piercing blue eyes seemingly intent on her face, and she couldn't help glancing away. Surely he was only talking about the natural beauty of this planet, and nothing else.

But....

Jillian picked up her wine glass and took a large swallow. This was a darker, heavier red than the merlot they'd had the night before. She wondered where he'd gotten it. From the stores at The Hollar, the restaurant across the street? Or had he reached out much farther than that, to the abandoned wine shops and wine tasting rooms in Albuquerque, only some thirty miles away?

All she did know was that he couldn't have gotten it from anywhere in Santa Fe.

"It is very beautiful here," she said, her tone as neutral as she could make it. "Or at least certain parts of it. You probably wouldn't find the Sahara Desert quite as inviting."

"No," he agreed. "And I doubt it will ever be settled again. There is far too much land available in the more hospitable places in the world."

Yes, that was sadly true. Because of the information the Santa Fe djinn had shared with the community in Los Alamos, Jillian knew there were approximately twenty thousand djinn altogether in existence. Of them there was the much smaller subset of the One Thousand, the djinn who had protested the extermination of humanity and who had saved precisely one thousand human beings. But the One Thousand were segregated from the others of their kind, kept in small communities consisting of djinn and their Chosen. She didn't know how many of such communities actually existed, since that particular fact hadn't made it to Los Alamos. Maybe Zahrias, the leader of the Santa Fe djinn, didn't know, either. It was enough that he and his people were safe.

But the other djinn, the ones who had wanted this world for themselves—they'd already begun to spread across the globe, each taking a piece for themselves. It sounded as if the djinn elders had something to do with who got which piece, although the mechanisms for how all that worked hadn't been fully explained. All she did know was that a djinn who had a Chosen had to stay with his or her community; they couldn't set up a homestead someplace and live away from the others with their human partners. The house where Jessica Monroe and her partner Jace lived sounded as if it was somewhat outside Santa Fe, but not so far that it was completely outside the boundary of the land grant the community had been given.

"Why Taos?" she asked then, and Aldair lifted an eyebrow at her.

"What do you mean?"

"Well, your group was in Taos first before they moved to Santa Fe. So why there?"

His shoulders lifted, and he reached to pick up his wine glass. "That was Zahrias' decision. I do not know why. Not a very good choice, as it turns out, since the elders did not ultimately approve of the location. But as to why certain djinn of the One Thousand ended up in one place and not another...it was because of their Chosen. Those partners would have suffered enough shocks, and so every attempt was made to have them settle in the same region where they had lived before the world changed."

That did make sense. To lose everyone you'd ever known and loved was an unimaginable blow on its own. But to be taken from the place you were familiar with and brought someplace else entirely to live— that would have been almost too difficult to bear. Yes, she was from Albuquerque and had only visited Los Alamos a few times, but it still didn't feel completely strange to her. The seasons, the vegetation, the shapes of the mountains—they were close enough that she had been able to adjust fairly well. But if she'd had to go to some other country altogether...Russia or Japan or South Africa...it would have been so much harder.

Thinking of Taos only made her wonder once again about Aldair's Chosen. He must have had one, and yet he didn't seem to miss her very much. Only a single mention of her, and that just in passing. Surely he must have loved her. That was one thing Jillian knew very well. The djinn in Santa Fe were utterly devoted to their human partners. So why was Aldair so differ- ent? Because he'd been sent into exile, and thought he would never see her again? Even if that were the case, shouldn't he be trying to get back to her, now that he had escaped? Yes, he would have to avoid the Santa Fe djinn, but their presence shouldn't have been enough to keep him away if he truly cared. She knew Jack would have moved heaven and earth to be with her again if he'd been in a similar situation.

Did she have the courage to ask the question? Then again, how could she not ask? If he had admitted to being one of those in Zahrias' group, then he must realize she would want to know what had happened to the woman he had saved and brought to sanctuary in Taos.

To gather her courage, Jillian sipped at her wine again. Across the table from her, Aldair had returned to his steak, but she could sense from a certain tension in his shoulders that he was anticipating what her next words might be.

"What about your Chosen?" she asked. "What happened to her?"

"That I do not know for sure," he replied, although his gaze wouldn't quite meet hers. He had to be hiding something. Precisely what, Jillian couldn't guess. "Her name was Katelyn, and she came from Roswell. But—"

"Katelyn?" Jillian repeated, wondering if she'd heard him correctly. "Katelyn Fonseca?"

Those brilliant blue eyes flared with surprise. "You know her? How is that possible?"

"I don't know her well, but yes, I've met her." Talk about your coincidences. Watching as Aldair's brows drew together, Jillian went on, "She came to live in Los Alamos about a year ago. Julia told us she'd lost her djinn partner earlier that winter, but she didn't go into a lot of detail, only said that everyone had decided she would feel more comfortable being in Los Alamos rather than in Santa Fe, surrounded by djinn who might remind her of her loss. And Katelyn never talks about it. But eventually she bounced back, found her rhythm in the community. She's with Shawn now."

Hardly any alteration of Aldair's expression. "Shawn?"

Jillian swallowed. Shouldn't he have reacted much more to hearing that the woman he'd once chosen was now with another man? But since she'd embarked on this discussion, she knew she had no choice but to continue. "Shawn Gutierrez. He's been running things ever since Julia left to be with Zahrias. We also have a sort of town council, but he's the one who casts the deciding vote."

"Ah."

Just that single syllable, which could have meant anything. Jillian picked up her fork and ate a mouthful of mashed potatoes, since she really was at a loss as to what she should say next. Maybe she should let it go. Was it even possible for a djinn to relinquish his claim on a human woman? She had no idea, because she'd never encountered this particular situation before. For all she knew, Aldair's exile to the outer circles had also cut his connection to Katelyn, making her a free agent.

Jillian gazed across the table at Aldair. He still wore that tight, closed-off look, so she was having an even more difficult time than usual trying to read his expression. But since she'd raised the topic already, she figured she might as well plow ahead.

"So you didn't know? That is, I'd heard there's supposed to be some sort of connection between djinn and their Chosen—"

"She was no longer my Chosen," Aldair said abruptly. "I went into exile. Her destiny was her own after that."

So Jillian's guess had been correct. She didn't feel any particular satisfaction in knowing that, however, not when it was clearly a sore subject with Aldair. "And you're not—you're not going to try to get her back?"

"Why would I do that? She's decided on the path her life will now take. I will not interfere. Besides," he added, after he picked up his wine glass and swallowed a large mouthful, "I am beginning to realize I might not have made the wisest of choices when it came to selecting her."

As he spoke, his eyes locked on Jillian's, and a shiver worked its way through her body. Was he saying what she thought he was saying?

No, she had to be flattering herself. Katelyn Fonseca was five years younger than she, a tawny-haired young woman with striking dark eyes and the perfect bone structure of a fashion model. In no way could Jillian ever think that she might be a more attractive candidate for a djinn's Chosen than Katelyn. Anyway, she was too old. All Chosen had been twenty-five years old or younger when their djinn selected them, while Jillian was twenty-seven at the time the Dying had swept across the earth. Not that she could have ever gone willingly with a djinn, not when her heart had broken into a million pieces in that moment when she realized Jack was never coming home, that the Heat had taken him, too.

"Has that happened with anyone else?" she asked. "That is, to have a djinn and their Chosen separate and go on with their lives?"

"That I do not know." His voice sounded even enough as he made his reply, although Jillian could tell he really didn't want to continue this topic of conversation for much longer. "Certainly not in the Santa Fe community. That is, you told me of Lindsay, who is now with Miles Odekirk, but that is different. Her djinn partner died. It is not as if he is still living somewhere, seeing her with a new man."

No, that was an entirely different matter. "I suppose not."

"And our djinn communities do not communicate with one another. Or at least, mine did not while I still lived among them. It was always intended that they would be their own little islands, surviving separately from the rest of the djinn and their Chosen. The elders did not give their reasoning for this, but I think it was partly that they did not wish for the One Thousand to join together and become a force of their own. At any rate, because of that isolation, I cannot speak to what may or may not have happened in any other communities."

Spurred by a sudden impulse, Jillian reached across the table and laid her hand on his. Only for a moment, just to show her sympathy, but almost as soon as she had done so, she wondered if she'd done the right thing. Aldair didn't move, but the warmth of his skin against hers was almost too much to bear. She said, "I'm sorry," and moved her hand away, going to lift her wine glass as if that was what she had intended all along.

"Don't be sorry," he replied. "There is nothing to be sorry about."

And he went back to his plate, gaze dropping from hers so she had to attend to her own meal, even though right then she didn't feel very hungry, despite the excellence of the food. But she forced down mouthful after mouthful, determined that she would show the meal the respect it deserved. She owed Aldair that much, even if she had developed a clear case of foot-in-mouth disease tonight.

Eventually, they had both cleared their plates, and only a few inches of wine remained at the bottom of the bottle. Aldair lifted it and poured half into Jillian's glass, and the remainder into his own. As he set down the bottle, the jukebox, which had been playing quietly in the background the whole time, switched over to an old standard, sung by a woman Jillian didn't recognize, but who had a husky, whiskey sort of voice.

Aldair rose from his seat and extended a hand. "Dance with me."

He couldn't be serious. Did djinn even dance, especially to human music?

But he looked serious. Deadly serious. Jillian wasn't sure how he would react if she declined. She wanted to. Or at least, part of her wanted to say no. The other part, the one that had shivered at the heat of his touch and couldn't stop remembering what it had felt like to have his mouth against hers, wanted to very much.

Almost without thinking, she got up from her chair and took his hand. "I'm not a very good dancer."

His mouth twitched in amusement. "I have seen this kind of dancing. It does not require a great deal of skill."

Well, she couldn't really argue with that statement. When it came to slow dancing, about all you had to do was hold on to each other and shuffle around the dance floor a bit.

So she let him pull her into his arms, and didn't dare look up into his face as they began to move slowly to the music. It felt good, though—felt far better than she wanted to admit to herself. And she'd always loved this song. It must have been the wine, but she found herself softly singing along.

*"Just remember, darling, all the while*
*"You belong to me."*

Then, to her mortification, she realized the music had stopped, that Aldair was staring down at her with an inscrutable expression on his features. At length he said, "You have a very lovely voice."

Blood rushed to her cheeks. "No, I—"

"You do. Far more pleasant than the woman on the recording." He glanced over at the jukebox and then looked back at Jillian. "Why have I not heard you sing before this?"

Despite herself, she couldn't quite keep herself from grinning. "Well, it's not exactly as if I've had much of a chance to sing lately."

"True. I should give you more opportunities."

The warmth in his voice was impossible to miss. Jillian knew she should do or say something to defuse the situation, but damned if she could think of anything. Realizing that the jukebox remained silent, she ventured, "Um—it's kind of hard to dance when there's no music playing."

"True." He paused then, blue eyes still fixed on her face. "Perhaps the time for dancing has passed. We have been dancing around one another, don't you think?"

Not sure how to respond, Jillian could only allow herself a single cautious nod. That seemed to be enough for Aldair, though, because he let go of her hand so he could raise his own to push back a loose strand of hair from her face. Then he moved his hand downward, ever so slightly, so he might cup her cheek.

A shiver went through her. That curiously gentle touch was enough to send heat flaring along every limb. His eyes still watched her, as if gauging her every reaction. Was he waiting for her to protest, to pull away? She knew she should. She should do something to stop him.

Somehow, though, she couldn't find the strength to do anything except stand there.

"Ah." One syllable, an acknowledgment of something she hadn't wanted to face.

Then he bent and placed his mouth against hers.

Sweet fire, racing all through her body. It had been so very long since she'd felt anything like this, waking parts of her that had felt dead for the past two years. His tongue touched her gently, tasting of wine and something else, perhaps only his own exotic djinn flavor. She didn't know, and right then didn't much care, only wanted him to keep on kissing her.

But he shouldn't be kissing her. This was wrong— so wrong. She wasn't his Chosen. She wasn't anyone who would have ever caught the eye of a djinn. And how could she let him embrace her like this when it had been his people who destroyed all of mankind?

Who had killed Jack.

With a gasp, she thrust herself away. Shock and anger flared in Aldair's eyes, but she knew she had done the right thing.

"I'm sorry," she gasped. "I can't. I just—I can't."

And with those words she fled from him, running as if her life depended on it. Maybe it did. But she bolted out of the Mine Shaft and out onto Main Street, wondering when he was going to give chase, and what she should do when he caught up with her.

He didn't, however. She ran all the way home, then hurried inside and went to her room and shut the door. Her entire body shook, and she grasped the corner of the dresser for support as she attempted to catch her breath. The silence of the house around her rang in her ears.

Why hadn't he pursued her?

## CHAPTER ELEVEN

For a long, long moment, Aldair stood in the middle of the bar at the Mine Shaft tavern, hands clenched into fists at his sides. He had to do that, because otherwise he knew he would have taken to the air, would have made sure he got to the house before Jillian did, so he might confront her over her foolishness.

Then, when the angry beating of his heart had subsided somewhat, he crossed over to the table where they'd sat and lifted his wine glass so he might drain the meager remnants at the bottom. Not satisfied, he reached over for Jillian's abandoned glass and drank the little bit of wine it still contained.

Still not enough. Well, he was in a bar, after all.

One of the bottles hidden under the counter sailed out and landed in his outstretched hand. No need for a corkscrew; he merely made a twirling motion with one finger, and the cork spiraled up and out of the bottle, landing on the floor.

No need for a glass, either. Aldair raised the bottle to his mouth and took a long swallow. This wine wasn't nearly as good as the one he and Jillian had shared at dinner, but then, savoring its vintage wasn't the reason he drank now.

He had been so sure of her. Just the look in her eyes, the warmth in her smile as she gazed at him. And then when she had reached over to lay her hand on top of his, he had seen the gesture as more than simple sympathy for the perceived loss of his Chosen. He had truly thought Jillian had intended to send him a subtle signal that such contact was welcome for her.

And she had agreed to dance with him.

For a few exquisite moments, he had held her, felt the warm curves of her body pressed against his. Her voice, too—that had been a surprise. Sweet and soft and low, just as lovely as she herself was. All in all, he had had no reason to think she didn't want him just as much as he wanted her.

The damnable thing was, he could almost swear she had been just as lit with desire. Something had stopped her. Misguided loyalty to that damnable husband of hers? Right then, Aldair thought it a good thing that this paragon, this Jack, was already dead. Otherwise, Aldair would have been tempted to kill him.

Very well. He had miscalculated here, and would have to think of the best way to approach Jillian all over again. He would not have called her shy, but clearly there was some part of her that she kept well hidden. Otherwise, she would not have given all the signs of attraction, and then backed away as soon as he acted upon them.

Patches, who had been sitting off to one side the entire time, came over and leaned his head against Aldair's leg. Although he would have thought that being bothered by a dog was the last thing he wanted right then, still he bent down and stroked behind Patches' ears, glad of the chance to think of something besides this last disastrous encounter with Jillian Powell.

"Women," he muttered, and Patches looked up, expression hopeful. Well, there was a little steak left over.

He went back to the table and sat down, then set the wine bottle in front of him. The dog watched these movements closely, waiting for his chance.

"Here you are," Aldair said, feeding a morsel of leftover ribeye to the dog. That offering elicited some fierce tail wagging. Good that Patches at least could enjoy the remainder of the evening. "Any advice?" he went on. "For clearly I don't seem to know what I am doing."

More tail wagging, and Aldair fed some more steak to the dog. What was Jillian doing at this very moment? Hiding in her room, relieved that an angry djinn hadn't come chasing after her? Or did she wonder precisely why he hadn't made any pursuit?

He had wanted to, but until he could think of exactly the right thing to say, such an effort would only be an exercise in futility. Also, right then he didn't want to admit that he had elicited her sympathy by telling her a series of lies. Yes, it was true enough that he had no attachment to Katelyn Fonseca, his supposed Chosen...but what he had neglected to mention was that their attachment had been severed long ago. It was not his exile that had caused their separation, but his pursuit of revenge. She had been captured by Khalim's men, but he had not bothered to rescue her. Indeed, he had allowed her to be taken by Ali, Khalim's cousin. Why worry about her eventual fate, when at the time Aldair had been so certain that he would have Jessica Monroe soon within his grasp?

These unpleasant truths were ones he had no intention of divulging to Jillian. Now she was only skittish and perhaps a little frightened, not sure what she should do about her attraction to him. Because Aldair knew she was attracted. She simply couldn't quite accept the fact.

But if she knew of everything he had done...if she ever learned the truth...then that attraction would

vanish as if it had never been. And he would not allow
that. Yes, his true goal was still attempting to find a way
that he might live freely in the world, and perhaps also
to finally get his long-delayed revenge on Jasreel.

Now, though…now Aldair began to realize that
he wanted very much for Jillian to share that life with
him. Surely once she heard how he had been treated,
how his miserable half-breed of a brother had ruined
his life, she would understand. She would stand with
him and lend her strength to his.

If, of course, she ever intended to speak to him
again.


The only sign of Aldair's return was the slight creak of
the stairs as he walked up them. She hadn't heard the
front door shut, or heard him moving around on the
ground floor. Actually, she rather thought he was coming up the stairs in the usual way because he wanted
her to know he was home. Otherwise, he could have
simply zapped himself into his own room.

She'd taken off the heavy necklace he'd given her,
had climbed into one of her borrowed tank tops and
yoga pants. And she'd lain down in bed and closed her
eyes, but she knew she wouldn't be able to sleep. Not
with her heart still racing, her blood still pounding in
her veins. Not with her heart and her body so at war
with one another.

Would he knock on her door as he had the day before, attempt to speak with her? Or would he realize she was a lost cause and go straight to bed?

Jillian didn't know which would be worse.

She barely dared to breathe as she lay there, listening to his heavy footsteps. They paused on the landing for the longest time, so long that she almost got up herself and went to the door, just because she didn't think she could bear the suspense any longer. At last, though, he moved away and his door shut—but softly, as if he didn't want to make enough noise to wake her.

Shit.

The opportunity lost, she rolled over on her side and stared at the closed door a few yards away from her. She could see it very clearly because of the bright moonlight pouring through the thin curtains at the window—the bronze finish of the door's round handle, the various "eyes" of the knotty pine. Every detail seared into her brain as she lay there for what felt like an eternity.

*You can get up and go talk to him, you know,* she thought.

That inner voice sounded so rational, and yet she knew she could never follow its advice. Hadn't she fled from him because she knew that any sort of connection between them was wrong? How could she defile Jack's memory by being intimate with one of the beings who'd wiped almost every trace of humanity from the surface of the earth?

But Aldair wasn't one of them. He couldn't be. He'd had a Chosen; therefore, he must be one of the "good" djinn.

On the other hand, how good could he have been if he'd been sent to the outer circles? Jillian doubted that sort of punishment was handed out to people who'd been found guilty of the djinn version of jaywalking, or shoplifting.

Damn it to hell.

Almost without realizing what she was doing, she pushed back the single sheet that covered her and went to the door. Laid her hand on the knob and let her fingers rest on the cool metal for a long, long time— so long that she felt the bronze begin to warm to her touch. Then she pulled in a breath, and another, and opened the door.

Aldair's room was not so very far away, just down the hall, but right then it felt as if it was more like a mile. Eventually, though, Jillian got there, and hesitated once more. Maybe he hadn't heard her get up and come over here. Maybe she could just tiptoe back to her room and act as if she'd never suffered such a terrible lapse in judgment.

But no, she wasn't going to be that kind of coward.

She raised her hand and knocked on the door. "Aldair."

He opened it so swiftly that she wondered if he'd been waiting for her. Even in the gloom, she could see the angry flicker of his blue eyes. "Jillian."

*You've come this far. Just say it.* She swallowed, then said quickly, "I want you to tell me."

"Tell you what?"

"Why you were exiled."

He didn't speak. He only stood there, just a few inches away. His chest rose and fell, and she realized he wasn't wearing the shimmering djinn robes from dinner, but a pair of loose dark pants and nothing else. A candle flickered somewhere in the room behind him, washing a warm glow over the impressive contours of his chest and arms.

At last he said, "Why?"

She swallowed. "Because I need to know."

Another long pause, while her heartbeat thudded in her ears and she wondered if he was going to slam the door in her face for her impertinence. "I will tell you...if you will tell me something."

How like him to ask for something before he would agree to do anything himself. But she was the one who had come to his door as a supplicant, so she supposed she had better meet him halfway. "If I can."

"Why did you run from me?"

Damn it. She bit her lip and glanced away, saw the lacy outline of the aspen tree outside the hallway window cast into sharp relief by the bright moonlight. "Because I was afraid."

Aldair made an exasperated sound. "Afraid of what?"

"Us. You."

He was silent then, clearly weighing her words. Then he said, "You have no reason to be afraid."

She couldn't hold back the little hiccup of laughter that rose in her throat. "Oh, I think I do."

"Because of Jack?"

"Partly. And because of everything else."

Aldair seemed nonplussed by her reply. His head tilted to one side as he gazed down at her. Was her expression even that visible in the half-lit corridor? Possibly. Maybe djinn could see better than regular humans.

But then he gave a slow nod. "Let us go downstairs. This is not the sort of talk to have while standing in a hallway."

And he moved past her so he could head down the stairs. Jillian trailed behind, not sure whether she should be relieved or not. Yes, it seemed as if he was about to finally tell her the truth, but what if it was a truth she didn't want to hear? What if he revealed himself to be truly as terrible as she'd feared?

Or worse, what if she found out that he hadn't done anything particularly horrible, that he wasn't one of the "bad" djinn and so not someone she needed to avoid? What then?

Heart pounding in her breast, she followed him into the living room. He sat down on the couch, while she settled herself on the love seat. No way would she sit next to him. That felt far too dangerous.

The pair of candles sitting on the mantel flared into life. Jillian startled, then told herself to relax. It was better to do this with some kind of light, wasn't it?

Although she would have preferred the more impersonal nature of the light fixture overhead.

A shadow slipped past her feet, and she started again before realizing it was just Patches, coming down to be with his people. He must have been sleeping in Aldair's room.

At the same time, a tall, slender bottle and a pair of small cordial glasses appeared on the coffee table before them. Aldair reached for the bottle, saying, "I thought this might help."

She didn't bother to protest as he poured a small measure of dark, heavy liquid into each glass. All right, it could have been too much wine that allowed her to lose her mind and let Aldair kiss her, but she didn't think so, even if it would have been a lot easier to blame her loss of control on the alcohol, rather than the weakness in her own heart.

"Thank you," she said as he handed one of the glasses to her. "What is it?"

"Late harvest pinot noir," he replied. "Something of a rarity. Much more nuanced than port, or brandy. You must let me know what you think of it."

Where he'd gotten such a thing, she had no idea. Maybe he had magicked it here out of some wine shop in Albuquerque. She allowed herself a cautious sip. The flavor was intense, sweet, but with a tartness to it as well, very different from the one time she'd tasted port and judged it not for her, too thick and syrupy. This wine had a lightness to it, for all its concentrated taste.

Jillian thought she liked it, which meant she had to be careful. It would be far too easy to keep sipping away and have it loosen her tongue and her inhibitions, while Aldair indulged her weakness and somehow managed once again to avoid telling her any of the things she needed so desperately to know.

"It's fine," she said.

"Just fine?"

She slanted a glance up at him as she set the small cordial glass down on the coffee table. "I like it better than port. Okay?"

One eyebrow went up. "Okay." He clearly didn't seem to harbor the same reservations about drinking the potent dessert wine, for he drained what was in his glass and then poured himself some more.

He didn't seem inclined to say anything else, and impatience stirred within her. Had he brought her down here merely to see if she would get drunk enough to surrender to his kisses? If that had been his plan, he was going to be sorely disappointed.

She crossed her arms and wished she was wearing something more substantial than a tank top. No, Aldair didn't seem to be paying much attention to the amount of cleavage currently on display, but she still would have felt a lot more comfortable in a baggy T-shirt.

"So?" she prompted, and his mouth tightened.

"I do not think it is a story you will much enjoy."

"Maybe not. All the same, I want you to tell me. I can't—" She hesitated, and wondered how much honesty he could take. For her, though, there was something raw and honest about sharing a kiss, about opening up enough to allow even that small intimacy. She shouldn't dance around who she was, what she felt. "Maybe for you a kiss isn't a big deal. It is for me, though. I need to know more about the man I was kissing."

"The djinn you were kissing," he corrected her, and she lifted her shoulders.

"If you like. But I won't—I *can't* do anything else without you telling me the truth."

Even in the dimly lit room, she could see the way his body tensed. And what a magnificent body it was, painted in shadow and light, the muscles appearing more heavily sculpted because of the way the glow from the candles moved over his skin. But she couldn't let herself be distracted by appearances. Not any more than she already had been, anyway.

"The truth," he said at last, his tone heavy. "Whose truth, Jillian? For I am sure that what I believe to be the truth is different from the truth as Zahrias, the leader of the Santa Fe djinn, might have seen it, or as the elders saw it...or even as my bastard of a half-brother saw it."

"You have a brother?" she asked, startled, and then wondered why she should be so surprised. After all, the djinn had their own families; it wasn't as if they sprang full-blown into the world. Zahrias himself had a brother who sounded as if he was his closest friend and confidant.

"Unfortunately, yes. He is there, with the djinn of Santa Fe." Aldair drank some more of the pinot noir, nearly half the small glass he held. That couldn't be a good sign, but Jillian didn't protest, only sat quietly on the love seat and waited for him to continue. "My father took a fancy to a human woman, once upon a time, and sired a son upon her."

"What about your own mother?" Jillian asked.

"My parents had gone their separate ways many years earlier. It is not the djinn way to stay with one partner for millennia, although when they agree to have a child, they also agree to remain together until their child reaches maturity, which is twenty of your years."

She supposed that was something, especially when you considered how many human marriages split up long before the children were grown. At the same time, she didn't much like how the djinn apparently didn't value long-term relationships. Was that how Aldair viewed his possible future with her, something transitory, to be enjoyed for a time until it was no longer convenient for him?

No wonder she'd run away. Maybe her heart had already guessed at something her mind hadn't quite grasped.

"What about the djinn and their Chosen?" she asked. "I got the impression that they were supposed to be bonded for all time."

"They are," he admitted. "That is an entirely different situation, one that has no bearing on the relationships djinn have with other djinn."

"Ah," she said, although she still didn't quite understand how the djinn could treat relationships with humans so differently from how they viewed liaisons with their own kind. Anyway, she decided to leave that aside for now, to return to the topic of Aldair's brother. "So your brother is half-djinn?"

"Yes," Aldair replied, mouth twisting with distaste. "But when a half-breed is raised in the djinn world, he develops his powers just as any other djinn might. For some reason, my father took a fancy to my brother, showed him unnatural favor—including gifting him with wealth and properties that should have been mine."

Well, that sounded like a terrible thing to do. Even so, she couldn't see how that would be enough to make Aldair view his brother unfavorably—which he must, judging by the sour expression that passed over his handsome features whenever he mentioned his half-brother. Shouldn't Aldair's anger have been reserved for his father instead?

"I guess that wasn't very fair," she began, but he immediately cut her off.

"It was the very opposite of fair. I protested, said that it was not right that I should be promised these things, only to have them taken away. But he told me that I should have a good enough inheritance from my mother, where my brother's human mother could give him nothing. My father said I should understand."

"I'm guessing you didn't."

A flash of blue fire from Aldair's narrowed eyes, and for a second an odd, harsh draft blew across Jillian's exposed arms and shoulders, as if the djinn was so angry that he'd allowed his powers to disrupt the air currents in the room. "Why should I understand? He made a promise, and he broke it. He preferred to show favor to his half-breed son rather than to me, his firstborn."

She wondered what on earth she could say then. Clearly, Aldair had been nursing this hurt and anger for many, many years. Probably far longer than she'd been alive, when you took a djinn's enormous lifespan into account. Thinking she should steer the conversation away from the subject of his half-brother, she ventured, "But your exile?"

Aldair scowled. "I wanted my revenge on him."

Back to that again. "Shouldn't your anger have been directed at your father? It seems to me as if your brother didn't have much to do with it."

"You know nothing." Jillian matched Aldair's scowl with a frown of her own, but he didn't seem to notice, only continued, "Do you not think I did not try to appeal to my brother's better nature? But no, he only said that our father's wishes were clear enough, and he would not go against them. He certainly had no desire to do what was right."

She decided to let it go. Since she hadn't been there, she couldn't really comment on what might have passed between the two brothers. An only child herself, she wasn't sure what she would have done in a similar situation, caught between a parent's misguided generosity and the very real resentment of a sibling. "Okay, so you wanted to get something of your own back from your brother. How did that lead to being banished to the outer circles?"

No reply at first. Aldair reached for the bottle of late-harvest wine, then seemed to think better of it, for he stopped mid-movement and instead clenched his hand into a fist. "Among the djinn, oaths are binding. I broke an oath I had sworn, and that was enough."

"What kind of oath?"

"What does it matter?" he said angrily. "The elders saw fit to punish me, and I was exiled. That is all you need to know."

"Are you kidding me?" she burst out, not caring whether she angered him further. "You haven't told me anything, except that you're someone who breaks his promises."

"Some are meant to be broken, for they mean nothing."

How in the world was she supposed to reply to that? More importantly, how could she ever trust someone who didn't honor his promises? "You don't really mean that, do you?"

He pushed himself up from the couch and stalked over to the window, then drew the curtains aside so he could gaze out onto the moonlight-drenched yard. "Yes."

She'd heard enough. Jillian found herself rising from her seat as well, although she didn't approach him where he stood by the window. Instead, she told him, "Well, I suppose I shouldn't be surprised. You said you would tell me why you were exiled, and you're going back on that promise as well. So I guess I'll say good night."

Aldair turned then, brows still pulled together. "I did tell you."

"You told me something so vague that it didn't mean anything at all. I'm guessing it had something to do with this brother of yours, and I suppose that's one of the main reasons you don't want to go anywhere near Santa Fe—you want to stay well out of his orbit. All right, I suppose I can understand that. But...." She let the words trail off as she attempted to decide whether she should just leave it there, or whether she should tell him what she'd really been thinking. However, avoiding the truth would make her nearly as bad as he was, wouldn't it? "But I'm not going to be a party to it. Tomorrow morning I'm heading back to Los Alamos. I won't tell anyone about you. I promise that—and *I* keep my promises. But I don't see any point in staying here."

In a flash, he was away from the window and at her side, one hand gripping her arm with fingers that felt like a band of steel around her bicep. Voice silkily quiet, he said, "I believe I have already impressed on you the importance of your remaining in Madrid."

A trickle of icy sweat moved down her back, but Jillian forced herself not to react, to remain still and calm in his grasp. "Yes, you did. And I told you I wouldn't reveal your whereabouts to anyone. Why can't you just accept that?"

"Because I see no reason to."

Jaw clenched, she responded, "What are you going to do—tie me to a chair or something?"

"If I must. Although there is no reason for me to be that extreme. There is no place you could go on foot where I could not catch up with you long before you even began to get close to Santa Fe."

Which was only the truth. She'd seen how he could take to the air, cover so much more ground than a person afoot. Yes, she might be able to beat him if she were driving a car, but all the cars in Madrid had been sitting neglected for almost two years. Their batteries had to be dead. She could no more use one of them to effect her escape than she could fly.

"Fine," she said, fury boiling in her as she saw a gloating smile touch his lips. "You win. But don't bother inviting me to any more romantic dinners. That ship has sailed, Aldair." To emphasize her point, she jerked her arm from his grasp. He let go, still smiling.

"As you wish, Jillian."

If she had to look at that horrible smile for a single second longer, she was going to scream. She turned on her heel and swept out of the room, hurrying up the stairs so she could give the door to her bedroom a satisfying slam.

As soon as she was alone, though, her whole body began to shake. Her arm throbbed where Aldair had held her, and she reached over with her left hand to rub the tender skin. There would be a bruise tomorrow, she was sure of it.

And then she sat down on the bed and stared blankly at the shut door. Would the djinn keep her prisoner in here? Or would he still allow her to roam around the town, confident in the knowledge that he could always track her down, no matter where she went?

For some stupid reason, she recalled the way his hand had cupped her cheek back at the tavern, the way he had kissed her so gently. How could he be so tender then, and yet such a raging asshole now?

*Because he's Aldair,* she told herself. *It's all about him and what he wants. You probably don't even count as a real person to him. How could you? You're just a mere human, and he's an almighty djinn.*

Tears burned in her eyes, but she wouldn't let them fall. No way. She would not allow that selfish bastard to make her cry.

If he wanted a prisoner, fine. But he was about to discover that she wouldn't be a very pleasant one.

## CHAPTER TWELVE

DEAD SILENCE FROM UPSTAIRS. ALDAIR WASN'T quite sure what he had expected from Jillian, but after that one slammed door, he could hear nothing from her at all. Was she weeping, or merely sitting on her bed and contemplating all the ways she might get her revenge on him?

Although he told himself it did not truly matter one way or another, he found himself hoping that he had not made her cry.

He blinked the bottle of late-harvest pinot and its accompanying glasses into the kitchen, then did the same thing to bring himself to his room, for in that moment, he did not much feel like climbing the stairs. However, he left the door open so Patches might enter and take his favored spot at the foot of the bed.

At least, that was the reason he gave himself for not shutting the bedroom door. Of course it could not be because he rather hoped Jillian would approach at some point, so she might apologize for threatening to leave.

No, she would never do such a thing. He had seen the true fury in her eyes, even though he did not think she had any real reason to be so angry. Had he not told her that he was exiled because he had broken an oath? What else did she need to know?

Indeed, he thought he had been rather clever about handling the matter, since he had been able to reveal the reason for his banishment without going into any of the details behind his punishment. She would not have to know about his plans to possess Jessica Monroe so he might ruin his half-brother's happiness, or how he had thrown in with Khalim and his followers when his plans went awry. His revenge on Jasreel was something the elders might have overlooked, for in general they did not meddle with the personal lives of the djinn community. However, joining up with Khalim was the true reason he had invoked their wrath, since by doing so he had gone back on the oath all djinn had sworn not to bring any harm upon the Chosen. Khalim had injured one Chosen and killed another, and that was enough to make all his followers share equally in his guilt.

But it seemed clear enough that Jillian did not think him clever at all. No, she had accused him of breaking his promise to her. Why that should matter so much to her, he did not know, unless she had begun to harbor feelings toward him, and now felt doubly betrayed. It was true that she had responded to his kiss much more favorably than he had hoped—until realization set in, and she fled from him.

Frowning, he settled into his bed, and then heard the soft click of Patches' toenails on the wooden floor out in the hallway, quickly muffled as the dog crossed over onto the rug. Aldair dangled his arm over the side of the bed. A few seconds later, the dog pushed his cold, wet nose into Aldair's palm, and settled down so his master might stroke his ears.

The presence of the dog was some comfort, but of course it could not begin to match the pleasure Aldair would have felt in having Jillian in here with him. That was how he hoped the evening would end—that they would eat and drink, and perhaps dance, and at the end he would take her in his arms and bring her up these stairs, and lay her down in his bed so he might make love to her. Taste her enticing flesh and make her his.

But she had proved herself to be far too stubborn, and apparently in possession of far too many scruples, for such a thing to happen. He did not believe her to be the sort of person to hold a grudge, but he also did not know how long she might allow herself to burn with righteous indignation.

No matter. She would calm down sooner or later, and then he could continue with his pursuit of her. In a way, her anger with him added a fillip of anticipation to the entire situation. For when she finally did succumb, her surrender would be all the more delicious, since he would then know how much she'd had to unbend to allow herself to be his.

Yes, he thought he could wait some time for such a pleasant outcome.

*You will not talk to him,* Jillian told herself as she got dressed the next morning. *Or at least, you won't talk to him unless it's strictly necessary, like asking where a certain item is located. Things like that.*

On the surface, that resolution sounded easy enough to carry out. But she'd never been one to sulk. Neither had Jack. They rarely fought, and the few times they'd had disagreements, they'd basically fallen over themselves to patch things up so they wouldn't go to bed angry.

Last night, though, she'd been so furious with Aldair that it had taken her hours to fall asleep, and even then she'd tossed and turned, unable to shut off her racing brain. She wasn't used to that, either. Usually, she could fall asleep fairly easily. But Aldair's high-handed way of dealing with the situation had upset her to the point where she wasn't sure if she'd ever been this angry with anyone in her entire life. Some kind of gratitude, to make a prisoner out of the woman who'd been his means of escaping exile, just because she didn't want to stay in his insufferable presence a second longer than she absolutely had to.

Just to spite him, she resolutely ignored the pretty clothes she'd gotten from the boutique, and climbed into the baggy jeans and shapeless T-shirt she'd found in the previous owner's dresser in the master bedroom. Coupled with the running shoes she'd worn with her Los Alamos clothes, they made a fairly drab outfit, one that hid her body nicely. No more letting Aldair get an eyeful of her bare arms and feet and ankles, and a decent helping of her cleavage as well. She also pulled her hair back into a tight ponytail instead of letting it fall around her shoulders.

All in all, she looked pretty damn unappealing by the time she was done, which of course was the whole point.

Jillian emerged from her bedroom to the warm, dark chocolate scent of mocha java drifting up the stairs. So Aldair had made coffee. Whether he'd made enough for the both of them remained to be seen.

She took in a single bracing breath, and then headed down to the kitchen. As she entered the room, she saw the djinn sitting at the table, a mug of coffee and a plate of toast in front of him. Off to one side,

Patches wagged his tail in greeting, but he apparently wasn't willing to give up his spot in case Aldair might offer a piece of crust.

Her captor's gaze flicked toward her, and his mouth tightened as he appeared to take in her baggy attire. However, he didn't say anything, only gave her a single nod of acknowledgment before he lifted his coffee and took a sip.

Well, he wasn't exactly acting friendly, but she hadn't expected him to. What was more important right then was the almost full carafe of coffee she spotted when she looked away from him. So he hadn't stooped to that sort of petty spitefulness at least.

So what? she asked herself as she fetched a mug from the cupboard and poured herself some coffee. He's still keeping you a prisoner here. He doesn't deserve a medal just for not starting off the morning with a snarky comment.

True enough. Even though in general she liked to drink most of her coffee before she started eating, the silence in the room felt awkward, so she got the loaf of bread out of the breadbox, cut herself several slices, and put them in the toaster oven. The whole time she could feel Aldair's gaze on her, but he didn't speak.

Just as she was pulling the toast out of the oven, he said briefly, "That won't work, you know."

She didn't turn around, but began to methodically spread butter on her toast. "What won't work?"

"The clothes. Do you think I can't remember what your body looks like...feels like?"

Hot blood rushed to her cheeks, but she told herself that he was just trying to upset her. He might know something of what she looked like, or felt like, but certainly not everything. Not even close. "They're comfortable," she said evenly. "I thought I'd do some work in the garden today...it's not as if I have anything better to do."

"What work? I have cleared the weeds. It is far too late in the year to grow vegetables. And it is much too hot for you to be spending an appreciable amount of time out there."

"I'll be the judge of that."

"What do you think to accomplish by making yourself faint from the heat?"

She wouldn't flatter herself that he actually cared. This time she did turn around, but she took a bite from the piece of toast she held before replying, "I'm not the fainting type, Aldair. I'll be fine."

His mouth twisted. "Suit yourself. Just don't expect to have me carry you up the stairs when you do make yourself weak from exhaustion."

"No worries there," she said in falsely sweet tones. "I would never expect you to do something so chivalrous."

His eyes glittered, and he opened his mouth to make some kind of a retort. But then he shook his head, as if he realized he could say nothing to change her mind. He reached for his coffee and drained it, and in the next instant he disappeared, a faint *pop* sounding in his wake, as if the air had rushed in to fill the space he'd just vacated.

Typical. Of course he wouldn't stick around to continue the argument. At the same time, Jillian knew she couldn't feel terribly relieved by his absence. He might not be in the house, but he would be around somewhere. Watching. Making sure she didn't try to leave. Or rather, she could try, but she wouldn't get very far.

To be truthful, she really didn't want to work in the yard. She'd mentioned the project because she knew it would annoy Aldair. But now that she'd made such a fuss about the whole thing, she knew she'd have to put in a couple of hours, just to save face. If there was even a couple of hours' worth of work to do out there. He'd been pretty effective in using his djinn abilities to clear the area, to get rid of the weeds while leaving the prettiest of the wildflowers intact.

But maybe she could clear out the remains of the vegetable garden. As far as she could tell, Aldair had left that alone, probably because you couldn't see much of it from the house.

First, though, to finish her coffee and toast, and then wash off her plate and mug and put them back in the cupboard. With Aldair gone, she had to take care of the clean-up the old-fashioned way, but she didn't mind too much. There was something vaguely comforting about the ritual, of making sure the kitchen was spotless before she stepped outside.

Or maybe she'd only been stalling because she really wasn't looking forward to the next few hours.

Patches ran outside as soon as she opened the back door. Once again, the day was almost brutally clear, the sky pure blue. She couldn't see a single cloud. It was likely some clouds had begun to build up around the Sangre de Cristo range to the northeast, but buried in this valley, she wouldn't be able to see any of them until they began to drift in this direction.

As the dog roamed around the perimeter of the garden, sniffing away happily, she went to the shed and took stock of the equipment it contained. Several shovels, a spade, trowels, and a weed whacker, although no lawnmower. Well, she doubted there had been a lawn here to mow even back before the home's owner died and the place had gone to seed.

Jillian also saw a contraption apparently designed for using a propane flame to burn out particularly pesky weeds. While she thought such a thing might be useful, she also didn't want to take the risk of starting a fire she couldn't put out...especially now that she couldn't rely on Aldair to help her.

No, that probably wasn't particularly fair. He'd been acting like a world-class jerk, but even he wouldn't be stupid enough to let her burn down the house, especially since it was probably the nicest dwelling in the entire Madrid area.

She picked up the lighter of the two shovels and headed out to where the remnants of the vegetable garden were located. It did seem as if the squash had probably hung on the first year, but now all that remained were some dried-up leaves and desiccated runners that looked more like a bunch of dead snakes instead of the remains of a vine.

Even though it wasn't quite past nine in the morning, according to the clocks in the house, the sun already felt like a physical weight on the back of her neck as she began to turn the dry earth under. Sweat trickled down her forehead, and she wished she'd thought to look for some kind of hat in the house. Surely the woman who'd lived here before had used something to protect her head while she worked in the garden.

If she had, then such a hat was probably stowed in the closet in Aldair's bedroom, and no way would Jillian risk going in there. She'd just have to grit her teeth and bear it.

She wasn't wearing a watch, so she had no real idea of time passing, only the subtle movement of the sun overhead. Patches soon got bored with nosing around the garden and went to lie down in the infinitely more comfortable shade of the porch. At one point, Jillian thought that perhaps she should stop, but she'd settled into a rhythm. Besides, she was concentrating so hard that she'd almost forgotten about Aldair, had let everything slip from her mind except the ground immediately before her and the rapidly growing pile of discarded weeds and dead plants.

The landscape wavered in front of her, and she stopped, leaning heavily on the shovel. Loose strands of hair had plastered themselves to her sweaty forehead. She still didn't have any idea what time it was, but from the way the muscles in her arms and shoulders were screaming, maybe she was due for a break.

When she began to walk back toward the house, she was dismayed by how her knees wobbled. Surely she was in better shape than this? But while she kept herself fit by walking pretty much everywhere she went in Los Alamos, it was so much cooler there than it was here. So much of her work had been done while sitting down, not breaking her back outside.

She stumbled and nearly fell as she began to make her way up the porch steps. In the next instant, even though she hadn't seen where he'd come from, Aldair was beside her, a steadying arm around her waist.

"I see you have done exactly what I feared you would," he said, his voice rough with anger. Or was that worry?

"I'm fine," she said, and tried to pull away from him. But the arm encircling her waist clearly wasn't going anywhere.

"Are you? For I just saw you nearly fall. That is not what I would call fine."

More protests rose to her lips, but clearly Aldair didn't intend to listen to them. Before she could even blink, he had whisked her in that unsettling djinn way from the porch to the blessed coolness of the living room, where he sat her down on the couch. A second later, a glass of ice water was being pressed into her hands.

She wasn't so foolish as to decline the drink. Instead, she lifted the glass to her lips and took a long swallow, followed by another. The cool liquid spilled down her parched throat, going all the way down, sending relief to her overtaxed body.

"Thank you," she said.

He didn't smile. Those hard blue eyes were fixed on her face. "You are very pale. You could have made yourself ill."

"Just too much sun. I'll be fine in a bit."

"So at least you admit that you are not fine now."

Jillian didn't want to admit anything, least of all that she had been stubborn and foolish. Never in her life had she experienced any kind of problem with being out in the sun, but then, strolling around the county fair in upper eighty-degree temperatures wasn't quite the same thing as experiencing that same kind of heat while shoveling under a defunct vegetable garden.

"It might have been a bit much," she said at last. "Next time I'll wear a hat."

"There will be no next time," he said in that high-handed way of his. "For I will make sure there is nothing left for you to do here, if this is what you plan to do with your idle time."

Oh, the nerve of him! So apparently it wasn't enough for him to keep her trapped here—now he also was telling her what she could and couldn't do to prevent herself from going insane from boredom?

If she spoke, she worried about what might come out of her mouth. As infuriating as he was, Aldair commanded powers she still didn't fully understand. Getting into a shouting match with him—if she could even find it in herself to engage in that sort of behavior—wasn't just foolish. It might be downright dangerous.

So she kept her gaze studiously away from him as she swallowed some more water, right before she set the glass down on a coaster and stood.

"Where are you going?" he asked.

"To my room," she said coldly. "I'm tired. Or are you also going to dictate when I can and can't lie down?"

"No," he said, and now she noticed a glint in his sapphire-colored eyes, as if he was amused by her reply. "I think it would be good for you to rest."

*And would you stop me if you didn't?* she thought then, but she didn't reply. Instead, she turned away from him and headed up the stairs. Her knees were still shaky, and she had to hang on to the banister to basically haul herself along, but she was damned if she would ask him for any assistance. He'd done enough already.

As she went, she thought she could hear him chuckling softly. So her pitiful act of defiance had amused him. Her entire body stiffened, but she forced herself to keep going. The last thing she wanted was for him to see how much he'd gotten under her skin.

Bastard. And to think she'd actually let him kiss her.

Well, that certainly wasn't going to happen again.

## CHAPTER THIRTEEN

Dinner time came around, but Jillian didn't emerge from her room. Aldair didn't think it a good idea for her to go without food, even if she was being so infernally stubborn, and so he put together a tray of the grilled trout and rice and vegetables he'd conjured for their evening meal, and left it outside her door. Patches eyed the tray with a good deal of interest, but Aldair threatened him with being tied up on the porch all night if he should touch Jillian's food, and the dog reluctantly backed away and left it alone.

Well, the bribe of another bone could also have had something to do with his good behavior.

Aldair ate his own meal and washed it down with some light white wine, a New Mexico blend called Shining River that he'd found in the wine rack in the kitchen. The combination was quite delicious, but he found he couldn't enjoy it the way he had wanted to. Not with Jillian so obviously avoiding him.

Foolish woman. Perhaps he should have left her to faint on the porch. Perhaps that would have shown her that her stubbornness would only hurt her in the end. But he did not think he could have allowed himself to do that. He did not want her to be injured, or ill.

What he wanted...well, unfortunately, she did not seem terribly inclined to give him what he truly wanted.

After his lonely dinner, he retired to his room with a map he had found in one of the town's shops. That was where he had gone while Jillian labored away in the garden—back to the touristy part of Madrid, to see if he could locate any more useful items. He was not so far away that he could still not sense her presence, although he knew she would not try to escape. Not yet, anyway. Perhaps as her captivity wore on, she would grow more desperate, and would risk his wrath in an attempt to get away.

Or perhaps she would come to realize that he had no intention of hurting her. Rather the opposite. Surely if enough time passed, she would soften toward him.

At the moment, however, that outcome did not seem terribly likely.

Scowling, he spread the map out on the bed and sipped at a glass of wine as he studied the markings on the heavy paper. Yes, as Jillian had said, Madrid was approximately thirty miles south of Santa Fe. It was a distance that should protect him, as long as none of the djinn in the former capitol decided to roam southward. But then, why would they? They had everything they needed in the town that had been given to them.

Still.... He had spent enough time with that contingent of djinn and their Chosen while they were in Taos to know that they did not have to adhere strictly to the town's borders when it came to the territory they might call their own. They were given an area to settle in, one that could spill over into the surrounding lands. That was why his hated brother was still safe in the compound he had taken for his own, one several miles outside Santa Fe proper.

Even given those parameters, though, Aldair doubted the djinn in Santa Fe would venture as far away as Madrid. He should be quite safe here, for as long as he needed to stay.

That was the real question, however. How long could he really stay here? If he had had Jillian to distract him, then perhaps he could have endured in this hidden corner of the world for some time. But she certainly gave no sign of wanting to share his company any more than she absolutely had to.

*That is how she feels at the moment,* he told himself. *It does not mean her feelings cannot change tomorrow, or a few days hence. We do have everything we need here.*

Well, more or less. This might have been the finest house in Madrid, but that, he feared, was damning with faint praise. In the otherworld, he had lived in a house of marble, with courtyards where water from their fountains played and plants grew in an imitation of Earth's beauty. He had built that house himself, over a span of many years, but it was foolish to go to such effort when this world offered so many empty homes that were ripe for the taking. While he probably could not have anything quite so fine here, he knew that Santa Fe possessed many elegant residences, and he thought Albuquerque probably did as well. But had any of his fellow djinn settled there? He had been away for so long that he knew he had missed a good deal.

Did he dare do any cautious reconnoitering? Perhaps. Not right away, though. He would do some more exploring in the countryside immediately around Madrid, just to see if Jillian would remain where she was. Once he was certain she would not bolt if he went off for an extended time, perhaps at that point he would feel comfortable enough venturing farther afield.

For really, what did she have to run to?

She ate the dinner he'd left for her, simply because she knew it was foolish to deprive herself of a meal out of pique. After she'd crept out to the bathroom and readied herself for bed, she'd fallen asleep almost immediately, and slumbered for almost ten hours. Clearly, her body was trying to tell her that she'd overdone it. Of course, all the assorted aches she experienced when she woke up the next morning would have been proof enough of that.

No point in trying to annoy Aldair with the same baggy clothes. Besides, they were dirty and needed to be washed. She put on a flowy skirt and a tank top, and let her hair fall free. All the same, she waited until she'd watched the djinn go out the front door, Patches tagging along, before she allowed herself to go downstairs.

Oh, the blessed relief of having him gone so she could pour herself some coffee and sit at the kitchen table to drink it without having him watch her the entire time. Jillian hadn't realized what a weight his gaze could be, not until she was free to do as she wished.

All right, not entirely free. She wasn't about to fool herself that he wasn't still keeping an eye on her in some way. She'd heard how the djinn could sense when mortals were around, even if they weren't directly in their line of sight. So changing into something more practical and heading for the hills really wasn't in the cards.

Instead, she savored her coffee, made some toast, and then fried herself an egg. No, it wasn't as good as the breakfasts Aldair had conjured, but she didn't mind. The savor of being by herself more than made up for any lack of flavor.

Afterward, she cleaned up the kitchen before wandering out to the porch so she could sit on the bench there. The weather felt somewhat cooler today, with clouds already forming overhead. It seemed as if they might be in for another round of monsoon storms. She was fine with that. Anything to keep the heat at bay.

She wondered where Aldair had gone, then immediately wanted to chide herself for even caring. Wasn't the important thing that he was somewhere else?

True, but she knew sooner or later they'd have to do something to get past the uneasy detente they were currently sharing. They couldn't go on like this indefinitely.

*Yes, and I'm sure he's just waiting for you to cave in so he can pick up where he left off the other night. I have no doubt that he believes you're going to succumb to his charms sooner or later.*

Fat chance. If she ever found it within her to move on with someone who wasn't Jack, that someone sure as hell wouldn't be Aldair al-Ankara. She'd want someone good and kind and understanding. Maybe she had been too quick to shoot down Brent Sanderson. Yes, he was more than ten years older than she, and his looks couldn't be described as much more than "pleasant," but he was a good man. She could have done a lot worse. Looks weren't everything. After all, Aldair was drop-dead gorgeous, but he was also one arrogant bastard.

As if her thoughts had conjured him, he appeared then—not in the djinn way, appearing out of nowhere, but walking up the driveway, Patches at his side. His dark hair waved in the breeze, as did the loose, flowing garments he wore. The half-hearted sunlight still was able to glimmer over the exposed muscles of his chest and stomach.

All right, maybe she needed to revise her stance on that whole "looks aren't everything" notion.

"You are feeling better this morning?" he asked, somewhat formally.

"Yes," she replied. "It looks as if you and Patches are having a good morning, too."

"We went for a long walk. This pleases him, I think. And I wanted to see more of the town's outskirts."

She wondered what he had been looking for. Not that she'd gone on many rambles in the area, but from what she'd seen, there just wasn't much to be found. A few homesteads on the borders of the town, none of them as nice as the one where they were staying. At the northern end of town, an old ball field, one she thought she'd read had been built back in Madrid's mining days, although it was still used for festivals and such. But still, not much that a djinn would find interesting.

"It's a nice day for a walk," she said, and stopped herself there. The last thing she wanted was for him to start in on her again for her foolishness in the hot sun yesterday.

As it was, he seemed to be thinking about the same thing, for the slightest of frowns pulled at his brows as he shot a quick glance upward at the overcast skies. To her relief, however, he didn't make any more comment than that. Instead, he slung a fabric bag off one shoulder and extended it to her.

"I found this for you."

Mystified, she took the bag from him. It was made of patchwork fabric, some of the pieces embroidered. Not djinn work, though; the bag looked similar to others she'd seen in boutiques that specialized in imports from India. She opened it, and saw that inside were several pieces of mesh cloth, already marked with designs for needlepoint, along with skeins of the fine wool thread needed for that sort of project.

Her heart caught. Maybe there were other things she could have done to fill her time, but this—this was familiar, something that would help to soothe her soul and spirit. "Th-thank you, Aldair."

He shrugged, his expression almost too blank. "I recalled that you said you practiced these sorts of needle arts. I found these items in one of the houses. Perhaps it will be a...less risky...form of amusement for you."

She almost wanted to argue, to tell him that she could manage her own amusements very well, but she held her tongue. Here he'd done something thoughtful for her. Throwing it in his face wouldn't help the current state of affairs at all. Hadn't she just been think-ing that their situation couldn't go on like this forever?

"Well, it will definitely help me stay cool," she said. "In fact, I think I'll go inside and get started now."

"Good. Patches has had enough exercise for the morning, I think, so I will leave him here with you."

"You're going back out?"

Piercing blue eyes met hers, and she looked down quickly, pretending to fiddle with the strap of the bag she held. "Yes," he said. "I hadn't quite finished."

She didn't dare ask him, *Finished with what?* Instead, she made herself nod, then added, "Well, keep an eye on the weather. I think it's going to rain sooner or later."

"No worries. I am a djinn of the air. I always know when a storm is coming."

And then he was gone, disappearing into the air that was his element. Jillian's breath caught, although she tried to tell herself she should be used to that sort of thing by now. Down by her feet, Patches shifted, then gazed imploringly up into her face.

"Well, kid," she said. "Looks like it's just you and me for a while."

Matters did seem to improve somewhat after that exchange. The gift of the needlecraft seemed to have mollified Jillian. Or at least, it gave her something to do, something that made her happy. No doubt she found comfort in its familiarity, when the rest of the world had changed so utterly for her.

Even so, he did not try to presume on the small change in her attitude. He could tell that she chafed at being kept here, even though she had made no further arguments for him to let her go. But he thought he had also learned something of her temperament during the time they had spent together. While she did not seem afraid to stand up for herself when necessary, she was not the sort of woman who thrived on conflict, and indeed did what she could to avoid it. They achieved a somewhat fragile peace as the week wore on, and he made sure not to upset that peace.

What he did do was continue his explorations in the local area, finding at first a hamlet off to the northwest called Cerrillos, a town even tinier than Madrid. Nothing lived there except a pack of stray dogs, all of whom looked healthy and strong, if not terribly thrilled to see him. He let them alone, once he'd determined there was nothing left in the place that could aid him and Jillian.

After that, he ranged south, finding miles and miles of open land, with the occasional ranch or other settlement to break up the monotony. No survivors here, either, which surprised him not at all. Even if anyone in these places had lived through the Dying, they had either possessed enough wits or luck to join the rest of the Immune in Los Alamos, or they had been picked off by the djinn whose role it was to scour the Earth of any humans who remained after the Heat had done its work.

It was also clear enough to him that this area had been deemed unworthy to be settled by djinn, for he sensed no others of his kind, no one at all. Emboldened, he finally ventured all the way to Albuquerque, where he encountered a most unusual sight. The miles and miles of urban and suburban sprawl were utterly devoid of any signs of life that went on two legs, and yet at the city's center, he saw evidence that someone had been at work here—an earth elemental, if his eyes and his instincts did not deceive him. Almost all the buildings in that area had been knocked down, except one tall edifice that appeared to have once been a hotel. Open grassland waved around it, dotted with indigenous shrubs and trees, and a stream meandered past before ending in a small lake. Wildflowers, fed by the monsoon rains, bloomed everywhere.

If he didn't know better, he would have said that one of his fellow djinn had begun reconstructing the city into something that pleased him better, only to be interrupted in that work. Who—or what—might have interrupted that unknown djinn, Aldair couldn't begin to guess. Once a land grant had been given by the elders, it could not be taken away. It was supposed to be eternal.

But clearly no one lived here now. Aldair wandered into the hotel and saw that it was furnished with the sort of splendor a djinn might very well want to claim for his own, with carved ceilings above and grottoes where fountains once played. For a moment, he wondered if he might bring Jillian here, for certainly this was a place that appealed to him far more than the glorified farmhouse where they currently dwelled.

However, after pondering the idea for a moment, he decided it would not do. If this place had once belonged to another djinn, then that meant it was not entirely off the radar, to use a human phrase. Someone else might happen along, or perhaps the djinn whose land it originally had been might return to inspect his or her property.

Aldair went back out to the street and stood on the bit of sidewalk that still remained. All around him was utter silence, save the whisper of the wind in the tall grass. Again he sent his senses questing outward, but he felt nothing—certainly no humans, and no djinn, either.

Looking to the north and east, he saw the impressive bulk of the mountain range known as the Sandias. Nestled among its foothills he could just make out the glint of windows, indicating that homes must have been built there. Large ones, too, if his sense of perspective meant anything. Perhaps one of those properties might warrant a closer look. It was hard to tell for sure from this distance, but it seemed as if they were set fairly far apart. Private. And perched up there, they would have a commanding view of the valley where most of Albuquerque lay. It would make for quite a defensible position.

Nodding in approval, he took to the air once more, letting the wind's currents help bear him to his destination. As he flew, his thoughts strayed to Jillian. If he found the perfect hideaway for the two of them, would she come willingly? Or would she view the change of location as another chance to escape?

Only time would tell, he supposed.

Aldair had been gone a long while. Over the past week, he'd begun to disappear for increasingly lengthy periods, but still something had kept Jillian from trying to make a run for it. Maybe it was only because she never quite knew when he would reappear—and he did so at the most unexpected times—making it difficult for her to determine how best to plan her escape.

And also...well, she really didn't want to admit to herself that she wasn't quite as eager to get away from him as she had been only a few days earlier.

They had both been civil, Jillian because she knew her time here was going to be much more exhausting if she continued to fight with him every second of the day, and Aldair because—actually, she didn't know for sure why he was being so nice. He'd brought her the needlepoint supplies, and that helped a great deal to pass the time, but it was more than that. He asked her what she would like for dinner, brought wildflowers to decorate the table, invited her along for his evening walks with Patches if it wasn't too hot. The whole time, Jillian had to wonder if this was just another stratagem for getting into her pants. But he'd been such a gentleman that she began to doubt her own judgment, and to ask herself if she was inclined to think the worst of him because, in a way, that would make things easier for her. Disliking him was so much better than the alternative.

*You are not going to let yourself fall for him,* she told herself sternly as she refilled the water in a cream-colored pitcher of heavy ceramic that held several exuberant bunches of sunflowers, brightening up the dining room table. *Yes, he's handsome, and yes, he's been decent the past several days, but that's all it is. It's just*—she broke off as she racked her brain for the word—*it's just propinquity. You've been thrown together in close proximity, and now you're manufacturing an attraction because it seems like the logical thing to happen.*

Then she wanted to laugh at herself. Psych 101 did tend to resurface at the oddest times.

Underneath, though, she couldn't ignore her unease, as if she knew logic had nothing to do with any of this. Logic would have made her seek an escape the second she thought she had enough time to get away safely. Instead, she lingered here, doing her best to ignore what her irrational heart was trying to tell her.

As she waited for Aldair to return, a certain restlessness sent her upstairs. She went into the room that had once been the owner's studio and looked at the paintings there, both finished and unfinished. It would have been convenient if Jillian herself had been an artist; she would have had something else to occupy her time, and there were certainly ample supplies here to keep her happily painting and drawing for months and months, if not years. Unfortunately, she didn't have an artistic bone in her body, except a certain eye for color, a talent that helped with the needlepoint and certainly when decorating the townhouse she and Jack had shared. But knowing which pillows would look best with your couch didn't exactly make you Picasso.

Up until now, Jillian had mostly ignored the room that once served as an office here in the house. She certainly wasn't going to attempt to get past the password that protected the big iMac there, even if her talents had extended to computer hacking. Snooping around a dead woman's computer was just wrong. The same went for the contents of her desk.

However, on the desktop was a stack of office supplies, as if the home's owner had recently gotten a shipment of the stuff right before the Heat rendered all that sort of thing useless. All right, not entirely useless; the stacks of Post-it notes and boxes of staples probably could have been put to good use up in Los Alamos, where they did tend to go through office supplies at a rate that couldn't possibly be sustainable.

What caught Jillian's eye, though, were the two refills for the desk calendar, both of them still wrapped in plastic. One was for the year already past, and so she ignored that one. But the other could still be of some use. She pulled off the cellophane and inserted the stack of calendar pages into the little plastic holder, lining up the holes in the paper with the metal loops that held it in place. And then she began flipping through the calendar, thumbing ahead to what she hoped was today's date. She knew the lab accident had happened on August 27th, because Miles always wrote the current date on one of the whiteboards there—probably to help him keep track as of his progress. And, ticking the days off on her fingers, she realized she had been here in Madrid for a full week. So she flipped the pages over, leaving today's date to stare up at her.

September 2nd.

Her heart seized in her chest. Had she really been so oblivious that she hadn't realized the day was coming around once again?

September 2nd. It would have been Jack's thirtieth birthday today. A day they'd planned for, talked about. She'd joked and said he'd be her old man, since he was a year and a half older than she was. And he'd just grinned and told her he'd be honored, since the only thing he wanted was to grow old with her.

The numbers on the calendar blurred before her eyes. Damn those tears, always threatening when she least expected them. She blinked, swallowing huge gulps of air, but somehow that didn't seem to be good enough to prevent a sob from forcing its way up her throat. She couldn't breathe, couldn't do anything except push herself blindly away from the desk so she could get out of that office and down the stairs.

Fresh air. That's what she needed.

The day had been another overcast one, the skies lowering, distant thunder echoing off the hillsides even though no rain had yet fallen. Now, though, as Jillian stumbled down the porch steps, the first drops of rain hit her face and arms, cold, stinging. Lightning flashed, with thunder following just a few seconds later, so loud that it seemed to reverberate in her very bones.

Here it was Jack's birthday, and she'd been grappling with the knowledge that somehow she'd let herself fall in love with a djinn. A *djinn*. They'd destroyed this world. They'd been responsible for Jack's death and the deaths of so many others. Her parents. Jack's younger brother, and her in-laws, and everyone else she'd known and loved or even liked. How on earth could she be so selfish as to think it was all right to give one of those creatures her heart?

The rain began to fall in earnest, soaking through her clothes, plastering her hair to her forehead and neck and shoulders. But she hardly noticed. She staggered down the drive toward the highway, ignoring the rain, ignoring the blinding flash overhead as lightning pierced the sky once again. The thunder that followed was so loud, she clapped her hands to her ears.

Even that didn't stop her, however. She knew she had to get out of here. She had to get out before Aldair came back, Aldair with those blue, blue eyes that seemed to see every part of her, with a mouth that promised everything she knew she should be trying to avoid. If she let Aldair kiss her again, she'd forget herself. She'd forget Jack, and she knew she couldn't let that happen. Because if she forgot him, he'd be truly gone, since there was no one left to remember who he was, who he'd been.

Water was beginning to flow in little rivulets across the highway as the rain pounded down, so heavy she could barely see the buildings in "downtown" Madrid. But that was where she had to go. Through Madrid, and beyond. If she could just get to Santa Fe, the djinn and their Chosen there would help her get all the way home to Los Alamos. But no, Los Alamos wasn't really home. No place had been home. Not since she lost Jack.

She wouldn't think about how the house here on the outskirts of Madrid had begun to feel like home, with Patches and Aldair and their quiet daily routine. She couldn't think about that.

Was she going crazy?

Maybe. And the only way to stay sane was to get the hell out of here.

She kept walking.

## CHAPTER FOURTEEN

ALDAIR COULD FEEL THE STORM CELL BUILDING off to the northeast. Over Madrid? Possibly. From here in Albuquerque, it was difficult to tell exactly, what with the bulk of the Sandia Mountains in the way. He had found a house he liked very much, one built on its own promontory in the foothills, with architecture that would not have been out of place in ancient Toledo— tile roofs and hidden courtyards, and hanging lanterns of dark wrought iron. It was beautiful, and far more to his taste than the rustic homestead where he'd been living for the past week. Would Jillian think it beautiful if he brought her here?

The best way to know for certain was to ask her.

Since he knew his destination, he blinked himself from the house above Albuquerque directly into the

living room of the home in Madrid. Cool air surrounded him at once—almost too cool, for the air
conditioning had been set at a certain temperature to
keep the house comfortable in the summer heat, but
the storm that raged in the little mountain town had
made the air outside almost cold.

Patches was sitting at the front door, looking
despondent. Immediately, Aldair went over to the dog
and bent so he could scratch behind his ears. "What is
it?" he asked. "Does the thunder frighten you?"

A shake, and then Patches scratched at the door-
frame and whined softly.

A thin trickle of cold that had nothing to do with
the air conditioning made its way down Aldair's spine.
"And Jillian? Where is she?"

Another whine.

Aldair turned from the dog and called out into the
depths of the house, "Jillian!"

Only silence in reply, just as he'd feared there
would be.

He blinked himself upstairs and hurried over to
her room. The door stood open, so he could see the
bed was neatly made. A quick peek inside the closet
told him that all her clothes were still there, except the
ones on her back. The necklace he'd given her lay across
the top of the dresser, but that in and of itself would
not have normally worried him. She did not wear the

piece all the time, although she did tend to put it on for dinner, as if to dress up whatever she was wearing.

And yet, somehow he knew she was gone.

Cursing under his breath, he blinked himself outside. Almost at once, the rain pouring from the skies soaked through the silk garments he wore, but he cared little for that. A djinn could not take a chill the way a human could, and he could use the winds to dry himself just as soon as he returned indoors.

Because he did not know exactly where Jillian was, he could not send himself directly to her location. He was forced to fly along the highway, heading north since that seemed the most logical direction for her to have gone. Santa Fe lay to the north.

No sign of her in the small section of Madrid where the shops and restaurants lay. He kept going, ignoring the crackle of lightning overhead and its answering thunder. Even if he should be struck directly, he would take no harm. At the same time, he could feel the way the storm cell had settled itself over the town. It clearly did not intend to go anywhere for some time.

There. Just beyond the northern outskirts of the small settlement, where steep hills loomed to one side and the incongruity of a sports field lay to the other, Aldair spotted a slender figure laboring up the incline. As he watched, she reached down to fiddle with one of the flimsy sandals she wore. It must have broken, because he saw her fling it away, followed by its companion. Then she squared her shoulders and resumed her pitiful march.

No. He would not allow her to walk on that stony road in her bare feet with the rain pouring down all around. It was painfully clear that she had made her attempt to get away, but he cared nothing for that now. He must get her inside, get her warm. Only then would he begin to ask for answers.

After pushing himself forward through the rain, he overshot her by a few feet so he could come to rest directly in her path. Even through the pouring rain, he saw how her eyes widened as he descended to the blacktop in front of her.

"No," she said. "No."

Not exactly the welcome he had hoped for, but he also wasn't terribly surprised. After all, she had been trying to escape. "Jillian, you are soaked through. Let me take you back to the house."

At once she shook her head. "No. I can't go back there. I won't."

Had she lost her mind? With her face soaked by the rain, it was difficult for him to tell, but she appeared to have been weeping, teardrops mixing with raindrops so it was nearly impossible to distinguish one from the other. What could possibly have happened to upset her so? He hadn't been gone so very long, not more than a few hours at most.

He reached out to take her by the arm, but she shook her head and backed away.

"Don't touch me."

This was getting ridiculous. Even as impatience and anger flared, he told himself he should not frighten her. She obviously wasn't thinking clearly at the moment.

As he watched, she put her hands to her face and sank to her knees on the rocky highway, rain beating on her bedraggled hair. Her entire body shook—from cold, or some kind of internal torment. He didn't know for sure. All he did know was that he had to get her out of there.

Ignoring the muddy rivulets pouring across the highway, he went to his knees beside her, then reached out and drew her close. For a few seconds, her entire body went tense, as if she meant to resist him once more. Then she collapsed against him, sobbing in a hopeless sort of way that made him wonder once again what could have possibly brought her to this state of agitation.

But he would worry about that later. For now, it was enough that she had not fought him. His arms tightened around her, and he blinked the two of them away from that abandoned stretch of road, back into the house—into the master bath, where he set her carefully on the countertop so he could fetch one of the towels that hung from the rack there and wrap it around her shoulders. At the same time, he summoned

the gentlest of winds to spin their way about her, drying the dripping masses of her hair.

She stared at him, eyes wide, almost the same
color as the storm clouds that hung over the valley.
"Aldair—"

"Shh," he said, then took a corner of the towel so
he might wipe away the last of her tears. Once he was
done, he let go of the towel and cupped her face in his
hands. Her skin still felt cool, but at least she wasn't as
icy-cold as she'd been a moment ago. "Let me warm
you."

And he brought his mouth to hers, tasted salt on
her lips. For a moment she went utterly still, and he
worried she would rebuff him once more. But then her
mouth opened to his, and she was kissing him back,
kissing him with the kind of wild abandon he had
hoped for but wasn't sure she would actually be capable of. He pulled her close, ignoring her wet clothes,
since he knew the touch of his body would dry them
soon enough.

They stayed locked in that manner for what seemed
to be the sweetest of eternities. At length, though, she
pulled away, her hand going to her mouth. "I can't
believe I did that," she whispered.

"My dear," he said. Strange, because he had never
used that endearment before, not with any of his previous lovers. But it felt right to him, just as the touch of
her lips to him had felt more right than anything he'd

ever done. Whatever had upset her, he must find the means to comfort her as best he could. "Why should you not believe it? It is not the first time I have kissed you—and I very much hope it will not be the last."

Those words did not appear to reassure her. She shook her head, then pushed herself off the counter so she might stand up. Aldair contemplated stopping her, but decided it was better to let her have her freedom—for now. His entire body throbbed with need, and yet he knew he must step back for the moment. She was so fragile...so very, very fragile. If he bent her the wrong way, she would snap, and he feared he might never be able to repair the damage.

Her eyes would not meet his. "It was wrong. This... this is wrong."

"My dear, why? I have already told you that I no longer have a connection with Katelyn, and you told me that she is now partnered with one of your men in Los Alamos. So how is it wrong?"

"Because of who you are. *What* you are." She shook her head and passed a hand over the skirt she wore. It was no longer dripping wet, thanks to the winds he had called to help dry her off, but he could tell it was still damp. "Can I—can you let me change, please? I'll meet you downstairs when I'm ready."

He wanted to protest, to tell her they would have this out now. Part of him rankled at her words. "What" he was? Were they back to that?

But he could tell from the set of her mouth that arguing with her would be a very bad idea. Better to give her a few moments to herself. Perhaps then she could gather her thoughts, calm down. She still hadn't told him what had upset her so greatly, what had sent her running out into the rain and the storm.

He needed to know.

So he nodded, and said, "Of course. I'll be waiting for you in the living room."

She didn't exactly smile, but the expression of relief that passed over her face was obvious enough. Since she already stood close to the door of the bathroom, she slipped out then and hurried across his chamber and on into her own bedroom, just before she closed the door behind her.

Aldair let out a breath. And then, because there was little else he could do, he went downstairs to wait for her.

Jillian leaned her head against the bedroom door. Too bad it wasn't one of those big metal bank vault doors, the kind that could withstand everything up to plastic explosives. Then she could lock herself in here and never come out again.

No, that would be cowardly. She still couldn't quite explain the meltdown that had led to her running into the storm, but grief was a strange thing. It could lie in wait, lurking in the shadows, waiting for that perfect moment of vulnerability when it might rise up again to overcome you.

The shock of realizing it was Jack's birthday...the conflict over her feelings for Aldair...well, she supposed it wasn't so terribly surprising that she'd totally lost it.

But why she'd let the djinn kiss her afterward...why she hadn't stopped him...she didn't know if she really wanted to analyze that particular reaction.

She pulled off her damp clothes and laid them across the top of the dresser so they might finish drying out all the way. Her underwear went in the hamper in the corner, and she quickly climbed into some fresh panties and one of her borrowed bras. No skirt, though; she'd laundered the jeans she'd been wearing when she'd been zapped out of the lab, and so she climbed into those, although she did put on one of the pretty tops she'd gotten from the boutique in town. The sandals she'd worn for her escape attempt were long gone, so she fetched another pair from the closet.

Her gaze fell on the turquoise necklace Aldair had given her. No, she couldn't wear that. It would be giving far too much of a signal. Only her silver hoop earrings, the ones that had come with her from Los Alamos. A quick hop over to the bathroom so she could run a comb through her nearly dry hair. That was a handy trick, she had to admit—a djinn was much better than one of those hot-air dryers that used to populate public restrooms.

Her reflection in the mirror didn't exactly inspire confidence. She looked pale and tragic, although at least she hadn't been wearing any makeup, so she didn't have to worry about runny mascara. Apparently the artist who'd lived in this house hadn't used cosmetics, so there hadn't been anything Jillian could have borrowed. She'd been going bare-faced ever since she got here, although Aldair didn't seem to mind too much.

Okay, no more stalling. He was waiting for her, and it would be rude to keep messing around up here when she really didn't have anything else she could do to repair her appearance. It would be hard as hell to look him in the face and tell him the truth, but she would. He might enjoy evasion, but that wasn't her style. Once he knew what she was thinking and feeling, he would have to let her go. Why in the world would he keep her around after he learned that he had no hope of ever being with her?

That sounded very noble. If only she didn't keep feeling the touch of his lips against hers, the exquisite gentleness of his fingers as he'd cupped her face....

No. No.

She wouldn't think about that.

She couldn't.

One step at a time, she descended the stairs. Cool air moved against her face, but it wasn't as cold as it had been when she'd left the house. Aldair must have adjusted the temperature on the thermostat. Rain still pounded on the roof, and lightning still flickered out-side. The clouds were so low, the day so dark, it felt as if nighttime was approaching, even though she knew it had to be a few hours off.

He'd turned on one of the lamps in the living room. She could see its warm glow as she approached. And there was Patches, lying on the rug in front of the fireplace, even though of course no fire burned in the hearth.

A pitcher of water and two glasses sat on the coffee table, along with a mug of tea, which sent up a faint tendril of steam. A flicker of surprise moved through her; she'd thought a bottle of wine was more Aldair's style. But maybe he wanted to make sure they were both completely sober for this discussion.

Somehow, she made herself move into the living room, then sat down on the love seat. Aldair watched her, his expression grave. While she'd been changing, obviously he'd changed, too. The new outfit was a dark charcoal gray, with an edging of deep cobalt blue on the open robe. The colors were more somber than what she'd seen him wear previously, although she supposed she shouldn't be too surprised. They hadn't exactly met here for a cocktail party.

Without speaking, he lifted the mug of tea and extended it to her. She took it from him, then drank. The liquid was warm as it coursed down her throat, soothing. Yes, that was a little better.

"You are feeling improved?" he asked.

"Yes, thank you." She wrapped her hands around the mug, holding on to it as if it were a lifeline rather than a simple mug of tea. Its warmth helped to take the last of the chill away from her body. "I—I suppose you think I've completely lost it."

"I don't know," he said frankly. "I suppose that is for you to tell me. I had thought...." The words trailed off, and he shrugged. "For now, it is not important what I thought. Please, tell me what happened."

How often had Aldair said "please" in his long, long life? Probably not very often at all. He didn't seem the type. And that was part of the problem, wasn't it? How could she have developed feelings for someone who was the complete opposite of the kind of man she'd always found admirable?

She set the mug down on a coaster and knotted her fingers on top of her knee. "It would have been Jack's thirtieth birthday today."

An eyebrow lifted slightly. "And this upset you."

"Of course it would! Thirty is a big birthday for us mere humans, you know. We'd talked about saving up for some kind of trip—maybe to California—although he didn't know about taking time off during the school year. And...." Jillian paused then. "I guess it just hit me. Or it sneaked up on me. But I thought of everything we'd planned, everything we were supposed to do, and how it was all gone, just like that."

"That would be difficult."

She risked a quick glance over at him. Aldair's expression was still somber, so she couldn't really tell if he truly meant what he'd just said, or whether he'd uttered a few words of sympathy because he thought that was what she expected.

But of course, what she'd just told him wasn't everything. Not by a long shot.

"And also...." Again she had to stop and attempt to gather her thoughts. Oh, why had he returned when he did? Another hour, and maybe she would have been far enough away that he couldn't risk catching up with her. Even as the thought crossed her mind, however, a pang went through her body. Would she really have been happy, knowing she would never see him again?

Maybe not happy. But a whole hell of a lot less tormented.

She shifted on the love seat, and wished he wasn't so close. Yes, he sat on the couch and not directly next to her, but still, his presence seemed almost overwhelming—the rich brown hair waving around his face, the sensual lines of his mouth, the glint of those blue eyes in their frame of thick lashes. And she didn't dare let her gaze move away from his face, because his body was even more distracting.

"I know this might be hard for you to understand," she said, forcing herself to go on. "That is, you had a Chosen. You were surrounded by couples made up of djinn and humans. To all of you, that sort of pairing isn't so strange. But I—" Her mouth was suddenly dry, and she reached for one of the glasses of water he'd set out so she might keep herself from coughing. "I never thought I would be in this kind of situation. In fact, I sometimes wondered how the Chosen could bear to be with a djinn at all."

His mouth thinned somewhat, but his tone was even enough as he responded, "What, because we are so repulsive?"

"Not in body," Jillian said honestly. "But in deed."

"Not all of us are responsible for what happened. You know that."

"I know it intellectually. But I guess I have to won-der—did all of you One Thousand really work that hard to try to stop what happened?"

A spark of anger lit deep within those blue, blue eyes. "We did what we could. We managed to save a thousand of your people. Without us, humanity would have been utterly annihilated."

"Not utterly," she said. "Thanks to Miles Odekirk." She didn't bother to add, *And no thanks to you djinn.* There was no need to. From the way Aldair's nostrils flared and his jaw set, she could tell he'd gotten the message.

When he spoke, however, he sounded calm enough...almost too calm. "Yes, Dr. Odekirk did pro-vide quite a service to the survivors of New Mexico.

But that doesn't negate what the djinn of the One Thousand did, either." He stopped there, and his gaze slid away from her.

Jillian didn't have a great deal of experience when it came to dealing with lies and misdirection, but once again she got the sense that Aldair was holding something back. In the past, his evasions had annoyed her, but now, with her heart and soul as bruised and raw as they were, that furtive sideways glance was enough to set her blood boiling. "Oh, yes, I suppose it was all very noble. I can't comment on that, since I wasn't one of the fortunate few. But you tell me, Aldair—was it a sense of cosmic responsibility that led you to choose Katelyn Fonseca as your partner, or was there something else going on? Because I keep getting the feeling that there's a whole hell of a lot more to the story than what you're telling me."

For a long moment, he said nothing. His fingers clenched his silk-clad knees, the fabric rippling with the movement. Then, still without responding, he bent forward so he could lift his glass of water and take a drink.

Watching him, Jillian once again experienced the sting of unwanted tears in her eyes. Clearly, it didn't matter what she said or what she thought—he had secrets he would never divulge. Even if they somehow managed to get past her problems with him being a djinn, it wouldn't matter in the end, because he kept some part of his heart locked away, something to be kept from her at all costs.

She stood, and he stared up at her in surprise. "What are you doing?"

"I'm going up to my room," she replied. "And in the morning, I'm walking away from here and going to Los Alamos. And don't you try to stop me this time."

After delivering this ultimatum, she turned so she might leave—only to have him rise to his feet as well. His hand closed on her wrist. "Don't go."

Her jaw clenched, but she didn't try to pull away. There was no point in getting into a struggle with him. He was so very strong. "Let go of me."

"I will—if you will stay and talk to me. Please."

There it was again. *Please.* Reluctantly, she stared up into his face. His expression wasn't particularly pleading, but something in those eyes seemed to have altered. They were wide open, almost naked in their earnestness.

"All right," she said, relenting, then added as she saw relief begin to spread over his face, "but only if you will tell me the truth."

"The truth about what?"

"Everything. You've been hiding far too much. I'm like an open book to you, practically, but I can tell you haven't given me the whole story. Not even close."

At first, he didn't respond. Then, slowly, he let go of her wrist. "You will not like it."

"Let me be the judge of that. Because...." She had to stop herself there, because inwardly she wrestled with what she needed to say as opposed to what she should say. "Because I know it's foolish to deny there's nothing between us. I felt it upstairs when we kissed—"

"As did I," Aldair cut in, his gaze softening as he stared down at her. "I am glad you recognized it as well."

"But," Jillian went on, "I'm not going to let that chemistry completely take over my brain. Not when so much is at stake. I know the djinn thing is my hang-up, because clearly there are plenty of human women who are very happy with their djinn partners. But I expect honesty of the man I'm with, whether he's djinn or human. So tell me what you've been hiding all this time, and then...."

"And then?" he prompted.

"Well, I guess we'll just have to see."

## CHAPTER FIFTEEN

COULD HE DO IT? COULD HE BARE HIS SOUL TO HER, knowing that once she learned the truth about why he had chosen Katelyn Fonseca, why he had been with the djinn in Taos at all, Jillian would most certainly reject him. Her soul was too good and pure to accept a man such as he, even when her kisses scorched like those of a fire elemental.

On the other hand, if he refused to tell her the truth, then she would walk away. And he could do nothing to stop her this time, because she had offered him a way for them to move forward, and he had been too much of a coward to do as she asked.

He pushed out a breath, and knotted his fists at his side. Throughout his life, he had always done as he wished, and had not allowed the needs and desires of others to impede his path. Now he would have to set all that aside, humble himself before her. And still his sacrifice might not be enough.

Jillian stood there, watching him carefully. Ah, how beautiful she was, with that mouth which just begged to be kissed, and with those wide, smoky gray eyes. Yes, those eyes were still a little reddened from her weeping bout earlier, but he found that did very little to mar her appearance. Had he ever found a djinn woman so lovely? At the moment, he rather thought he hadn't.

Better to risk all, on the chance he might have her, rather than ignore her request and know that she would walk out of his life forever.

"Very well," he said at last. "But please—do sit down. I think that is best."

She nodded, then resumed her seat. Aldair noticed that she still seemed very tense, as though she knew she would not like what she was about to hear, and so had already steeled herself against it.

Wise woman.

He also sat down, and sent one irritated glance toward the water that sat on the table before returning his attention to Jillian. In that moment, he longed for some wine to give him courage, but making the substitution now would be far too obvious. He would have to force himself through this unaided.

Then he might as well get to it.

"I told you of my brother," he said.

"Yes. How your father favored him, and how you wanted to take your revenge." Her head tilted slightly. "But you didn't say how."

"Through Katelyn, to start."

"Katelyn?" Jillian repeated, looking confused. "What did she have to do with it?"

"Very little, save as a means to an end." He stopped there, steeling himself. The expression of puzzlement on Jillian's face had already started to shift toward worry, and he had only just begun to tell the tale. "You see, when we knew the time to unleash the Heat was nearly upon us, those djinn who wished to save their humans made their selections for their Chosen. I had not fully decided what I was going to do—"

"You mean you didn't care whether you saved someone or not?" she asked, worry now turning to something rather like horror. "But you said—"

"Let me continue." He did not like to cut her off in such a way, but he knew he had to keep going, that if he stopped he might not have the nerve to continue. It was bad enough already, for Jillian now looked at him like some creeping insect she had just discovered in her bedchamber. His blood went cold, but he made himself say, "As I told you, I was not sure what I planned to do. But then I heard that my brother Jasreel—"

"Jasreel?" she interrupted. "You mean Jace? The djinn who's with Jessica Monroe?"

"Yes," Aldair replied. He realized then that this was the first time he had uttered his brother's name in Jillian's presence. "You know him?

"Not exactly. I've met Jessica, though, and—" Jillian stopped herself there. "That doesn't really matter. I guess it just startled me. I suppose if I'd really thought it through, I would have connected you by your last name. But I think I've only heard it once, and that time in passing. Anyway, please go on."

Well, at least she didn't know his hated half-brother very well. That was something. Aldair nodded, and continued, "As I was saying, I had heard that Jasreel had selected a woman for himself, and I thought that would be a very good way of taking my revenge upon him—to claim the same woman he wanted as my own."

"You didn't love her, though."

"No. She is a very beautiful woman, however, and I thought I would do well enough with her. But because Jasreel and I had claimed the same Chosen, the elders decreed that we must battle one another for the right to have her."

Jillian appeared to absorb all this while wearing a faint frown. "So…I assume he won, since you were with Katelyn instead."

Oh, the ignominy of having to admit to such a thing, especially to Jillian. Aldair's fists clenched, but he managed to keep his tone level enough as he replied, "I am still not sure he did not cheat in some way. But yes, the elders believed that he came out ahead in that conflict, and so he claimed Jessica Monroe as his own."

"Well," Jillian said, "she is very beautiful."

"Nowhere near as beautiful as you."

That comment elicited a raised eyebrow and a disbelieving look, but Jillian made no other reply. Perhaps she simply did not want to waste time on foolish arguments when the meat of the story still lay ahead. "So you moved on to Katelyn Fonseca."

"I did select her as my second choice. But my true goal was merely to be accepted as a member of the Taos community, so I might be close to Jasreel and Jessica, and therefore wait until another opportunity presented itself. Which it did soon enough, for Jasreel was captured by your people in Los Alamos. I thought then that perhaps this could all be resolved with no further conflict, for Katelyn had disappeared as well not long before that, when she went out with a scouting party to learn more of the people in Los Alamos."

"But she was never in Los Alamos," Jillian protested. "That is, I never heard anything about it."

"You did not hear anything because it was not Captain Margolis and his men who captured her. She was taken by Khalim and his followers, and given to one of Khalim's cousins as a prize."

"That's...horrible." Jillian's face had gone white, and she crossed her arms, hugging herself, as if she had suddenly taken a chill.

This was where Aldair wished very much he could leave off, for he would have to admit that he had felt very little concern as to Katelyn's fate. He had never loved her, only used her. At the time, he had been so consumed by his own desire for revenge on Jasreel that the thoughts and feelings of one human woman mattered very little to him. Now, though, he could only reflect on what he had done to her and realize how shameful, how cowardly, his own behavior had been.

"Yes," he said briefly. "Although when she went missing, I truly had no idea what might have become of her. I only thought that with both her and Jasreel gone, then I could take Jessica as mine. Indeed, I went to Zahrias, the leader of our community, and asked him to intercede on my behalf. He would not go so far as to simply hand her over to me, although he did try to convince her that there was no way to save Jasreel, and that if she became my Chosen, she could still remain in the community. Of course, she would have none of it, and went on to rescue him." Despite his own efforts to keep his face as expressionless as possible, he could feel his mouth twisting as he thought of Jessica's devotion to the hated Jasreel, of how she absolutely refused to take him, Aldair, as her replacement lover.

"But you couldn't let it go, could you?"

"No," he replied. How well Jillian already knew him. Of course he could not abandon his revenge. He merely had taken it in another direction. "I left the Taos community and went to join Khalim and his followers."

"But...." The confused look was back, although somewhere behind it Aldair could detect some of that same worry and horror, as if she knew the answer to the question and yet could not prevent herself from asking it anyway. "Wasn't this Khalim person behind the attacks on Taos? Didn't he hurt one of your Chosen and kill another?"

Aldair let out a heavy breath. "And more than that, for he also attacked Katelyn's scouting party, and killed the men in the group and took the women hostage. He cared nothing for the compact all djinn had agreed to, that the Chosen must be sacrosanct, and no harm brought to them."

"How on earth could you ever join up with someone like that?" Now Jillian had shrunk back against the cushions of the love seat, as if she needed to put even that meager distance between them. "He was a monster."

From the tone of her voice, Aldair guessed she must think that he was a monster, too. Well, she wouldn't be the first person to believe such a thing of him. "I was angry, and not thinking clearly. I—"

"And did you even try to get Katelyn away from those djinn?"

"No."

Dead silence. Jillian's mouth worked, and she looked away from him, staring off into the opening that led to the dining room. The sunflowers he had brought her still sat on the table, incongruously bright notes in the storm-darkened house.

At last she said, "I'm not sure I want to hear any more of this."

Exactly what he had feared. Well, what had he expected—that she would nod in understanding and forgive all his heinous deeds? For now, seeing them through her horrified eyes, he realized how dreadful his actions had been. He had not attempted to save Katelyn from Ali, Khalim's cousin, for he had not cared about her. Indeed, he had not cared about Jessica, either. He had only wanted her because to possess her would hurt Jasreel so terribly.

"That is your choice, of course."

Jillian rested an unsteady hand on the love seat's cushion, then used it to push herself upward. However, she did not leave the room, as he had both expected and feared. Instead, she moved to the window and stared out into the storm. Rain lashed the window, blurring the landscape outside. "I don't understand," she said then, her voice faint, shaky. She cleared her throat and went on, the words a little stronger this time. "I mean, I guess I'm trying to reconcile the person I've spent time with this week with the man you've just described to me. How can you—how could you—?" Her voice broke there, and she clenched her fingers on the windowsill, apparently using it to hold herself up, to prevent her knees from giving way.

He rose from the couch and went to her. However, he took care to remain a safe distance away, even though in that moment he only wished he could take her in his arms and hold her, tell her that he had changed, that he was not the same man who had left Katelyn to the wolves and had tried to steal the woman his brother loved more than life itself.

But he was the same man. Or rather, the anger and the resentment that had driven him to such actions were as much a part of him as the affection he now knew he felt for this woman, this mortal. Whether she could learn to accept all of him—well, he could not know the answer to that.

"It is difficult," he said. "I can make no excuses, for that will not change what I did. Nothing can change any of it. But all I did was succeed in making Jasreel and Jessica's love stronger than ever, and it seems Katelyn has found her own happiness as well, with this man Shawn Gutierrez who leads your community. And I—I told you that I was banished for breaking an oath. The oath I broke was the one I had sworn to keep all the world's Chosen safe, for by casting my lot with Khalim, I was a party to his crimes as well. That was why you found me there in the outer circles. The elders and the people of Taos—and now Santa Fe—thought

I had been given a just punishment. This is why I have done my best to avoid them. For if they learn of where I am, then they will most certainly send me back. And that is what I cannot bear. Yes, I can endure the outer circles again if I must. What I cannot bear is the thought of being there for all of eternity, and never seeing your face again."

Tears glistened in Jillian's eyes. But she didn't move, stayed where she was, gripping the windowsill as if it was the only thing that held her up. When she spoke, the words came out in a cracked whisper. "Aldair... you are making this so hard for me. I can't—I—" She stopped there, pulled in a gasp of a breath. "I want to hate you. I should. But...."

"But?" he repeated. He didn't want to hold hope in his heart. Hope hurt. And yet, she still stood there. She hadn't run away. Surely if she despised him, wanted nothing more to do with him, she would have fled the room.

"But...." Another of those pauses. He could almost see the thoughts darting through her mind as she attempted to decide what she should say. "But I also know that holding on to hate is not the way to move forward. I'm not sure I can ever truly forgive the djinn for what they did. I guess what I'm trying to figure out is whether I can forgive you for what you did." She stared out at the sodden landscape past the window, where the stalks of the sunflowers were bent almost double by the force of the rain and where new little rivers had formed in the bare dirt of the front yard. "Do you promise me—do you *swear*—that you had nothing to do with the Heat, with letting it loose on the world?"

At least that was one thing he could do, without reservation. "I do swear it," he said quietly. "I will admit to you that I did nothing to stop it, either. Not that I could have. The decision had been made, and far more of my people wished for the world to be cleansed than they wished to preserve it as it existed. But although my motives were far from pure, I did keep Katelyn from perishing in the scourge that followed the Dying."

Jillian's full mouth twisted into a crooked smile. "So I guess you did the right thing for all the wrong reasons."

"Yes, I suppose you could look at it that way."

She nodded, but didn't reply. Again he got that sense of her mind rushing at full speed, trying to process everything he had told her. Weighing what he had done.

And if she found him lacking, if she found the small kindnesses he had shown her could not possibly make up for all the dreadful things he had done before they met…what then?

*Well, you will set her free,* he told himself. *Bad enough that you tried to force Jessica, when she came to you to save the people of the Taos community from Khalim. You will certainly not do such a thing to Jillian.*

Whether he would have actually taken Jessica to his bed, Aldair couldn't say. For all his other crimes, he had never forced a woman. His partners had always come to him willingly. But he had been so driven by his desire for vengeance, he could not truly say whether he would have stopped himself at the last moment. Luckily, he had not been compelled to make that decision for himself, since the elders had interceded and taken Jessica away before anything could happen.

It still bothered him, that he did not know for sure what he would have done.

Jillian let go of the windowsill and faced him. Without speaking, she reached out and took both his hands in hers. Her fingers felt very small and cold and fragile, and he wished he could draw her closer so he might fold her in his arms and warm her properly. However, he knew he did not dare to make such a gesture. She would have to approach him, if that was what she truly wanted.

To his surprise, she let out a rusty little chuckle. "I've been fighting with myself the past few days, you know. I didn't want to acknowledge what I'd begun to feel for you. And now, hearing what you had to tell me...." She shook her head so her loose hair fell over her shoulders, rich and brown against her lightly tanned skin. "Part of me was almost relieved, because you'd given me the best excuse in the world to walk away. After all, how could I possibly be with someone capable of such things?"

"I see," he said, as calmly as he could, even though her words sent another chill through him. He began to pull his hands from hers, but her fingers tightened immediately, preventing him from stepping away.

"No, you don't, Aldair." Lifting her chin, she gazed up into his face. "But then I thought of how it would feel to never see you again, to have you gone completely from my life. And—and I realized something. Jack died almost two years ago, and ever since then, I've been dead, too. Dead inside, because I was too frightened to let myself live again. I fought those feelings for you because I knew that meant I wasn't dead. You made me feel alive. Even when I wanted to strangle you," she added with a rueful smile.

Her words brought him more hope than he could have hoped for. At the same time, though, he willed himself to be cautious. She had not yet said that she wished to stay. She had not said the words he had always thought of as a trap, but which he longed for now like nothing he had ever longed for before...not even vengeance on his brother.

He waited, because this was her moment, and the last thing he wanted was to speak and ruin it.

Now her fingers weren't quite as cold, although they still felt cool to his touch. She moistened her lips before saying, "I have to forgive you, Aldair. I *have* to, because that's the only way I can admit to being in love with you."

Such a surge of warmth came over him then, he knew he could do nothing but reply in kind, although he had managed to avoid saying those words his entire life. "I love you, Jillian. God witness these words, for I have never said them to anyone before. How could I, when I had to wait through the centuries for the perfect moment when I could be with you?"

Her eyes filled with tears, and she managed a gasping little breath, right before she said, "Why, that's quite a line, Aldair. Is it true?"

"Of course it is true," he replied, somewhat indignantly. Here he had just bared his soul to her, and she was questioning his veracity?

"Prove it," she said, moving closer. Those stormy eyes were locked on his, filled with a warmth he would have been a fool not to recognize.

And whatever else he might be, Aldair was no fool. He bent, and claimed her sweet, sweet mouth with his.

## CHAPTER SIXTEEN

OH, THIS WAS MUCH, MUCH BETTER. WITH ALDAIR kissing her like this, his arms pulling her close so he might send his own heat through her chilled body, she didn't have to think about anything other than how amazing he felt, how wonderful he tasted. How those lips of his touched hers and made her amazingly, thrillingly alive.

Was it wrong? Maybe. But right then she realized she just didn't care.

And when he drew her away from the window, pulled her down onto the couch, she didn't resist. She wanted this. God, how she wanted this.

Strong fingers grasped the bottom of her tank top and pulled it over her head, then reached for the clasp on her bra. Dimly, she wondered how a djinn even knew how human undergarments worked, but then she didn't have time to think about anything else, because his hands closed on her breasts, caressing, moving over the sensitive skin so masterfully that she gasped aloud.

"You are sublime," he whispered. "So lovely, so perfect."

She wanted to argue she wasn't perfect at all. How could she be, compared to a djinn? But then his mouth closed on her nipple, suckling, and the wave of arousal that passed over her was so strong that she almost climaxed then and there. One of his hands remained on her breast, but the other moved lower, finding the button of her jeans so he could undo it, and then pull down the zipper.

Right then, she wished she had put on a skirt—it would have made this a lot easier. She helped as best she could, wriggling out of the snug jeans as Aldair worked them down, followed by her underwear.

*Just like a couple of high school kids going for a quickie on the couch,* she thought, but she realized she didn't mind so very much. She was with him, and whether on the sofa or upstairs in his bed, she knew it would be amazing.

He paused so he could shrug out of the open robe he wore, then undid the drawstring of his pants and let them fall to the floor. Jillian had already felt him pressed up against her, but seeing him now, seeing the size of his arousal, she couldn't help letting out a small gasp. Jack certainly hadn't been lacking in that department, but Aldair....

Her fingers seemed to go to him of their own accord, wrapping around his shaft so she could feel his heat, his strength. He groaned, and pressed up against her, his hand slipping between her legs, dipping into the delicious warmth at her core.

Oh, God, yes. There. Right there.

She clung to him with one hand as her other caressed him, the delicious little shivers flooding through her telling her that it wouldn't be all that long now. How could she possibly hold out, when he was making her feel this way?

The orgasm broke through her like a storm surge cresting over a sea wall. She had to let go of his cock then, because she needed both hands to hold onto him as she climaxed, everything in her shuddering apart and then coming together again.

"Aldair," she gasped, and his lips were warm against her face as he replied,

"My love. My darling. Yes. Let it go."

She'd never come like that before. How could she, when she'd never gone so long without release? She held on to him, and felt warm winds blowing around them, lifting them up from the admittedly cramped quarters of the sofa. With wondering eyes, she gazed up into his face, then down at the floor, some six or seven feet below them. Good thing the house had ten-foot ceilings. "What...?"

"I want to make love to you like this, as an elemental of the air. Does it frighten you?"

Without hesitation, she shook her head. "No. It's marvelous, like being held up by a cloud. Anyway, I know you would never let me fall."

"No, my love," he said, and kissed her. "I will never let you fall."

And he began to move down her neck, kissing her the whole way, pausing to caress her breasts for a moment, but she knew then what he intended to do, knew that he wanted to love her in the deepest, tenderest way he could. His tongue touched her, slowly, languorously, as if he wanted to savor her like the world's rarest delicacy. All she could do was lie back on those cloud-like winds, let them hold her up while he made love to her with his mouth, until another of those mind-blowing orgasms moved through her, this time with such force that she had to cry out, had to give voice to the pleasure that throbbed in every single nerve ending.

The last of those delicious shudders hadn't finished flowing to her very fingertips before he raised his head and moved upward along her body, skin pressed against skin, until she sensed him pushing against her, pushing into her. He was large, but he slipped in easily enough, filling her, causing her to gasp and wrap her legs around him so he could go even deeper, become one with her.

She locked eyes with his, found herself drowning in those brilliant blue depths, the only ocean she would ever need. They rocked together, finding their rhythm, until she knew she was close again—as was he, by the way his breath sped up and his amazing eyes finally closed, lashes heavy and dark against his cheekbones. And then at last the climax overtook him, and he shuddered into her, even as she rode him for those last few seconds so she might come as well. For the longest moment, they clung to one another, neither of them speaking.

Then at last he kissed her, and smoothed a lock of damp hair away from her brow. "My love," he said. "My perfect, wonderful Jillian."

"I love you, Aldair," she whispered, and she knew she meant it. Was this a betrayal of Jack? She didn't know. She only knew that her heart now belonged utterly, irretrievably, to Aldair al-Ankara.

He did not lower them to the sofa, but instead blinked himself and Jillian up to the master bathroom, so they might revel in the warmth of the shower together. Which they did, with Jillian running her soap-slick hands over him, as if marveling at the feel of his muscles beneath her fingers.

Well, she was welcome to marvel away, if it meant he could stand there and gaze at her, at the lush contours of her body as the water of the shower beat down upon them. She was so perfect, breasts larger than he had imagined, waist slender, but defined by the rounded curves of her delicious bottom. Aldair resolved then that she should never wear those terrible baggy, borrowed clothes again. They were a crime against her beauty.

At length they emerged from the shower and dried one another off. He hardened at her touch, and she shot him a sly look up through her lashes. "If we start all over again, then what was the point of the shower?"

"Because it felt good," he said. "Just as this will."

Before she could protest, he had gathered her up in his arms and taken her over to the bed, where he kissed her over and over, his fingers finding the warm wetness at her womanly center. Then he lifted her so she might straddle him, all her delicious heat surrounding him as he caressed her breasts, bringing him to a climax in what he might previously have thought was an embarrassingly short amount of time. Now, though, he could only think of it as a compliment to her charms.

She didn't seem to mind. After resting against him for a long moment, her cheek pressed up to his chest, as if listening to his heartbeat, she slipped off and lay next to him, the curve of her hip and leg lining up with his own body, a perfect symmetry.

He touched the silky fall of her hair, marveling at its softness as it slipped through his fingers. How exquisite she was. For the first time, he experienced a rush of pity for her late husband, that he must be taken away from her perfection.

However, Aldair knew better than to voice such a sentiment aloud. He did not want to disrupt the perfection of this moment with any mention of the man she had lost. Instead, he pressed a kiss to her cheek and said, "It grows late. Are you hungry?"

She stretched, a graceful catlike motion. He could feel himself stir, just watching her, but for the most part, he was sated. Right then, he thought it better if they satisfied another kind of hunger.

"Now that you mention it, I am," she said, smiling. "I had to stop and think about it for a minute." A shift in her position so she could look toward the window, at the rain which still fell outside. "I suppose I lost track of time, especially with the storm making it so dark. It's definitely sticking around. Strange—usually these monsoon storms blow in and blow out in less than an hour."

"I like it." Which was only the truth. He'd always enjoyed the crash of thunder, the glare of lightning, feeling the movements in the air currents and the transient energies that powered the storms.

"So do I. It makes everything feel cozy." She reached over and gave his hand a squeeze, then slipped off the edge of the bed and stood. While Aldair missed the warmth of her body pressed up against his, he did have to admit that she provided a much better view when standing there like that.

Not that she remained in that spot for very long. "I need to get some clothes on," she said, then went out and down the hall to her room.

He would have to do something about that. Now they had become intimate, she should share this room with him, and bring her belongings here. Ah, well. That was a subject he could bring up over dinner.

Since there was no point in him remaining in bed, he got up as well and summoned a fresh outfit to wear, this one in royal blue with silver embroidery. Perhaps he could convince Jillian to try djinn garb as well. He thought she would look especially beautiful in a close-fitting tunic of deep blue, the neckline cut low.

When she emerged from her room, he saw that she wore one of the spangled skirts she'd found here in Madrid, along with a tank top in a soft pink shade. It hugged her curves well enough, and he was pleased to see that she'd put on the turquoise necklace he'd given her. She was so beautiful, glowing and happy, that right then he didn't believe her appearance could be improved any more, not even by djinn clothing.

They went downstairs, where Patches met them with some uncertain tail wags. No doubt he'd been attempting to determine what all those sounds his masters were making might mean, but as soon as Jillian got out the dog food and dumped a respectable amount of kibble into his bowl, all of Patches' uncertainty disappeared. He set to his meal as Aldair turned to Jillian.

"What would you like for dinner?"

"I can have anything?"

"Well, within reason," he said. "It is easier if I don't have to reach too far away to assemble my components."

"Oh, I'm not asking for pufferfish sushi or anything like that," she replied with a smile. "I suppose it's the weather, making me want something familiar. Comfort food. Pot roast and gravy and potatoes."

"That should be simple enough." Indeed, he had consumed such meals during his time spent on Earth, when no one had thought him anything other than the human he'd pretended to be. "And you're right—the weather is suited for this sort of thing."

She came over and kissed him on the cheek. "Perfect. I'll go set the table."

Aldair didn't stop her as she went into the dining room, even though he could have also prepared the table at the same time he conjured the meal. For some reason, he thought she wanted the comfort of that particular ritual, of telling herself that much of her life was normal, even though so many other things had changed.

As they had changed for him as well. He had never thought his heart one that would surrender, and yet here he had given it to a human woman, one not deemed worthy of being Chosen because she had been too old when the Dying swept through the world's population.

Too old. Aldair wanted to laugh. From certain comments she had made, he guessed that she had only been twenty-six or twenty-seven at the time of the Heat. Hardly decrepit. And yet...

...and yet, he knew she would continue to age, that although she was young and beautiful now, she would not stay that way forever. Not unless he made her his Chosen.

He had done that for Katelyn, although the bond between them was broken when she was captured by Khalim's men. When he selected her, he had been so consumed by revenge that he hadn't stopped to consider all the ramifications of their relationship, that if his plans to take Jessica away from Jasreel turned to nothing, he would be saddled with a woman he didn't love for all eternity. The universe had spared him that particular fate, it seemed, but now he must make a far more conscious decision.

Not that he had to think about the matter for more than a few long moments, while Jillian put out the placemats and the napkins and flatware, then fetched plates and wine glasses from the cupboard. She was humming under her breath, a happy, pretty sound, although he didn't recognize the tune. As he listened to her, Aldair realized he did not want to think of a future that did not include her. Even if that future was forever.

He would just have to think of the best way to ask her.

Jillian couldn't remember the last time she'd experienced such a sense of well-being. Not since the Heat, that was for sure. Too much grief, too much doubt and worry. No, she'd never been ill, except for a very minor cold last winter, but she'd also never felt good, hadn't felt like her old self. How could she, with Jack dead and the world she knew gone?

*Well, you did just have some pretty spectacular sex,* she thought as she arranged the candles on the sideboard. *That's always a decent mood elevator.*

But she knew it was far more than that. Yes, the sex had been amazing—Aldair clearly knew what he was doing—but if it hadn't been with him, that was all it would have been. Just sex. With Aldair, though...she had practically felt the love flowing from him, seen the admiration in his eyes as he gazed at her.

And he'd said that he loved her. Never in a million years would she have expected him to reveal so much of himself. Yes, there were terrible things in his past, dreadful deeds and decisions that she couldn't begin to justify. But the man she loved here and now seemed light-years away from that angry, vengeful person.

Maybe his time in the outer circles had tempered that part of him, burned it away.

Or maybe it was something to do with her, with the way they'd interacted over the past few days, making him stop to think about the choices he'd made. Jillian would like to believe that, although she thought the true change had come from within, rather than without.

"Table's ready," she told him as she came back into the kitchen.

"Good," he replied. "For I have just finished selecting the wine. Now we can go sit, and I will bring the food to us."

Yes, the miracle of his djinn powers, whisking an elaborate meal into the dining room with no more apparent effort than the blink of an eye. It took only about that long as well; Jillian had barely seated herself before the tabletop was filled by a delectable roast on a platter, and a gravy boat full of a dark, rich-smelling liquid, with various bowls containing roasted potatoes and vegetables and salad set around the main course. And bread, too, the warm, golden smell of fresh-baked rolls rising from a basket off to one side.

*Good thing I worked off so many calories earlier,* Jillian thought, repressing a grin. Aloud, she said, "This all looks incredible."

"I hope it is enough comfort food for you."

"Oh, I'm pretty sure about that."

They were silent for a few moments as Aldair dished up the food, then uncorked the bottle he'd brought with him and poured a decent measure into each of their glasses. Once he was done, he lifted his wine glass and said, "I would like to salute the most beautiful and wonderful woman in the world."

Blood rushed to her cheeks. She'd never been that good with compliments, especially ones as hyperbolic as the accolade Aldair had just delivered. "Well...."

"I think you are the most amazing woman I have ever met, and I have lived a very long time," he cut in. "So I think you should defer to my judgment on this."

At those words, what could she do but shrug and laugh? After all, it was only the truth...partly, anyway. Aldair had lived a very long time—longer than she probably wanted to contemplate—and so of course his experience must be quite broad and varied.

Should she ask him exactly how long he'd lived? No, what would be the point of that? She knew he had to be hundreds of years old, possibly even thousands. When the gap was so wide, it barely counted anymore.

"I think you're amazing, too," she said.

He smiled, but she noticed how the smile didn't quite meet his eyes. "More amazing than Jack?"

Surely he couldn't be jealous of a man who'd been dead for almost two years. Then again, this was Aldair.

She'd seen his good side, saw the passion and fire within him, but she also knew that same fiery nature lent itself to extremes of emotion. "This isn't a competition," she said gently. "Anyway, I haven't asked you about the women who came before me."

"That's because they meant nothing—a few hours of passion, nothing more." He lifted his wine glass and swallowed some of the cabernet it held, but slowly, as if he was evaluating its flavor. "But you were married to Jack. I've heard you speak highly of him. So it is a very different thing."

She supposed it was. But what she'd felt for Jack certainly didn't change her feelings for Aldair. "A wise man once said that comparisons are odious. So I'm not going to begin to compare the two of you. I loved Jack. I won't lie and say I didn't. But he's gone." She had to pause there and pull in a breath, because even now the thought of it hurt. Not merely in the sense of what she herself had lost, but what the world had lost as well. His would have been a steadying presence in this post-Dying world. "I've spent too long thinking I might as well have died with him. You are wonderful, Aldair, because you've made me want to live again."

At those words, some of the worry left his eyes, and he set down his glass so he could reach over to her and lay his hand on top of hers. Those fingers were long and strong and warm, and at their touch a melting little shiver passed through her. Yes, he was amazing, with the way he could awaken her body with such a whisper of a caress.

"Thank you, Jillian," he said. "I am not sure that I deserve you, but I will endeavor to do so. And that is why...." A hesitation, as if he wrestled with something he didn't know how to say. Then he went on, "That is why I would very much like to make you my Chosen."

Shock rippled through her, and she held herself very still. Aldair's hand was a weight on top of hers, not oppressive, but still, very much there. If she pulled away, he would think the worst, think she was rejecting him.

Yes, he had told her he loved her, but to go from that to saying he wanted to spend all of eternity, now to the end of time with her? That was a leap—a leap of faith, if nothing else. They had only spent a week together. Yes, a week where they were constantly together, practically in each other's laps, but still....

"I...I don't know what to say."

"What is there to say? We care for one another. I do not want to see you age, or become ill. As my Chosen, you will share my health, and my years." His expression clouded as his lips compressed. "Or was your talk of love something that only arose from the heat of the moment, and you fear that it can't possibly last?"

"No," she said at once. She needed to set him straight when it came to that notion, no matter what else happened. "What I said—what I told you—it's not the sort of thing I say lightly. Only one other man has ever heard it from me, and he was my husband."

Something about the set of Aldair's shoulders seemed to relax slightly. "Then I do not see what the problem is. Is not everlasting youth and unending life something humans have dreamed of since the dawn of time?"

Jillian couldn't argue with that. Except...she'd never been the type to yearn for more than what she'd been given. Her only dream had been to spend a long and happy life with Jack, and that when she passed from this world, to have known she'd had children who could carry on after she was gone. The children had been denied her, as had that life she'd dreamed of.

Children. She hadn't even thought about it, caught up in the moment as she'd been, but right then she realized she'd had unprotected sex with Aldair. Twice. A tremor went through her, even as she tried to tell herself the chances of becoming pregnant were fairly remote, since her last period had ended just a few days before the lab accident that sent her on a collision course with Aldair al-Ankara.

"It's something some humans have dreamed of," she admitted. "I always thought a life well-lived was better than a life that lasted forever."

"Well, now you can have both."

Would it be a life well-lived, this life that her djinn offered her? Hard to say, when they were living here like fugitives. Yes, she'd enjoyed parts of her time here in Madrid, the quiet peace of this valley, the way she and Aldair and Patches had become an odd little family. But she knew that what they had here was terribly fragile.

"And a family?" she asked. "Have you ever wanted children?"

Those piercing blue eyes caught hers, and held. "Not until now."

A shiver went through her. "So you would be willing to have children with me."

"As many as you like." One of his eyebrows lifted at an ironic angle, and he added, "Not that we have started our family yet, in case you were wondering. Among the djinn, we must decide consciously to procreate. Until that moment, lovemaking is simply that—shared pleasure, nothing more."

She didn't find anything particularly "simple" about sex with Aldair, since it was the most mind-blowing sex she'd ever had...even more so than when she'd been with Jack. It had been good, even great sometimes, but when Aldair made love to her, it was as if she'd been transported to a different plane.

And now he was offering her the family she'd been denied, and eternal life at the very pleasant physical age of twenty-eight. What woman could possibly turn down such an offer?

Not she. Jillian knew she wasn't brave enough for that.

"Yes, Aldair," she said softly. "I would love to be your Chosen."

## CHAPTER SEVENTEEN

HE HAD HOPED THAT WOULD BE HER REPLY, BUT until the words left her lips, he couldn't be sure. She might have said she needed more time, and he would have had to respect her wishes.

But she looked at him with her gray eyes shining, and said that she would be his Chosen. So whatever doubts and fears she might have harbored earlier, they appeared to be gone now. And he would have to endeavor to prove himself worthy of her.

"I want to do it now," he said.

Her eyebrows lifted. "Now? Won't dinner get cold?"

Perhaps she was teasing him, ever so slightly. He found he did not mind so very much. "I only need to say a few words. And besides, have you not noticed that the meals I create for us never grow cold, no matter how long they might sit on the table?"

A curve of her lovely lips, and she shook her head. "I'm afraid I haven't been that observant. I suppose all the times we've sat down together, you've been distracting me."

Ah, well, he could not complain about that. "I will do my best not to distract you in the future."

"No, I like it. I'd worry if you weren't distracting me."

He could only shake his head at that comment. All the same, he didn't want to be sent off track himself. As he'd told her, the words that would bind her to him as his Chosen were not so very many. He cleared his throat, then met her gaze as he said, slowly and deliberately, "I claim this human woman as my own. Jillian Powell will be forever known as my Chosen, and we are now bound together for all eternity."

A small silence fell after he had uttered those words. Then Jillian said, "So...that's it? I'm now your Chosen? Am I supposed to say something?"

"No—the binding of a Chosen is done by the djinn. And yes, you are now Chosen. I told you, there are not so very many words involved."

She glanced away from him and down at herself, as if expecting to see some material change in her person. "I don't feel any different."

"Nor should you. But my being is now bound with yours. While you do not have any true djinn abilities, you will never age a day beyond the age you are now, and you will never become ill. And if you should suffer some injury, it will heal quickly, and not impede you in any way."

A breath escaped her lips, and she reached for her glass of wine so she might take a large swallow. "This is...a lot to take in."

"Yes, I can imagine." He offered her what he hoped was an encouraging smile. "But you have all of time to learn what it means to be Chosen."

This was all insane, wasn't it? Just a few hours earlier, she'd tried to walk out of Aldair's life, had convinced herself that she couldn't possibly allow herself to have any feelings for him. And now she was irrevocably his, wedded to him mind, body, and spirit, forever.

Well, maybe not irrevocably. He'd relinquished his claim on Katelyn somehow. So how did Jillian know for sure that he wouldn't do the same thing to her?

*Because he wouldn't,* she told herself fiercely as they returned to their neglected dinner. *He said he never cared for Katelyn, and he said he loves me, has never loved anyone before. That means a whole hell of a lot.*

She watched him from beneath her lashes as he ate. How handsome he was. But it was more than those ridiculous good looks—she now saw something relaxed about him, as if he'd been holding on to a certain tension ever since they'd come here to Madrid, and now he could finally let it go.

Although maybe not all the way. Her thoughts returned to what she'd been brooding over earlier. Yes, she was bound to him now, but the alteration in their relationship didn't change the fact that he was still, for all intents and purposes, a fugitive from justice. Maybe the Santa Fe djinn would never find them, tucked away here in Madrid...but what if they did?

"You are very quiet, my love," Aldair said then.

"Am I? Just processing, I guess." She set down the piece of roll she held and looked across the table at him. "I suppose I'm worried."

"Worried? Have I not reassured you that you are the only woman in the world for me?"

Despite her anxiety, Jillian couldn't hold back the warmth that flooded through her at his words. He sounded so sure of himself, so sure of her, as if their love and happiness was such an irrefutable fact that he was mildly surprised she could harbor any doubts.

"No, that's not what I meant. It's just—" She hesitated, glancing toward the window. Night had fallen by then, but she knew she looked more or less northward, toward Santa Fe. "It's just that they're out there. The Santa Fe djinn, I mean. I can't help worrying about what will happen if they find us."

"They will not," he said calmly, although she didn't miss the flicker of his eyes toward the window as well, as though something of her anxiety had communicated itself to him. "While they do have some space to roam within their territory, they would not come this far afield. No one will find us."

"Not even one of the other djinn?" she asked. Although she'd never seen them in action, she'd heard stories of what the skies above Taos had looked like when they boiled with angry djinn, those who had sworn to rid the earth of any humans who were not Chosen.

This time, Aldair did not answer right away. His fingers clenched on the stem of his wine glass, so tightly that Jillian worried he might snap it in two. Somehow, though, the fragile glass did not give way. Jaw tight, he replied, "They have no reason to come here. It is clear that everyone in this town died in the Heat, and there is certainly nothing worth plundering."

Well, except tens of thousands of dollars' worth of Native American jewelry in the various shops. But she supposed if those murderous djinn suddenly wanted to start loading up on turquoise, they could do so in the far larger boutiques and shops in Albuquerque. "You're sure?" she asked.

"Positive," he said, reaching with his free hand so he might pour more wine into her glass.

She wished his words could have reassured her. Unfortunately, she'd caught another of those furtive glances toward the window, and thought he might be just as worried as she.

Problem was, she didn't know what either of them could do about it.

Aldair would not allow Jillian's concerns to unsettle him. Not now, when they'd just discovered the joy of being in one another's arms. At least she had not offered any further arguments, had finished dinner as they speculated how long the storm would last, and then smiled in amazement and appreciation as he waved a hand and made all the leftovers on the table and all the dirty plates disappear, the uneaten food whisked away to be stored in the refrigerator, the dishes and glasses scrubbing themselves to sparkling newness as they returned to their respective cupboards.

And afterward they had gone up to his room— their room now—and made slow, languorous love for a good part of the night, exploring each other's bodies, kissing or simply holding on to one another. Finally, they fell asleep, sharing in their respective warmth, while the rain still pounded overhead, even though at last the thunder and lightning had disappeared as the heart of the storm finally began to move away.

The next morning, he was glad to see that Jillian did not bring up any of her worries from the evening before. Instead, she snuggled up to him and was all too glad to share the shower once more, after they'd finally pried themselves out of bed. And since the day was so sparkling and clear, with no hint of the storm that had drenched the valley, save some puddles in the yard and on the roadway, she suggested they go to the next town over, tiny Cerrillos, only a few miles up the road.

"Surely that will be safe enough, won't it?" she inquired.

"Of course," he said smoothly. "I went there myself earlier in the week. There is not much to be seen, but a change of scenery—at least, one so close by—should not be a problem at all."

To amuse her, and because he thought he might enjoy the novelty as well, he found an older but well-maintained motorcycle in an outbuilding of one of the houses. The battery was long dead, but a djinn could always supply the necessary charge. The Harley-Davidson roared to life while Jillian looked on with wide eyes.

"Do you actually know how to ride one of those things?" she asked.

"Yes," he said, which was no more than the truth. A djinn could do many things to amuse himself when visiting this world—dining in fine restaurants, going to the symphony. Or driving fast cars or riding motor-cycles. It all depended on how one wished to divert oneself. It had been some time since he had done so, but he knew he had not forgotten.

A djinn never forgot.

"Okay," she said, although her expression was still somewhat dubious. "But you might want to rethink your wardrobe. I don't think flowy robes are the best choice when it comes to tooling around on a Harley."

"You are right, of course." A flick of his fingers, and his silken robes and blousy pants had been replaced by jeans, a T-shirt, and a leather jacket. Heavy boots completed the ensemble. Even as Jillian's eyes widened in surprise, he snapped his fingers again. This time, it was her clothing that changed, the skirt and tank top and sandals morphing into a slightly more feminine version of what he himself wore.

"Wow, that's handy," she said. "If you could change my clothes so easily, why didn't you do so before, instead of having me pick through the boutiques or wear stuff that was two sizes too big?"

"You didn't ask," he replied with a grin. Noting her pained expression, he went on, "Also, at the time, we did not know one another well. It would have felt like taking a liberty. Now, though"—he shrugged—"it is the easiest way to outfit you for whatever endeavor you might wish to undertake."

"I suppose I can see that." Her eyes took on a certain glint. "Anyway, while I like your djinn clothes, I have to say that you're looking pretty damn fine in that leather jacket."

Her open admiration pleased him. He had always found human clothes to be rather blocky and unflattering, but if Jillian preferred them, he thought he could do with wearing jeans a few times a week. The jacket was another matter. Necessary for the ride, since even a djinn could be injured by a fall from a motorcycle, although the healing process would be supernaturally fast. But he had to admit that, with the bright September sun beaming down overhead, the thick leather was rather hot.

If Jillian was similarly uncomfortable, she made no mention of it. She climbed somewhat awkwardly onto the seat behind him without saying anything at all. Perhaps she had never ridden on a motorcycle before. From what she had said about her late husband, he did not exactly sound like the sort of person to own or ride one.

As Aldair adjusted the throttle and shifted into gear, she let out an excited little gasp. They could not go very fast here in town, not with this part of Highway 14 still choked with abandoned vehicles. However, it did not take so very long to weave in and out of the clumps of cars and SUVs, and in a few minutes, they were headed down the road at speeds high enough that he could feel Jillian's arms tightening further around his waist, her cheek pressed to his shoulder as they followed the curves of the highway to the turnoff for Cerrillos.

The last time he had come here, he had flown in djinn fashion, but the trip did not take so very long on two wheels, either. In just a few minutes they were slowly moving down the tiny hamlet's one paved road, past old adobe houses with walls two feet thick. Aldair saw a likely spot to park the Harley-Davidson under a pair of spreading cottonwood trees, and so he came to a stop there so Jillian could climb off and take a look around.

Which she did, eyes wide. "It feels so old," she said at last. "I mean, I know Madrid is old, but this feels even older."

"I believe it is, or parts of it, any rate. Turquoise was mined here long before they started taking coal out of the hillsides above Madrid." Jillian shot him a surprised look at that comment, and he added, "I have been reading some of the books from the gift shops, the ones on local history. At any rate, it makes sense that so many of the structures here in Cerrillos would be older."

She nodded, unzipping her jacket so she could drape it across the motorcycle's seat. Clearly, she thought it too heavy for the day as well. Her warm brown hair spilled over the tight-fitting T-shirt she wore, glinting with hints of gold in the bright sunlight. Aldair reflected then that perhaps there was something to human clothes, for those jeans did do a rather spectacular job of showing off the luscious curves of her hips and waist and rear end.

Perhaps he had been staring, for in the next moment she turned back to him, a smile playing on her lips. "Aldair, were you just looking at my butt?"

"If I was?"

She lifted her shoulders and let out a chuckle. "I guess I'd say that turnabout was fair play, since I was doing the same thing to you back in Madrid."

All he could do then was go over to her and give her a long, slow kiss, one that wakened the fire in his veins—and hers, too, judging by the flush that tinged her high cheekbones. Admittedly, Cerrillos was not the sort of place where he could imagine indulging in any midday romps, but in a way, that was better. Sometimes the long, slow burn was far more enjoyable, even if it meant some discomfort in the meantime.

Jillian pulled away as the kiss ended, then looked around again. "So, what's the plan?"

"No real plan," he admitted. "Although I did see a place at the edge of town where a creek flowed through. There are trees, and shade. After the rains last night, the creek should be flowing well."

"Sounds lovely. Lead on."

The place he had described was not quite a quarter-mile from where they stood, close enough that they walked there under their own power, rather than blinking over in djinn-fashion. As they passed under the enormous cottonwoods that overhung the creek, Jillian let out a sigh.

"Oh, that is nice. The sun is beautiful today, but it was starting to get a bit warm."

"And that is why I proposed this spot. Look, over there is a good place to sit down."

Which it was, a low, horizontal branch sturdy enough to bear both their weight. Only a few yards away, the creek chattered from within its banks, the water flowing fast because of the runoff from yesterday's rains. Aldair did not know where its source might be; he only knew he was glad of its presence on this warm late-summer day.

Jillian settled herself on the branch, and Aldair sat down next to her. Neither of them said anything for a moment, although she reached over so she could twine her fingers with his, then leaned her head on his shoulder.

Ah, yes, this was a good idea. It felt sheltered and safe in here, even more hidden from the world than tiny Madrid. The cool air touched his cheek and played with the hair at the back of his neck, and he allowed himself a sigh of his own.

"How did you find this place, anyway?" Jillian asked.

"When I was scouting the local countryside. It was easy enough to see Cerrillos itself, but then I noticed the line of trees and realized there must be a creek here. That day it was dry, because it hadn't rained for a while, but I thought the trees alone would provide a good respite from the heat." He tightened his fingers on hers, just a little, enough to show he thought his next words were important. "My love, we have done well enough in Madrid, and yet I cannot help but think perhaps we should discuss moving on."

"'Moving on'?" she repeated, and lifted her head from his shoulder. "But Madrid is safe. Where would we even move on to?"

"Yesterday, I found a house in Albuquerque. I—"

"Albuquerque? Wouldn't that just make it easier for the other djinn to find us?"

"Not necessarily. I could not sense any djinn in the city, nor any humans. It appeared as if there might have been one of my kind there once, but now the place seems utterly deserted. If it has been abandoned by the djinn, then they would have no reason to return there. Which makes it a very good choice for us."

Jillian didn't reply. She glanced away from him, at the cottonwood trees to either side, the pale purple and white wildflowers that grew at the base of their trunks. "You don't like it here?"

Was that the faintest trace of disappointment in her voice? Perhaps. He could see why she might have found herself attached to the house in Madrid. After all, it was where they had first explored their attraction to one another. But he hoped she would understand that a far better alternative waited for them in Albuquerque.

"It is not a question of liking it, precisely," he replied, choosing his words with care. "The house where we have been living has served us well. But it is not all that large, not really. You spoke of wanting to have a family. We would rapidly outgrow the place if we had more than one or two children."

Her brows lifted. "How many were you planning on?"

He couldn't help chuckling. "Only as many as you would like, my love. If that is only one, I will be happy. If it is six or seven, well"—he paused and shot her a wicked grin—"then I suppose I will manage somehow."

"That's a bit much, even for me. I say we start with one and then go from there." She'd worn a look of amusement up until that point, but it faded slightly. "But won't that be hard, to have a child without a hospital, without anyone to help?"

"It would have been," Aldair replied. He understood her concern, but the situation was nothing that should worry her. "But remember, you now have a djinn's gift of healing. Childbirth for one of us is nothing like what it would be for a mortal. That is, I assume the actual process is more or less the same, but with far less pain and a much shorter recovery."

"That's good." But although Jillian's words indicated she should have been relieved, she still appeared troubled.

"What is it?"

"I—" She bent and plucked one of the many-rayed purple flowers and twirled it between her fingers. "Is that really wise, though? To raise our children with no one else around. What would happen to them once they were old enough to really understand their isolation? It seems selfish to keep them from having any interaction with others."

While Aldair couldn't blame her for having these misgivings, he also thought perhaps she was borrowing trouble that might not occur for several decades. "My sins are my own, not theirs. When the time came, they could go out into the world—whether the world of the djinn in Santa Fe, or perhaps your own people in Los Alamos, if by that time Miles Odekirk has finally created a device that would not affect djinn adversely once they were inside its barrier. Because I will be helping to raise them, they will still come into their djinn powers, even if they are of half blood. So that will be their choice, I suppose."

"I suppose," she echoed, then glanced up at him and managed a crooked smile. "And I suppose I'm getting ahead of myself. Why don't you show me this house in Albuquerque? If you really think it's safe," she added.

"I know it is safe. There are no djinn in the area, and I have no reason to believe there will be. This world is vast, and there are—if you will beg my pardon—other places that would have been much more appealing."

From the way her mouth tightened, it appeared she wasn't overly pleased by this apparent slight to her former hometown. However, she merely shrugged and said, "I suppose so. I mean, if I had all the world to choose from, I'd probably want a place on the beach or up in a mountain meadow. So I'll believe you when you say no other djinn have settled in Albuquerque."

Relieved, Aldair pushed himself off the branch where they'd been sitting and extended a hand to Jillian so she might climb down as well. "We will take the motorcycle back to Madrid, and then we can go to Albuquerque."

"What, you can't just 'blink' it there, along with the two of us?"

"I could, but it is a large and heavy object. Also, the road that leads up to the house I found is steep and covered in gravel. The motorcycle might manage, but I think it wiser to leave it behind."

"Makes sense."

She held his hand as they left the cottonwood grove. Aldair could not help but marvel at the sensation of her fingers against his—so fragile-seeming, and yet so strong. *She* was a marvel, actually, every inch of her. And somehow she had agreed to be his.

They came around the corner of a high adobe wall, and Aldair found himself grinding to a halt, his fingers clamping down on Jillian's. For there, standing next to the motorcycle and inspecting it with an air of bemusement, were two djinn. He recognized one of them—Danilar al-Harith, Zahrias' younger brother. The other, a large hulk of a man, Aldair could not place immediately. Not that it mattered.

They had found him.

## CHAPTER EIGHTEEN

Although the breeze blowing around them was warm verging on hot, all of Jillian's veins suddenly turned to ice. She didn't know the two djinn who stood by the Harley—how could she? The only djinn she'd ever even caught a glimpse of was Zahrias—but that hardly mattered now.

What mattered was that they were here, staring at Aldair with expressions that held a strange mixture of astonishment and dislike.

"So we were right," said the younger and slighter of the two djinn, although he could only be described as "slight" when compared to his companion, who had to be around six foot six and had the build of a pro wrestler. "We sensed a djinn presence somewhere in these hills when there should not be one. How in all the heavens and hells came you to be here, Aldair al-Ankara?"

"A lucky accident, no more," Aldair said smoothly.

Jillian knew his current calm was only a façade, since she stood close enough to him to sense how tense he really was, wound tight as a watch spring. What would he do? Was he strong enough to overcome the two djinn who faced him? She didn't possibly see how, not when the one looked big enough to put Aldair through a wall, even if djinn powers weren't involved.

"You have broken your exile," the djinn continued. "You cannot be here."

"Am I hurting anyone?" Aldair returned. His tone was still deceptively mild, but a muscle worked in his cheek. "Have I done anything to disrupt your lives in Santa Fe?"

The two djinn looked at one another. For the first time, the larger one spoke. "That does not matter. Banishment is eternal. You still have much to answer for, Aldair."

"Answer to whom, Murrah al-Tayyar?"

"To my brother, first of all," the shorter djinn put in. "But I am sure the elders will wish to hear of this as well."

Aldair's hands knotted into fists. The wind around them picked up, swirling as a dust devil began to move toward the two djinn. At the same time, the ground rumbled, so sharply that Jillian nearly lost her balance.

She stumbled, and Aldair caught her by the wrist before she could actually fall.

"You cannot fight the two of us," the djinn went on. For the first time, his gaze flicked toward Jillian before returning to Aldair. "And do you really want to see any harm come to your woman?"

His grip on her wrist was so tight that another time, she might have protested. Now, though, she knew he clung to her like that because he was afraid of what might happen if he should let go.

"You will leave her alone," Aldair rasped, his stare so fierce, he might as well have been shooting blue laser bolts from those eyes.

"And we will," the djinn said. "If you come with us. Otherwise, I cannot answer for what might happen if we should have to exert undue force to subdue you."

For a long moment, Aldair did not reply. A tremor went through him, but one so slight that Jillian didn't think the other djinn could have noticed. The only reason she did was that she and Aldair stood so close.

At last, he released her arm and stepped forward. "Very well. Take me if you must, but leave her out of it."

"No!" Jillian burst out. She tried to move forward so she could stand next to him, but it was like hitting an invisible wall. The djinn who had been doing most of the talking must have deployed something like the force field Aldair had used that one night when she tried to storm out of the dining room. Furious,

she went on, "You can't do this. He—" And then she
stopped herself. She had been about to say, *He hasn't
done anything wrong.* But he had. Not to her. But to his
own people.

Clearly, they hadn't forgiven him.

The smaller djinn sent her a look that was almost
pitying. "I am sorry. But he must come with us."

A swirl of wind, another rumble of the earth
beneath her feet, and then all three of them were
gone—the two unknown djinn, Aldair. A few yellow-
ing cottonwood leaves drifted downward, clearly disturbed by the elementals' passing.

And Jillian was alone.

Aldair did not know this house. How could he, when
he had broken ranks with Zahrias al-Harith and his
people before they ever came to live here in Santa
Fe? By its size and understated opulence, however, Aldair
guessed this must be Zahrias' home.

Neither did he know the strikingly beautiful
blonde woman who stood at Zahrias' side, but he
guessed she must be Julia Innes, the mortal Zahrias had
taken as his Chosen. She stood next to her partner but
did not speak, as if she knew this was djinn business
and shouldn't interrupt.

The leader of the Santa Fe djinn wore a fearsome
scowl as he stared at the captive before him. Off to
one side stood his brother Danilar, along with Murrah

al-Tayyar, who apparently had remained behind just in case any brute force was required to subdue their prisoner.

"Aldair al-Ankara," Zahrias said heavily. "I had never thought to lay eyes on you again."

"I held that same belief," Aldair returned.

That reply appeared to do little to amuse the other djinn. His brow creased even further, and he crossed his arms. "How did this happen? And who was that woman my brother and Murrah found you with?"

"Leave her out of it," Aldair said immediately. If he must be sent back into exile, so be it, but he could not bear the thought of Jillian being a victim of Zahrias' over-developed sense of justice.

"I have no reason to bring her into it, unless you tell me otherwise."

How much should he tell Zahrias? For Aldair wished to shield Jillian, but at the same time, perhaps if he explained that he had done nothing wrong, that his return to this world was only by sheer accident and not any machinations of his own, then he might be able to make a credible plea for some kind of clemency.

A very small chance of that, but one he would have to try.

"It is because of her that I am here at all," he said. "She is one of the survivors from the Los Alamos community. Or rather, she was. Now she is my Chosen."

That revelation made Zahrias' dark eyes blaze, and flames flickered in and out of being around him, echoing his anger. "You had no right to do such a thing. You had a Chosen—"

"Who is no longer bound to me," Aldair cut in. "Actually, she is with the leader of the Los Alamos community. I am surprised you did not know that, considering how closely you apparently work with them now."

Aldair's reply did nothing to mollify Zahrias. Even as his eyes narrowed, Julia stepped forward and murmured something in his ear. So perhaps she was the one who paid attention to the relationships and liaisons in that community of survivors. Aldair could see why Zahrias might think such a thing beneath him.

"Very well," the fire elemental said. "It appears that much is true. So explain how this woman came to be your Chosen."

"That is a private matter," Aldair replied. "But, as I had begun to tell you, Jillian was one of the Los Alamos survivors. She—"

"Jillian Powell?" Julia asked, clearly startled.

"Yes, that is her name."

Zahrias said, "You knew her?"

"Only a little. She kept to herself. She always seemed...sad. She lost her husband in the Dying, and it seemed to hit her harder than most." This time, she was the one who frowned. "I honestly never thought she'd allow herself to be with anyone ever again."

"Well, apparently she relented," Zahrias said. "Although I must admit that I care little for her taste."

Aldair bristled, but he told himself that he must not give in to his anger. If he was calm and cool, then perhaps these djinn who stared at him with such judgment in their eyes would see that he had changed.

Jillian had changed him.

"As may be," Aldair said, an edge to his voice that he couldn't quite prevent. "At any rate, she was performing work for Miles Odekirk in his lab. We still don't know precisely what happened, but she had an accident as she was working on one of his newer devices. That accident propelled her into the outer circles, where I found her and kept her from dying."

Zahrias and the other two djinn exchanged startled glances. "A human survived the outer circles?"

"Just long enough for her to reverse the accident, and bring us back here. But we were not sent to Los Alamos, but rather to the small town the people here called Madrid."

"Where you hid yourself."

A swirl of angry air flared out from Aldair before he could prevent it. Both Danilar and Murrah stiffened, clearly prepared to act as Zahrias' bodyguards if necessary, although the leader of the Santa Fe djinn did not move a muscle.

"Would you have not done the same thing?" Aldair demanded. "Have you ever been to the outer circles, Zahrias?"

"Of course I have not. I have not transgressed as you have."

Well, Aldair would not bother to counter that argument. Zahrias always had been woefully perfect. "If you had, you might not judge me so harshly. But yes, we remained in Madrid. It seemed a safe enough place to shelter. I had no intention of coming to Santa Fe, of causing any trouble. Surely you must see that."

"It is true that you did not seek us out," Zahrias replied. "But I think your discretion stemmed from a desire to save your own skin, rather than any scruples which might have told you to leave us alone. At any rate, I do not believe I am the one who can judge you now. That is up to the elders. I will send Dani to speak with them, and I have no doubt that they will be here soon enough to pronounce their own judgment."

Danilar did not look especially pleased to be charged with this duty, but he made no protest, only bowed his head and said, "I will go now."

He disappeared almost as soon as he had spoken. No one present even blinked, not even Julia Innes, for of course she must be used to such comings and goings by now.

"And until they come," Zahrias continued, "Murrah and several other of my people will keep watch on you."

"What of my brother?" Aldair asked, for he found himself rather discomfited that Zahrias had not yet made any mention of Jasreel. How would his hated half-brother react when he learned that the prisoner was imprisoned no longer?

"He will be informed of your presence here. No doubt he will wish to be there to see the elders sentence you a second time. But for now, you must wait." Zahrias inclined his head toward Murrah, who stepped forward.

"This way," he said, pointing down a long hallway off to their left. Clearly, Aldair would be kept here in the house.

And why not? A prison cell meant very little to a djinn. It was only those who maintained a watch on him who would prevent him from escaping. He might as well wait here, kept close by against the arrival of the elders.

As Aldair followed Murrah down the hallway, however, he realized his own fate was not what occupied his thoughts.

What would Jillian do now? Could he trust Zahrias to let her be? Aldair realized he must, but that was not the worst of it. No, the worst was the very real possibility that he would be sent back into exile, and Jillian left here alone, the bond between them severed.

Perhaps she was strong enough to endure such a calamity...but he was not sure whether he himself was.

*Calm, you've got to stay calm,* Jillian admonished herself. If she lost it now, she'd be of no use at all to Aldair.

Unfortunately, taking deep breaths wasn't doing much to soothe the frightened beating of her heart, the shakiness in her legs.

At least she knew one thing, that her lover would have been taken to Santa Fe. It wasn't as if she'd have to scour the countryside looking for him. She knew exactly where he must be.

Okay, so that was one problem taken care of. The much larger one that remained was precisely how to get there.

She stood next to the Harley, staring down at it. Her ride with Aldair just an hour earlier had been the only time in her life she'd ever even been on a motorcycle. She certainly didn't know how to ride one.

*Well, you'd better learn fast. Because it's a long walk to Santa Fe, and this is the only working motor vehicle within miles.*

Okay. She let her hand slip over the chrome handlebars, moving down to the instrument cluster. This wasn't a new bike, and so it wasn't too high-tech. Speedometer, tachometer, gas gauge. Basic.

And she'd had an electric scooter back in college, so at least she knew how to ride something two-wheeled, even though this Harley bore about the same resemblance to her scooter that a WWI biplane did to an SR-71 Blackbird.

She also knew that a throttle on the right handlebar controlled the power, with the brake also on the right. How she'd picked up that piece of information, she didn't remember for sure, but it was something. Throttle up, down. The shifter was operated with your left foot; she'd watched Aldair do it as he manipulated the clutch with his left hand. He'd made the whole process seem easy.

Maybe if she was really lucky, she'd get a chance to ask him how he knew how to ride a Harley.

Gingerly, she threw one leg over the seat and settled herself on the padded leather. Her feet touched the ground, but just barely. There wasn't much she could do about that, though. Even with the motor silent, the big bike felt heavy, menacing. Sure, maybe she could get it running, but what would happen if she took a spill?

*You'd heal, because you're Chosen. Stop being a baby.*

Jillian turned the key in the ignition, then startled as the engine grunted to life. Her parents didn't like motorcycles, had thought even her scooter too much of a risk when she had to negotiate Albuquerque traffic

on her way to class. She could only imagine their looks
of horror if they'd ever seen her trying to ride a Harley.

All right, time for the throttle. She eased in some
gas, and the bike lurched forward as her feet dragged
along the ground. Damn. She'd forgotten about that
part. A little more throttle as she put her booted feet
on the footrests, and suddenly she was moving forward. Not very fast, just barely enough to keep the
Harley going down the street, but it was something.

Once again she throttled up, and this time she
could actually feel the breeze moving over her face. A
quick glance down at the speedometer told her that
she'd reached the lightning pace of seventeen miles an
hour. That was okay—if Santa Fe was roughly twenty-five miles from here, then she'd be there in about an
hour and a half. And maybe she'd be able to go up to
twenty or thirty once she was on the highway, at which
point she'd have to hope to God she didn't stall the
thing while trying to shift gears.

On second thought, thirty was probably pushing
it. It would be a lot easier to putt along in low gear all
the way to Santa Fe. But still.

She liked concentrating on the mechanics of not
crashing the Harley. That way, she didn't have to think
about what might be happening to Aldair right now.
Because whatever it was, she couldn't do a damn thing
about it. Not until she got there, anyway.

As she pulled out onto Highway 14, though, she had a panicked thought about Patches, who was still waiting back at the house in Madrid. She didn't know what she'd do about him, because he couldn't exactly fit on the Harley, but—

No, he'd be okay. They'd fed him his lunch and given him a fresh bowl of water right before they left on this expedition, so he'd be fine for a good long while. Bored, and wanting a walk by the time she got back, but....

If she got back.

Of course she would. The djinns' beef was with Aldair, not her. She didn't much relish the thought of leaving him behind to return to Madrid to take care of Patches, but she had no doubt that she would.

Probably.

Jaw set grimly, she headed north on the highway, gradually easing up to around twenty-two miles an hour, and somehow managing to successfully shift into second gear. Even if she'd felt more comfortable with the bike than she did, she knew it wouldn't be safe to go any faster than that. It wasn't as if this stretch of Highway 14 was like Interstate 40 back in Albuquerque, but there were still enough abandoned cars that she had to pay attention to what she was doing, slowing to a crawl from time to time so she could maneuver around them.

She didn't know Santa Fe like the back of her hand or anything, but she'd visited enough times that she remembered to follow the signs that guided her onto Cerrillos Road. Unlike the highway she'd just left, Santa Fe's main artery was completely clear, all the vehicles left behind now pushed off to the sides, if they hadn't been taken away altogether. After all, a lot of the trucks and SUVs in the Los Alamos motor pool had been collected from down here in the state's former capitol.

So she felt safe enough about going up to twenty-five as she passed the strip malls and gas stations and grocery stores on Cerrillos, at last angling off onto Paseo de Peralta, since she didn't know exactly where to go next. Downtown, sure, because that was where the djinn community here had concentrated. But that didn't mean she had a clue as to the exact location where they'd taken Aldair. Since Paseo de Peralta made a large loop around the downtown area, she figured the smartest thing to do was follow that loop until she ran into someone...hopefully not literally.

Which she almost did, just as she was about to pass Old Santa Fe Trail. All of a sudden, two burly djinn stood in the road in front of her, blocking her way. Jillian let off the throttle and grabbed the brake, and the Harley began to slide sideways.

*Oh, shit, I'm going to—*

"Crash" never made it all the way into her mind, because it was as if an invisible hand caught hold of the bike, preventing it from toppling over. At the same time, she felt herself lifted from the Harley's seat and deposited on the roadway. Gently, though—her teeth didn't even rattle as her feet touched the pavement.

"What business do you have here, mortal?" one of them asked.

"I—" The syllable barely made it out of her throat. *God, Jillian, try not to sound as if you're about to have a panic attack.* "I've come here to see Zahrias al-Harith."

The two djinn looked at one another. Physically, they were quite similar, with coal-black hair and dark eyes to match. Jillian wondered if they might be brothers. Then one of them frowned, and gave her a closer look, as if he'd just noticed something odd about her.

"Are you—are you Chosen? But how can you be? We know all of the Chosen in this area."

Of course they did. She wasn't about to confess her connection to Aldair, because she had a feeling that wouldn't earn her many brownie points with the pair who faced her now. Problem was, she didn't have a clue as to where any other djinn/Chosen communities might be located. Aldair had made it sound as if they were widely scattered, maybe only one per state, if even that many. So saying that she'd rode in from another of these enclaves wouldn't sound very plausible.

"I—I can't explain right now. I need to talk to Zahrias."

The two djinn looked at each other again. One of them raised an eyebrow. Were they communicating mentally with one another? Jillian knew that djinn could speak in such a way with their Chosen, although Aldair hadn't done so with her. Probably no need; it wasn't as if there was anyone else around in Madrid to overhear their conversations.

But then one of the djinn, the one with the expressive eyebrows, gave a shrug, as if he had decided that a lone human female wasn't much of a threat. "We will take you."

He stepped forward, and before she could even react, had slipped an arm around her waist. Not in any kind of forced intimacy, she realized, but because in the next second they had blinked out of the middle of Paseo de Peralta and stood in a walled garden riotous with late-summer blooms of roses and butterfly bushes and hollyhocks. Immediately the djinn let go of her and went up to the front door of the house that belonged to the garden, an imposing, updated hacienda-style abode with a tiled roof and a covered portico that appeared to run the length of the house.

To her surprise, the djinn rang the doorbell, just as any ordinary caller might. A moment or two later, the door opened, and Julia Innes looked out at them, her eyes widening in surprise as she recognized the visitor accompanying the djinn.

"Jillian?"

"Yes," she replied, trying to sound as if this was all completely normal, that being dropped out of the blue on one's doorstep was something that happened every day. "Can I come in?"

"Of course," Julia said, looking flustered and not much like her usual unflappable self. Or at least, she'd always seemed unflappable back when she was running things in Los Alamos. Since she'd been living here in Santa Fe for more than a year now, Jillian couldn't really comment on whether that aspect of the other woman's personality had changed or not.

But she supposed she was about to find out.

Julia stepped aside so Jillian could enter, then glanced back at the djinn who had brought her here. "Thank you, Hamidh. Zahrias and I will take care of this from here."

Hamidh nodded and bowed formally from the waist, right before he blinked himself away—maybe going back to performing guard duty on Paseo de Peralta. Jillian didn't have much time to think about it, because Julia was ushering her down the two-story hallway, saying, "I suppose I shouldn't have been so surprised to see you show up. After Aldair told us—"

"So he is here."

"Yes. Zahrias is having two of his men keep watch on him until the elders arrive." By this point, they had entered what had to be the living room, a space as imposing as the rest of the house, with its high ceiling and the obviously expensive abstract art that hung on the wall. Two couches of bone-colored leather faced one another across a coffee table of glass and bronze. Cool air from a central A/C unit flowed out of the vents.

Despite her worry for Aldair, Jillian couldn't help doing a few mental calculations as she gave a quick glance around—a hazard of working for several years in a real estate office, she supposed. What must this place have cost back when property values meant something? Two million?

Probably closer to three. Not that it mattered now. The Dying had rendered those sorts of considerations mostly unnecessary.

"The elders?" Jillian asked. "They're in charge of everything, right?"

"I think 'in charge' is probably a little too extreme. From what I've seen, they mostly try to stay out of the way, unless some kind of crisis comes up that absolutely requires their intervention. But please," Julia added, as if she'd just realized she wasn't being a very good hostess, "sit down. Can I get you something? Iced tea? Water? Lemonade?"

Considering how warm the day was, and how she hadn't drunk anything since she and Aldair had left the house several hours ago, all three of those sounded pretty good. But a little caffeine might not be a bad idea. "Iced tea would be great."

Julia smiled. "Just wait here. I'll go fetch it."

She left the room, heading down the hallway to the right, while Jillian was left to sit there and look around some more. Now that she'd had a chance to inspect them a little more closely, she got the feeling that the paintings on the wall had been done by the same artist whose home she and Aldair had appropriated back in Madrid. Talk about coincidences.

*Or maybe not,* she thought. *Obviously Natalie Marquez was fairly well known, and successful. It's not that big a surprise that some of her paintings might have ended up in a house like this.*

She didn't have time to speculate further and continue to distract herself, because in that moment Julia returned, a glass of iced tea in either hand. After giving one to Jillian, she sat down on the couch opposite hers, and fixed her with a very direct gaze. "So," she said. "You and Aldair. You want to tell me how that happened?"

*Not really,* Jillian thought. How could she begin to explain the attraction which had drawn the two of them together when she was still having a hard time understanding it herself? Anyway, this wasn't the time for confessions. It was the time to do whatever she must to make sure her lover was safe. So she shrugged and responded, "He didn't tell you anything?"

"He said you were innocent, that we shouldn't drag you into his problems. Not that we would have done anything like that anyway, but I have to say that Aldair al-Ankara acting selfless is a new one for me."

From Julia's tone of voice, Jillian got the impression that she didn't have a very high opinion of Aldair. Not really a surprise, considering what he'd already told her about his dealings with the djinn community here.

"But he did tell you how I helped him escape from the outer circles."

A shrug. "Yes, but he also made it clear that at the time you really didn't know what you were doing, that you were just trying to get out of there. As any other sane person would." Julia sipped her tea, then extracted a stoneware coaster from the bronze holder where it currently resided and set it down on the table. Her expression softened, and Jillian could see the concern in her big blue-gray eyes. "But…Jillian…forgive me for saying this, but Aldair?"

Even though she'd had a feeling this was coming, she still didn't much like the insinuation in Julia's voice. "He's not who you think he is."

At that remark, Julia's eyebrows lifted, and she crossed her arms as she settled against the back of the sofa. "Do you know anything about him?"

"I know everything."

The other woman's brows couldn't really rise any further, but she still managed to register sufficient astonishment as her eyes widened. "*Everything?*"

"Yes, because he told me. He told me all about trying to get his revenge on his brother. How he joined up with Khalim's people when his plans with Jessica fell apart. Everything. No sugarcoating."

"That doesn't sound at all like him."

"Maybe not, but that doesn't change what happened between us." Jillian leaned forward, hands clasped on her knees. Possibly there was no way to convince Julia of how Aldair had changed, but she knew she had to at least try. Julia's would be a far more sympathetic ear than Zahrias', that was for sure. If Jillian could get Julia on her side, then maybe there was some way she could convince the leader of the Santa Fe djinn that Aldair truly wasn't a threat anymore. "We weren't hurting anyone, living there in Madrid."

"Funny—he said basically the same thing. And I really don't think you were. But none of this is up to me. You understand that, don't you?"

Anger flared in Jillian, but she pushed it back as best she could. Actually, Julia really did look halfway sympathetic. But clearly she held the opinion that Zahrias wouldn't be swayed on the matter. And in the end, it really wasn't up to Zahrias, either, was it?

They were all waiting on the elders to arrive and pass judgment.

"I understand," Jillian said. "I don't like it, but I understand. Or at least, I'm trying to. But you all need to meet me halfway. Or don't you believe that people can change?"

Julia smiled, although there was something almost sad in her expression. "I didn't used to. Lately...I guess you could say I'm cautiously optimistic. But...." She paused, a small frown pulling at her fine brows, as if she wanted to say something but didn't know how well it would be received.

"But what?"

This time, the look Julia gave Jillian was extremely direct. It was the sort of look that made Jillian want to sit up straighter on the couch. "But—all right, I know we weren't close friends in Los Alamos. I got the impression that you really weren't close friends with anybody. That's okay—it was your choice. Word on the street was that you shot down any men who ever tried to approach you. Nicely, of course. But it seemed like you weren't ready to stop mourning, and now...." Her head tilted to one side. "How long were you there with Aldair in Madrid?"

"A week." That was probably a little better than falling into bed with someone after knowing them for a single evening, but not a lot of time to decide that you wanted to shack up for all eternity. Jillian could tell Julia was thinking about the same thing, although clearly she was too polite to say it. "I know it seems crazy. And I know you're all judging him for the terrible things he did—and I'm not excusing them, I'm not—but...." Jillian had to stop herself there. Because when you looked at the whole situation through eyes unblurred by love, she knew it did seem crazy. And it wasn't as if she was the sort of person who generally went for the "reformed bad boy" sorts of books or movies. God knows, Jack had been the very antithesis of a bad boy. At the same time, she could see why Aldair had been so angry, why he'd let that rage and resentment fester inside him for so long. She had to be glad that he'd somehow managed to get past it at last, even if he had done some very horrible things before they met.

"But....?" Julia probed gently.

"But he *was* punished. He spent eighteen months of our time in the outer circles. Maybe the elders won't think that was enough. But it's also not as if he didn't have to pay a price for what he did." Closing her eyes, Jillian recalled the nightmare landscape of that part of the djinn otherworld, of the bilious sky and toxic air, the way the winds felt as if they would flay the skin right off you, given enough time. "You have no idea what it was like there."

"No, and I don't want to ever find out. I've been to the part of the djinn plane where they actually lived,

and that was bad enough. So I'll take your word for it."
She stopped there, because in that moment, the sound
of male voices drifted down the hallway. "I think
Dani—Zahrias' brother—must be back. He was sent
to fetch the elders."

A nervous ache began in the pit of Jillian's stomach. If the elders were here, that meant it wouldn't be
long before they passed judgment on Aldair and then
returned to wherever it was they'd come from in the
first place. Had they remained on the djinn plane all
this time, or had they taken up residence somewhere
on Earth as well...maybe in a nice chateau on the Loire,
or possibly a multimillion-dollar mansion somewhere
in the cliffs above Malibu?

Not that any of that mattered. What mattered was
that she might never get to see Aldair again.

Two djinn entered the living room. Jillian recognized one of them at once—he was the slighter of the
two djinn who had taken Aldair away from Cerrillos.
The other seemed slightly older, although guessing
ages had to be a dicey thing when it came to djinn. He
was extremely handsome, with heavy dark hair drawn
back into a ponytail at the base of his neck and aristo-
cratic features.

He was also frowning in such a forbidding fashion
that Jillian couldn't quite help shrinking back into the
sofa cushions. After sending her a dismissive glance, he
returned his attention to Julia and announced, voice

thick with annoyance, "Dani has spoken with the elders. They told him they will not pass judgment in this instance, and so it is up to us to decide what to do with Aldair al-Ankara."

## CHAPTER NINETEEN

ALDAIR WOULD NEVER HAVE CALLED HIMSELF THE patient sort, but this waiting was particularly excruciating. Yes, he had been confined to what usually would have been a comfortable enough space, a largish bedroom with a sitting area that looked out over the property's lavish gardens, but he certainly was not comfortable now. Not with Murrah and Aziz leaning against the wall on the opposite side of the room, watching his every movement with narrowed eyes.

If only he had been able to see Jillian again, to comfort her and let her know how much he cared, no matter what happened. But he feared he most certainly would not be allowed to do such a thing. Most likely, he would be sent back to the outer circles, and she would be left to make her way in this world, alone again.

His heart ached at the thought...but it ached even more at the worry that she would move on from this, that she would return to Los Alamos and pick up the threads of her life, decide that perhaps life with a mortal man would not be so bad after all.

No. He would not allow himself to think of such things. There must be some way out of his current situation, even if presently he could not begin to guess what that escape might be.

A knock came at the door, and Murrah went to answer it. Julia Innes stood outside, worry and consternation mixing on her lovely features.

"Zahrias wants you to bring him to the living room," she said. "There's been a...development."

A development? What in the world was she talking about?

He assumed he would find out soon enough. Murrah and Aziz flanked him as Julia stepped out of the way so they might all head out into the corridor. The three of them followed her, past walls decorated with art niches that showed off rare pottery and ancient paintings on pieces of native sandstone.

And then they were in the living room. Zahrias was there, and his brother Danilar, but Aldair took them in with only a glance, for he spotted Jillian sitting on one of the sofas, Jillian, whom he had thought he would never see again.

Sparing not a single thought for his "bodyguards," he hurried forward, going to her. As soon as she spotted him, she rose and extended her hands. Even as their fingers twined around one another, he worried that Zahrias would give a command for Murrah and Aziz to haul him away from Jillian, but the command was never given.

"So," Zahrias said sourly, "it seems the lovebirds have been reunited."

At any other time, Aldair would have bridled at the disdainful note in the djinn leader's voice. Right then, however, he cared only that Jillian was here, that he was able to look down into her sweet face and see the glow in her shining gray eyes.

"Are you well?" he murmured. "How did you get here?"

"I drove the Harley," she said, smiling, although at the same time he thought he saw the glint of tears in her eyes. "Just luck that I didn't stall the damn thing. But I knew I had to come for you—I couldn't let them just take you like that—"

All words disappeared as he bent and covered his mouth with hers, tasted her sweetness. Ah, God, he had thought that he would never see her again.

"Ahem," Zahrias said.

At once, Jillian pulled away from him, looking somewhat shamefaced as she glanced over at the djinn leader. "I'm sorry," she said. "But after your men hauled him away like that, I was so worried—"

"Well, as you can see, your lover is hale and hearty. No harm has come to him." Zahrias stopped there, an unspoken "yet" hanging in the air. "But Dani has something he needs to say to all of us. Or rather," he added, "to the particular parties involved. Murrah, Aziz, thank you for your service. My brother and I will manage al-Ankara from here."

The two djinn didn't argue, but merely bowed and blinked out of the room.

"Very good," Zahrias said. "Dani, if you would tell us all what you just experienced?"

Dani wore a somewhat bemused expression, as if he was still coming to terms with what he must relate to the watching group. "As you requested, brother, I went to the palace of the elders in the otherworld. They still have their headquarters there, although I did see signs that at last they might be planning to remove here to Earth. At any rate," he went on hastily, as Zahrias' eyebrows lifted, apparently signaling his unconcern about the elders' current abode, "I did have an audience with them, and explained the situation. I said that we thought they must come down here and send Aldair back to the outer circles, for of course it is only they who have the power to access that accursed region."

"And it seems their answer was not what we expected." Zahrias' tone was even enough, but he frowned with some fierceness. Clearly, he was not pleased by what the elders had said.

"No, not at all," Danilar admitted. He sent an uncertain glance at Aldair and then Jillian, as if attempting to determine whether they had had something to do with the elders' capriciousness, although of course such a thing was quite impossible. "They expressed surprise that Aldair al-Ankara had been able to escape, but then, after conferring with the rest of his peers for a few minutes, Ibram, eldest of the elders, told me that if God had smiled on Aldair and allowed him to escape, then they would certainly not interfere with His judgment. He would not be returned to the outer circles, but allowed to remain here on Earth. Further, he said this was at its heart a personal dispute between the two al-Ankara brothers, and so it was for them to settle."

Hope sprang forth in Aldair's breast at hearing these words. If he was allowed to remain here, then he at least had a fighting chance. He permitted himself a quick glance over at Jillian; her hands were folded in her lap, and she held herself very still, but he could see how her eyes had begun to shine, how some color had returned to her cheeks. She might not have understood all the ramifications of the news Danilar had just related, but she understood enough to realize that her lover had been granted an unexpected reprieve.

"Settle how?" Zahrias asked then. The tension was clear enough in his voice. He did not like this ruling of the elders. No, he did not like it at all. "For Aldair and Jasreel have already met one another in combat on two separate occasions, and obviously being bested did not prevent Aldair from seeking his revenge time and time again."

Aldair opened his mouth to protest, then decided it would not do to argue that particular point once more. He would still contend that in their initial battle, Jasreel had cheated, and in their second confrontation, he most certainly had, by enlisting the aid of his Chosen. True, the elders had ruled her intervention fair enough, even though it certainly had not seemed that way to Aldair. But when he spoke, he attempted to sound as mild and unconcerned as possible. "I know that our dealings with one another have been...contentious. But please know that I no longer bear any ill will against my brother. I do not wish to interfere in his life. I am more than happy to return to Madrid with Jillian and let all of you alone."

"Is that even possible?" Julia asked then, entering the conversation for the first time. "That is, Jillian is your Chosen, Aldair. That is one thing the elders are pretty strict about—any djinn who has selected a mortal as their Chosen must live within a community. Or am I missing something?"

"No, you have missed nothing at all," Zahrias said. "The rules are very clear. But how can we have you here among us, Aldair, when you have perpetrated such wrongs against your brother? And not only him, but also Aidan, the Chosen of Lilias, who was disfigured by Khalim."

"I had nothing to do with that," Aldair protested. That was true enough, for he had not accompanied Khalim on the expedition that culminated in the ambush of Aidan and his hunting party. "But yes, I forget—guilt by association is enough for you, is it not?"

Zahrias scowled, and Julia broke in before anyone else could speak. "I believe you, Aldair. Not because I am so firmly convinced of your innocence," she added quickly, "but because Aidan would have told us if he had seen you among Khalim's men. But Zahrias is right—there is a good deal of bad blood here in Santa Fe that has nothing to do with your feud with Jasreel."

An uneasy silence fell then. Aldair saw how Jillian looked from Zahrias to Julia and then over at Danilar, as though in an attempt to discover how deep this bad blood actually went. Some of the color left her face, but she lifted her chin and said, "I'm not going to excuse what Aldair did in the past. And yes, he did tell me the truth, so you can all stop thinking that he somehow misled me, tried to make himself look better to me. Because he didn't. But still...." Her voice trembled for a second, and then she shook her head as if impatient with herself, and continued, "Isn't there such a thing as forgiveness among the djinn? Is there really no chance that you can allow yourself to believe he might have changed, that he might want to make amends for what he did?"

"Amends?" came a new voice from the doorway. "I don't think Aldair understands the meaning of the word."

Aldair looked away from Jillian and saw Jasreel standing there at the entrance to the living room, Jessica Monroe immediately behind him. Jasreel's mouth was tight with anger, and his dark eyes glinted ominously.

This probably was not going to go well.

Jillian had never met Jasreel, but she recognized Jessica at once and knew the man with her had to be Aldair's brother. There truly wasn't much resemblance between the two; if Jillian hadn't known better, she would have said Jasreel was of Native American descent, with his shining black hair and dark eyes and warm brown skin, and Aldair didn't look anything like that. But then, they were half-brothers. Maybe Aldair looked much more like his mother.

Without really knowing what she intended to do, Jillian rose to her feet. Somehow she had to make all of these djinn see reason, understand that remaining mired in the past wouldn't help any of them. "Hello, Jasreel," she said. At least her voice sounded calm enough now, despite that betraying shake of a few moments earlier. "And hi, Jessica." The other woman nodded, but she stood close to her partner, and her face didn't reveal even a ghost of a smile. "I know you have every right to be angry with Aldair. I know," she went on firmly, when it looked like Jasreel was about to open his mouth to speak, "because he confessed to me everything he'd done to you. And to you, Jessica. It was all horrible. But he's truly sorry for what he did. And if the elders think he's deserving of some mercy, maybe all of you should look for some mercy in your hearts as well."

"Is this true?" Jasreel demanded, not bothering to reply to her directly, but instead addressing the question to Zahrias. "The elders would not send him back to the outer circles?"

"I fear not," Zahrias said heavily. "It is a conundrum, for I know that none of us wish to go against the elders' wishes. But at the same time, I cannot see how we can allow him to live among us."

Jillian watched this exchange silently, heart pounding as she hoped against hope that Zahrias and Jasreel would relent, but then she knew she could hold back no longer. "So what are you going to do? Put him in your own jail? Force him and his brother to fight again?"

"I'm not sure you would have to force me," Jasreel said grimly, even as Jessica laid a placating hand on his arm.

"Look," she said then, "this has come as kind of a shock to us. Can we just...have some time to think about our options?"

"What options?" Jasreel replied. "Because the most logical thing would have been to let the elders put him back where he belongs, but since they apparently have allowed caprice to rule them in this matter, we're stuck with having to figure out what we can do with him."

They were talking about her partner as if he wasn't even in the room. Once again, Jillian could feel herself about to erupt, but Aldair forestalled her.

"I know this is difficult for everyone," he said. "Myself included, although I am sure you don't wish to hear about that. If Jasreel desires to meet me in combat, I will do so. However, no matter how angry he is with me, I know he is not a killer. And yet I know that is what it would come to, in the end. It would appear we have no other options."

Jillian's breath caught in her throat. Was Aldair really saying they had no choice but to have a duel to the death? She looked from Julia to Jessica, somehow knowing that it would have to be the women who stepped in here, who would need to be the voices of reason. Apparently even djinn had testosterone issues.

"I don't think we need to go there yet," Julia said. Her face was taut with worry, but she sounded calm and assured. Then again, it was easy for her to stay calm. It wasn't her lover's life on the line. "Can't we just, I don't know, table this for now? I'm sure Aldair won't mind if we put him somewhere overnight with a few guards keeping watch."

Judging by the slight alteration in Aldair's expression, the way his mouth compressed, Jillian thought he would mind. But that was still better than having to go out into the plaza and fight a duel right then and there. She had a sudden incongruous image of him and his brother going after one another with rapiers, like something out of *The Three Musketeers,* even though she knew that the djinn probably indulged in a far deadlier form of dueling.

"No, I do not mind," Aldair said.

"I think it's a good idea," Jessica put in. She, too, looked strained, and Jillian couldn't blame her. Yes, apparently her partner had prevailed against Aldair in the past, but maybe Aldair hadn't been desperate enough until now.

After all, back then he had only been fighting for vengeance. Now he would be fighting for a chance to be with the woman he loved.

In the end, they decided to put him in one of the cells under the former U.S. Marshal's building, where not so long ago they had imprisoned Richard Margolis, the former leader of Los Alamos. Normally, those barred doors and walls of reinforced concrete would have been of very little use in keeping a djinn captive. However, it seemed the Santa Fe djinn had one of Miles Odekirk's infernal devices in their keeping, and so they activated it and left him in the company of two human guards.

The effects were excruciating. To prevent the device from affecting any other djinn in the vicinity, they had raised the power level, which in turn shrank its area of effect. Aldair had thought the outer circles bad enough, but this—this was like having every ounce of energy drained from him while his head buzzed as if filled with a thousand angry bees, and every inch of his skin stung as though being pierced by a thousand needles at once.

Even more painful, however, was being separated from Jillian. She had begged to stay down here with him, but Zahrias would not allow it. "You will stay here as an honored guest in our house," he said, "for you have done nothing wrong, and Julia says you are a good woman. But I will not give any comfort to Aldair by allowing you to remain in his presence."

And so he had been hustled away and brought down here, and the device activated immediately afterward. The only comfort he could take was that at least it sounded as if they would treat Jillian well, would not hold his sins against her.

One of the guards was a young blond man, his once-handsome face now marred by deep scars on both his cheeks. Seeing him, Aldair knew this must be Aidan, who had been maimed by Khalim. No doubt he would be a very enthusiastic watchdog. The other young man Aldair did not recognize. Not that it mattered. In his current condition, with the device hammering away at his very being, Aldair barely had the strength to sit upright on the cot in his cell, let alone make any kind of an attempt at escape.

Nevertheless, he couldn't prevent himself from speaking as Aidan approached the bars of his cage. "I had nothing to do with that," Aldair said, gaze flickering to the scars on the man's cheeks.

"I know," Aidan replied. He sounded far less concerned than Aldair thought he himself would, if he had been maimed in the same fashion. "All the djinn who were there that day with Khalim—their faces are burned into my memory. Yours isn't one of them."

Even though Aldair knew that to be only the truth, he could not help but be slightly relieved. Yes, he had stayed back at the renegades' hideout at Ghost Ranch that day, for although he had joined up with Khalim, he had no stomach for the sort of "hunting parties" that the leader of the rogue djinn enjoyed so much. But it would have been easy enough for Aidan to claim that Aldair had been there, so he might enact his own personal revenge.

"Thank you," he said quietly.

The young man's shoulders lifted. "I'm not excusing the other stuff you did. But I'm also not going to hold you accountable for the things you didn't do." He grinned then, the scars on his cheeks pulling in what looked like a most uncomfortable way. "Besides, I'm not the one who has to look at my face all the time. In the morning when I'm shaving, but that's about it. And Lilias says she doesn't care."

"Lilias has a generous soul." That, too, was only the truth. She was not a djinn Aldair had ever desired—partly because Khalim was a former lover of hers, and he had a long memory and a habit of holding grudges—but he could not deny the gentleness of her spirit. That was why she did not stay long with Khalim, and certainly why she had selected a Chosen. She would never have allowed herself to give up the chance to save even one life.

"She does." Aidan's gaze flickered down toward the untouched tray of food in Aldair's cell. Yes, they'd locked him up, but they'd also provided a generous meal, for while Zahrias might be single-minded in his pursuit of justice, he was not a cruel man. "Aren't you going to eat that?"

"I fear I do not have much of an appetite."

"Still, you should eat." A pause, and Aidan glanced upward, as if thinking of the world of the Santa Fe djinn, a hundred feet above their heads. "I have a feeling you're going to need your strength tomorrow."

Aldair couldn't dispute that claim. He knew it was too much to hope that Jasreel would relent, would allow himself to set their differences aside. The last time he had faced his brother, they had squared off in an empty field a little outside the center of Taos. Would they do the same here, or would one of the open areas within the Plaza be sufficient?

And last time, he had been healthy and well. Now he would have to go up against Jasreel after spending the night being tortured by the device. If he was able to sleep at all, it would be a miracle.

"You are probably right," he said, and forced himself to pick up the fork and spoon a few mouthfuls of the spicy pork dish—something called carne adovada—into his mouth.

After all, even a condemned man was allowed his last meal.

Jillian rolled over onto her side and stared at the soft moonlight coming in through the bedroom window. At first she had thought that was what had been bothering her, and so she'd turned onto her other side so she could face the wall. But sleep eluded her there as well. Of course it wasn't the moonlight keeping her awake, but instead her jangled nerves. No matter what she did—breathing deeply, counting backward from a hundred, murmuring, "Go to sleep, go to sleep" over and over—nothing worked.

How could she sleep when Aldair might be dead in a few hours?

The horrible thing was, everyone had been incredibly nice to her. Danilar, Zahrias' kind-faced younger brother, had blinked her back to Madrid so she might gather some personal items and a change of clothes, and fetch Patches as well. The dog hadn't been too thrilled with being held tightly while Dani brought them back to Santa Fe, but he perked right up when allowed to explore the lovely gardens that surrounded the house Zahrias and Julia shared.

Now the dog was asleep on the rug next to her bed, with no idea that he might lose his adopted master the next day. Jillian wished she could find that sort of blissful oblivion, but she knew she wouldn't be that lucky.

When she'd tried to pick Julia's brain, to ask whether she thought Jasreel would go through with fighting his brother the next day, Julia had only shaken her head and said, "I really don't know. Usually, Jace is a pretty forgiving sort. But this feud with Aldair has been going on longer than we've been alive. He might just be glad of a chance to end it once and for all."

If she'd known Julia better, Jillian might have remarked sourly, "Thanks for the reassurance." But she had the feeling that Julia was only trying to be realistic, didn't want to sugarcoat the situation. The horrible thing was, no matter who won, someone else would lose. Jillian didn't wish any harm on Jasreel and Jessica. After everything they'd been through, they deserved a little peace.

Problem was, she believed the same thing about Aldair.

So she spent the whole night tossing and turning, trying in vain to find a position that would be comfortable enough to allow her a little rest. She did doze off sometime around five in the morning, only to wake a few hours later at the rich scent of coffee drifting through the house.

Her bedroom had its own *en suite* bath, and so she went in there to take a hot shower and try to make herself presentable. She didn't want to think that this might be the last time Aldair ever saw her, but if it was, she needed to make sure his final memory of her was a good one. The bathroom was equipped with a blow dryer, and also some makeup still in its packaging. Julia, of course. Somehow she'd slipped in that mascara and blush and lip gloss when Jillian wasn't looking.

Or, more likely, had Zahrias zap it into the drawer from the nearest drugstore.

As she got into one of her sequined skirts and tank top, Jillian glanced down at her left hand. The gold band Jack had placed on her finger gleamed there. She'd never taken it off, not once.

Her heart seemed to seize, and she made herself take a breath. Then another. She had lost Jack. Now she might lose Aldair as well. But if the worst happened, she wanted him to know that she was his completely, that she'd finally let go of the ghosts of the past.

Very gently, she eased the ring off her finger and set it down on the dresser, then went back into the bathroom to brush her hair a final time. Afterward, she followed her nose and headed toward the kitchen. As she entered the room, she saw Julia there, but no Zahrias.

"He and Dani have already gone over to the Plaza to mark out the area for the duel," she explained as she poured Jillian some coffee. Apparently noticing the stricken expression on Jillian's face, she added quickly, "That doesn't mean it's a done deal. There's still time to call it all off. But they wanted to be prepared."

"Of course," Jillian responded, voice flat. This didn't feel real. Maybe if she kept telling herself none of this was happening....

But of course it was. The kitchen, with its expensive maple cupboards and granite countertops, was certainly real, as was Patches over in a corner, greedily crunching away on the kibble Julia had put out for him.

Julia didn't say anything, only got up and put a couple pieces of bread in the toaster oven. How she'd figured out that was the only food her guest would be able to stomach, Jillian didn't know. But Julia had always been like that. She took care of people.

After her makeshift breakfast was over, Jillian went back to her bathroom so she could brush her teeth. Julia had already offered to let Patches out into the yard, so he was taken care of for the immediate future.

And then she came to the door of Jillian's room and said softly, "They're waiting at the Plaza."

The toast she'd just eaten congealed into a lump at the bottom of her stomach. "So Jasreel is going through with it?"

"It looks that way." A hesitation, and then Julia added, "I am so sorry."

Clearly, she didn't think Aldair had much of a chance. As much as she hated to admit it, Jillian couldn't help feeling the same way. She knew they'd used one of Miles's devices to keep Aldair from escaping, so he must be a mess this morning. If he couldn't defeat Jasreel when at the top of his form, how could he possibly hope to do so now?

And the thing was, she didn't want anything to happen to Jasreel, either. He was not a bad person. If anyone should be facing Aldair out in the Plaza, it should be their bastard of a father. He was the one who'd started all this.

After making sure Patches was safely inside and had plenty of water, the two women headed out to the Plaza. Since it was only a few blocks away, they walked.

The sun was warm, but the breeze surprisingly pleasant. Funny how much cooler it was here in Santa Fe, even though it lay only thirty miles or so from Madrid. But the elevation was a good deal higher.

As they approached the area designated for the duel, Jillian saw a large ring of people marking the spot. Her stomach tightened further, but she forced herself to pull in a breath. She was not going to allow herself to get sick here. No, she would hold it together and show Aldair that she believed in him, that somehow he would prevail. But that wasn't right. She didn't want either of them to prevail. She just wanted this all over, with everyone still safe and able to live their lives.

Zahrias nodded at them as they approached. "We are almost ready. We are only waiting for Jasreel."

Jillian glanced across the circle of onlookers and saw Aldair standing on the opposite side, flanked again by Murrah and Aziz. It seemed obvious enough that they'd been given guard duty because they were the two biggest djinn in the community.

Not that Aldair looked as if he was in any condition to attempt an escape. His face was drawn, deep shadows under his eyes that hadn't been there the day before. It didn't matter, though. He still looked handsomer to her than any man she'd ever known, and his bright blue eyes blazed with love and warmth as he gazed across the space that separated them.

"Can I speak to him?" she asked Zahrias.

"I fear not."

"But—"

"Really, Zahrias?" Julia interjected. At the moment, she didn't appear all too pleased with her partner. "You're not going to let them talk, even for a moment?"

His jaw hardened, but then he gave a reluctant nod. "One moment. And you will go with her, Julia."

"Fine." She turned and offered a reassuring smile to Jillian. "Let's go. It's better to do this before Jasreel shows up."

All Jillian could do was nod. She had no idea what she would say to Aldair. He would recognize any words of encouragement as only that—mere words. She couldn't do anything to help him. Right then, she wished she was a djinn, too, just so she could fight at her lover's side. But while he'd lent some of his abilities to her, enough that she would heal if injured and never get sick, those abilities didn't translate to striking down his enemies.

He did smile as she approached, and reached out to take her hands in his. "My love," he said. A quick glance at the watching crowds, and then he shrugged. Before Jillian could respond, he'd bent and laid his lips against hers. Only a brief kiss, just enough to feel the reassuring pressure of his mouth, but that was still sufficient to send her blood singing.

"Aldair," she whispered.

A brush of his hand against her hair. "Know this, Jillian Powell. There was only you. In this life, I have loved only you."

Tears rose in her throat, choking her. Then Julia was laying a gentle hand on her arm, pulling her away, because a sharp *pop* indicated that Jasreel had appeared in the Plaza. He stood next to Jessica, who kissed him, a hard, swift kiss, before backing away into the crowd.

The last time she had seen him, Jasreel had been wearing human clothes—jeans and boots and a T-shirt. Now, though, he had donned djinn garb, a flowing open robe in a sky-blue shade, bright against his warm-toned skin, the pants several shades darker.

He raised his voice and called out, "Aldair al-Ankara, I will see you on this field of battle once and for all. Your wrongs are too numerous to list here, but all those watching know what you have done, and support me in this endeavor."

*Not all,* Jillian thought fiercely, now back where Zahrias stood. She guessed that Julia had brought her there so the djinn leader could keep an eye on her.

Aldair stepped forward. They'd provided djinn robes for him as well, even though he'd been dressed for motorcycle riding when he was captured. Although he appeared straight and tall enough, Jillian could still see the weariness in him. He was in no condition for this fight.

And when he spoke, some of that exhaustion showed in his voice. "Jasreel, there is no need for this. You wish to fight a man who no longer exists."

"I don't think so, because I see him standing here before me."

He wouldn't give up. Jillian had been half holding her breath, hoping he would relent, but it seemed that centuries of conflict had finally worn him down to the point where all he wanted was an end. She didn't know if she could even blame him. Or rather, she wouldn't have blamed him...if the object of his ire was anyone rather than Aldair.

The two of them faced off in the center of the square. At once, a fierce wind began swirling around them, blowing in their hair, causing the silk of their robes to flap and billow. That wind took on a shape, coalescing into what looked like a miniature tornado, one that surrounded Aldair and caused him to stumble. Jillian sucked in her breath, frightened that he would lose his balance altogether. He had to be so weak after having that device beating on him all night....

But somehow he managed to remain upright, and even sent a second tornado spinning outward, headed straight for Jasreel. He raised both his hands in a blocking motion, however, one that deflected the tornado back at the one who had summoned it.

Aldair stumbled again, and this time, with both tornadoes bearing down on him, the force was enough to drive him to his knees. Jillian cried out, "No!" and began to take a step forward.

Julia caught her arm. "You can't interfere," she said, her voice soft but urgent. "I know it's dreadful, but—"

Right then, Jillian couldn't have cared less about djinn rules, or what was expected of her. No way was she going to stand there and watch the very breath sucked away from the man she loved. She wrenched her arm from Julia's grasp and hurled herself into the center of the fray, interposing herself between Aldair and his brother.

It was like being back in the outer circles. Her breath caught, and strangled, as the tornadoes whirled around her. Dimly, she heard Aldair crying out in protest, but she couldn't make out the words. She couldn't make out anything, except those blue, blue eyes of his, staring down at her, his lips forming sounds she couldn't hear.

If she could have chosen one last thing to see before she died, it would have been his eyes. Her mouth curved in a small smile.

The world went dark.

# CHAPTER TWENTY

At once the tornadoes disappeared as if they had never been. Aldair, already on his knees, reached for Jillian's limp body, cradling her in his arms. Above him, Jasreel stared down at them in consternation.

"Is she—?" he began, and then stopped himself, as if he could not bear to hear the answer.

Aldair lowered his face to hers, kissed her sweet, sweet lips. Ah, yes, there it was—the faintest hint of a warm breath against his mouth. He shook his head. "She lives. But barely."

"I—" Again Jasreel hesitated, his stricken gaze taking in the woman in his brother's arms. "She loves you. Truly loves you, enough so that she would interfere with our battle, even though she had no chance of prevailing. But she did not even hesitate."

"Yes," Aldair said, still holding her close, heart wrenched by the slack stillness of her features. "I cannot say that I deserve such devotion, for her heart should have been bestowed on a more deserving man. But there it is."

From the crowd, a dark-haired mortal hurried over. He knelt on the ground next to Aldair and said, "I'm Miguel, the medic here. Could I see her, please?"

Reluctant as Aldair was to hand Jillian over, he knew that this young mortal would have a far better chance of reviving his beloved than he would. So he nodded, and allowed Miguel to take her and feel her pulse, then open her slack eyelids so he might peer into her eyes. At last he nodded.

"I think she'll be all right. But we need to get her into bed so she can rest."

Aldair nodded. Miguel stood up slowly, Jillian's limp form in his arms. At once Julia and Zahrias hurried over. "Can you manage?" Zahrias asked.

"I think so, as long as I don't have to take her too far."

"To the La Fonda," Julia said quickly. "It's closest. I'll come with you."

The medic nodded and strode off toward a large building on the southeastern side of the Plaza, Dani moving swiftly to accompany them just in case Miguel needed some assistance. During all this, Jasreel had stood to one side, face somehow blank and worried at the same time, as if he didn't quite know what he should do now. He barely acknowledged Jessica, who quietly approached and paused next to him.

"It is up to you to decide what to do next," Zahrias said, turning back to Jasreel and Aldair. "Shall you continue the duel?"

"No," Jasreel said quickly, as if he had already made this decision, had come to his own inner conclusions.

Zahrias' brows lifted in surprise. Astonishment flooded through Aldair—but also a certain wariness. Of course he longed for this to be over. But he could not allow himself to hope too much. "You wish to wait until Jillian Powell has been healed?"

"No," Jasreel said again. His gaze flickered toward the djinn leader. "What she did—I never believed someone would sacrifice themselves for my brother. But she didn't care. It was obvious that all she thought of was trying to save him." He stopped there and ran a hand through his hair, a gesture Aldair recalled from the times in his brother's youth when he had been uncertain or nervous. "If she could do that for him, then maybe she was right. *Have* you changed?" Jasreel asked then, voice hardening as he looked at Aldair.

"I would like to think so. That was what I tried to tell all of you. But please—I must go see Jillian."

Zahrias' eyes narrowed. "Is this some trick, so you might now attempt to get away?"

Rage flared in Aldair, overcoming his weariness, his worry. "Send guards with me, if you like! But I must be at my Chosen's side!"

"Let him go," Jasreel said then. He still wore that slightly flummoxed expression, as if he could not decide how he was supposed to feel about what had just occurred. "I don't think he has any intention of running. And I think—I think we're all going to have to learn how to live with him."

"Are you saying what I think you are saying, Jasreel?" Zahrias appeared as if he couldn't quite believe what he had just heard.

"Yes," Jasreel replied, giving the leader of the Santa Fe djinn a reluctant smile. "The feud is over. Let him be one of us now."

Jillian's eyes opened slowly. At first she thought she was back in the guest bedroom at Zahrias and Julia's house, but after she blinked and her surroundings came more into focus, she realized this space was a good deal larger, the ceilings even higher. And the painted furniture—probably local—wasn't familiar at all.

But all those details melted away as she realized Aldair sat in a wood-framed chair that he'd pulled up to her bedside. The expression of worry he wore faded as their eyes met.

"How are you, my darling?"

"I—" How was she? Her chest and back ached as if someone had beaten her with a stick, but as far as she could tell, she seemed to be otherwise intact. Anyway, she knew she would heal quickly enough, thanks to the connection she and Aldair shared. "I'm fine."

"That was very brave of you," he said as he reached for her hand. His flesh felt warm and welcoming, and so wonderfully real.

"But...." Jillian glanced around again. The room was beautiful, but she halfway expected to see Murrah and Aziz still playing guard, standing off to one side as they watched their captive to make sure he couldn't get away. "You're here alone," she said flatly.

"Yes." His mouth twitched in a smile. "Would you have preferred more company?"

"No, of course not. But—"

"You're wondering where the guards are."

"Yes." How could he be so calm, so relaxed? She'd jumped into the middle of his battle with Jasreel because she hadn't known what else to do. Clearly, the forces the two djinn had been hurling at one another had also taken their toll on her, even though she was already beginning to feel better. But that didn't explain why they'd allowed Aldair to come in here unaccompanied.

"There will be no guards, because Jasreel and I have made our peace with one another."

"You...what?" Had she banged her head against the ground when she fainted? That would explain why Aldair didn't seem to be making any sense.

"Your self-sacrifice moved him, it seems." Aldair's fingers tightened on hers, and he rose from his chair so he might go to her, then bend and lay the lightest of kisses on her mouth. "He does not wish to fight me anymore."

Was this all a dream? It had to be, with the man she loved at her side, and the unbelievable news that his centuries-old feud had finally been put to rest. Somehow she managed to find her voice. "Well, good."

"'Good'?" Aldair repeated, chuckling. "Is that all you have to say?"

"No, but I guess I'm feeling a little out of it right now." She gazed up into his face. He appeared improved as well, the shadows gone from under his eyes, color returned to his face. "And how are you?"

"Much better, now that I know you are safe. And the effects from the device are wearing off more quickly than I had hoped." He winced then, as if he remembered all too well what it had done to him during those hours it had been operating. "Although perhaps not quickly enough."

Jillian gently released his hand so she could push herself up against the pillows. The room wavered a little bit, but then the balance centers in her brain seemed to take over, making everything reassuringly solid again. "So what happens now?"

"Well," he replied. "You will get better, first and foremost. Miguel thinks you should stay in bed for at least tonight."

"Oh, really?" she returned, then cast a significant glance at the empty space in the king-sized bed next to her.

"To *sleep*," Aldair said in mock-severe tones. "After that, we will have to look for a house."

"Here in Santa Fe." Once upon a time, she would have been thrilled at the prospect. She had always loved visiting here with Jack. But current circumstances might make hers and Aldair's residence in the former capitol a touch problematic.

"Yes, of course. Those are the rules. You are my Chosen, and we must reside with the community here."

"And everyone's okay with that?"

Once again he bent and kissed her, the caress much more lingering this time. Her body ached for him, nerve endings coming alive with need, but she knew that would have to wait. Not long, that was for sure. But probably this night, just to be safe.

"'Okay' might be slightly optimistic. I think they will grow used to the idea. And they will love you." He brushed a lock of wayward hair away from her face. "I will not lie—I think it will help that Jasreel and Jessica live outside Santa Fe proper, and do not venture much into town, according to what Zahrias has told me. It will not be that difficult to keep our paths from crossing, at least not until my brother has had more time to become used to the idea."

"You're probably right." And maybe with time, she and Aldair could become true members of the community here, just as tightly woven into its fabric as any of those who had been here from the beginning. It would be good, she thought, to not feel like an outsider, to truly be a part of things, rather than observing from the sidelines. That had been her own fault in Los Alamos, she knew. They'd tried to welcome her, but she would have none of it.

Things would be different here, solely because of the man who stood next to her and gazed down at her with all the love in the world in his eyes. She blessed the accident that had brought them together. The hand of God? She wasn't so conceited as to think she merited such special attention.

But if it had been...well, she would have to do her very best to prove she was worthy of such regard.

She smiled up at Aldair. "It will need to be a big house. You know, for those six or seven children."

He laughed then and bent to kiss her, his arms going around her so he might hold her close. And she clung to him, breathing his warmth into her, knowing the years to come would be filled with more warmth, more laughter.

And love. Oh, yes...always love.